D1547341

Donation from the library of
Jose Pedro Segundo
1922 - 2022
Please pass freely to others readers so
that everyone can enjoy this book!

Ivan Bunin

IN A FAR DISTANT LAND

SELECTED STORIES

Translated by ROBERT BOWIE

HERMITAGE

1983

Ivan BUNIN

IN A FAR DISTANT LAND
(Selected Stories)

Translations, Introduction and Annotations
by Robert Bowie

Copyright (C) 1983 by Robert Bowie
All rights reserved

Library of Congress Cataloging in Publication Data

Bunin, Ivan Alekseevich, 1870-1953.
     In a far distant land.

     I. Title.
PG3453.B9A15   1983   891.73'3   82-21296
ISBN 0-938920-27-8

Front cover: detail from
"Women on the Grass" (1916) by K. Somov

Published by HERMITAGE
2269 Shadowood Drive
Ann Arbor, MI 48104, USA

TO

J., J., R., and N.

Grateful acknowledgment is made to the following publications for permission to reprint the stories listed below, some of which appeared in slightly different form:

Russian Literature Triquarterly ("In a Far Distant Land," "Remote," "Indulgent Participation," "On the Night Sea")
The Colorado Quarterly ("Transfiguration," "The Idol")
The Literary Review ("An Unknown Friend")
Webster Review ("The Calf's Head")
Translation ("The Elephant")
The Denver Quarterly ("Temir-Aksak-Khan," "The Hare")

Acknowledgments

I would like to thank the many colleagues at Miami University and at the Translation Seminar (University of California at Santa Cruz, Summer, 1979) who read parts of this manuscript and who made valuable suggestions for changes. I would also like to express my appreciation to Miami University for two grants, one supporting translation of part of the manuscript, the other covering costs of typing and reproducing it.

CONTENTS

Ivan Bunin (1870-1953), the first Russian writer to be awarded the Nobel Prize for literature (1933), had one of the longest careers in Russian literary history. Having published his first poem in 1887, he continued to write poetry and prose works for another sixty years. His reputation as an exacting stylist was already well established in Russia before the Revolution and Civil War, which forced him into emigration in 1920. He spent the remainder of his life living in France but writing works set primarily in pre-Revolutionary Russia. In the collection of stories presented in this volume I have chosen to concentrate on what became most important in Bunin's fiction as he matured as a writer, the "eternal themes" of art, time, love and death.

The theme of romantic love is predominant throughout Bunin's work. He was both fascinated and perplexed by the enigma of human sensuality, especially by the sensual attraction of the female for the male; he once remarked about one of his favorite writers, Moupassant, that "he was the only one who dared to repeat incessantly that human life is ruled utterly by the craving for woman."[1] But at the end of a career dominated by the theme of sensuality and love, Bunin remained dissatisfied with literary treatment of love both in his own works and in other works of world literature:

> I am often amazed and saddened, even horrified . . . when I think about the stupidity, the inattentiveness toward women that was characteristic of me during the early years of my life in France (and even before that). *No one ever* has managed to write about that wondrous, ineffably beautiful something, utterly unique of all earthly things, the body of woman. And not only the body. One must, must make the attempt. I have tried—the result is filth and banality. I must find different words.[2]

The present collection is, in part, a reflection of Bunin's lifelong search for those "different words." Certainly he was aware that the enigma of romantic love and human sexuality can never be explained fully and adequately, but there is in Russian literature no more persistent search to understand that enigma than in Bunin's works.

It is difficult to place Bunin within any literary school; he has strong affinities with the great nineteenth century Russian Realist tradition and has been considered a kind of classicist for the perfection of his form. A preoccupation with romantic love suggests, of course, Romanticism, and Bunin is indeed a romantic in other ways, most prominently in his desire to transcend the bounds of the mundane in both life and art. Since his fear of death is inordinate, his emphasis on escape is not surprising, escape through romantic love, Eastern religions, idealization of a bucolic past, art. In a number of stories included in this collection Bunin blends the love theme with the theme of art and the creative consciousness. Most obvious in "The Grammar of Love" is the landowner Khvoshinsky's insane love for the peasant girl Lushka. But the story actually treats a strange *ménage à trois* since the creative dreamer Ivlev, an artist type modelled after Bunin himself, is shown in the process of becoming Khvoshinsky's alter ego. In a deliberate act of artistic creativity he relives Khvoshinsky's life in his own consciousness; the process is consummated when he buys *The Grammar of Love*. Ivlev assumes the identity of another dreamer like himself, falls in love with a figment of his own imagination, the "legendary Lushka," and achieves a creative, semi-insane escape into the other "being" described in the Baratynsky poem. Ivlev is also the protagonist of a later story, "In a Far Distant Land," in which he dreams the plot. As dreamer-narrator he views the action and creates it simultaneously, the ideal situation for the artist who would like to build the events of his own life in the way he constructs his fiction. In a distant dreamland (the title is the formulaic first line of a traditional Russian folk tale) Ivlev can create an ideal love for himself and calmly destroy any obstacle to that love (e.g., by "murdering" the old aunt in his dream). The story ends with the creative artist in the role of Pygmalion, worshipping his creation and asserting that this love is more real for him than any woman made of flesh and blood.

The story titled "The Mad Artist" (like the earlier "Noosiform Ears") has its roots in the horror that the First World War and the Russian Revolution aroused in Bunin. It deals with the limitations of art in a world gone berserk. One of Bunin's implications here is that art is rooted in the experiences of the artist and cannot be entirely separated from the world around him. The artist of the story wishes to "give birth" to a work of creative art that will be a surrogate for his stillborn son and will resurrect in the creative act that son and the artist's beloved wife. The work will also defeat the insane impulses of the times and save the world. But the artistic imagination refuses to lie, and the final creation embodies all the earthly horrors that the artist himself has lived through. In one of his best works on the art theme, "An Unknown Friend," Bunin puts his own ideas about art into the mouth of his heroine. This is a story about the complicated relationship between writer and reader, about artistic communication and the renewed creativity inspired by the right kind of communication. The woman reads a writer's stories, concocts a fictional image of that writer in her mind, falls in love with the concoction and begins writing love letters, in effect, to her own creation. She pleads for an answer but dimly realizes that if the real writer ever answered, her fictional reality would be destroyed. She has been inspired by art to create her own "art," and she falls in love with her own creation. It is not surprising to find this Pygmalion theme in the fiction of an artist as self-centered as Bunin. While writing his semi-autobiographical *Life of Arsen'ev,* he described how he had fallen in love with his own creation, Lika, about whom he began having dreams: "I once awoke and thought, Lord, this could really be the greatest love in all my life. And it turns out that she did not exist." [3] As suggested above, the "Ivlev cycle" of stories presents another Pygmalion, another artist in love with his own imaginative fancies. But despite the attraction of the Pygmalion myth for him, Bunin was not under the illusion that it could really work in life, where there are no goddesses around to incarnate statues; "An Unknown Friend," as "The Mad Artist," demonstrates the failure of solipsism in art. Communication is essential; if this solitary woman has no reader but herself, the process is incomplete. She needs a reader, but, paradoxically, that reader cannot be the artist who inspired her since he is the one she has invented. What complicates the issue even more is her attempting to substitute an invented love for an incarnate love. Notwithstanding the inclinations of the creative dreamer such as Ivlev (who represents, in large degree, Bunin himself), Bunin, a writer obsessed with carnality, is not one to believe wholeheartedly that the statue of Galatea, left unincarnate, is enough.

In his inordinate fear of death and his preoccupation with the flesh, Bunin resembles his idol, Lev Tolstoy, but he refuses to take social, political, or even moral issues as seriously as Tolstoy. He prefers to emphasize the metaphysical, above all the transience of life and the ways human beings adjust to the inevitable fact of their mortality. One reason why sensual love assumes such importance for Bunin is that it provides a brief transcendence of the imperfect world, allows one to forget one's mortality for a few seconds. But Bunin also seems to have understood early in life the affinity of sensuality and death. Many of his own adolescent experiences with love reinforced the ideas he derived from his reading of Romantic literature, especially the idea that death (often by suicide) is inherently akin to romantic love, that *eros* is inevitably linked to *libido* and *thanatos*. Already present in many of Bunin's early works, this *eros-libido-thanatos* linkage is later embodied in some of his best pre-Revolutionary stories (e. g., "The Grammar of Love," "Light Breathing") and in some of his most important works of the twenties and thirties ("Sunstroke," "The Case of Lieutenant Elagin," "The Consecration of Love," *The Life of Arsen'ev*). Romantic love leads directly to death in nearly every story he wrote in the forties, his last decade as an active writer. In the present collection the love-death theme is given detailed treatment in one of the longest stories of Bunin's émigré production, "The Consecration of Love." Quite clearly stated here is the central question of much of Bunin's art, a question that he realized had no definitive answer but had, nonetheless, to be asked: "What is love between man and woman?" Bunin simply does not believe in platonic love, and although he does believe that spiritual feelings can transcend the flesh, he would deny that romantic love can do without carnality. In his view carnality is at the basis of relationships between the sexes since human beings are ruled by natural animal instincts; whatever rational impulses we may have developed over the millenia since we crawled out of the sea in the person of our reptilian ancestors remain subordinate to these instincts. Prometheus hardly exists in the world of Bunin's art; Mother Nature is in control, constantly peering through the windows of the decrepit manor houses where Bunin's protagonists so often live, stretching out her arms to take these her children back into her bosom.

Furthermore, Mother Nature, or, more appropriately in regard to Bunin, the Mother Earth Goddess of ancient Russian folk psychology—*Matushka-syra-zemlja*—is not at all the benevolent type when it comes to love. She is interested only in doing her job, promoting propagation of the species and death, since, in the endless cycle of life, the old must be cleared away as the new are conceived and born. In "The Consecration of Love" Mitya is one of the creatures of the animal world mentioned by his friend Protasov, those who "pay the price of their own being for their first and last act of love." After the Earth Goddess has forced him to do what she has put him on earth for—to copulate—she is ready to absorb him, to mingle his flesh with her own and take him back into the serenity of the moist earth. Most astounding of all (for those of us raised with the philosophical and religious principles of the West) is that Mitya, like many of Bunin's protagonists, is secretly in love with Mother Earth. Subconsciously rejecting all of the precepts of the Enlightenment, Mitya is driven by his instincts to the sacrament of coitus-quietus, to a symbolic copulation (through copulation with woman) with the spirit of the earth, both womb and tomb of all earthly creatures. Bunin, as Freud, believes that *thanatos* exists in the energy of *eros,* that all living things are in mourning for the inorganic state and subconsciously yearning for their original condition of nullity. A Freudian death wish (which, however, he may have derived more from his knowledge of Russian folk psychology and his reading of Eastern religions than from Freud) is firmly ensconced in the souls of many of Bunin's characters, as in the soul of the author, whose fear and hatred of death is tempered by a secret wish to embrace it. The ruttish sensuality of some stories in the *Dark Avenues* collection, written when Bunin was approaching eighty years of age, more likely reflects his subconscious wish to come to terms with approaching death than (as some have suggested) the lascivious efforts of an old man to relive youthful sexual ecstasies in his creative imagination.

One of the strengths of Bunin's art is his willingness to face some of the darkest of contradictions in the human psyche, such as the love-death link and a tendency to fear death and embrace it simultaneously. Love as animal instinct, carnal love often leads to cruelty in the Bunin protagonist, even to such perverse sensuality as that of Sokolovich in "Noosiform Ears." But although he is repelled by Sokolovich's actions, Bunin is not one to shirk the fact, even the necessity, of human sensuality. After all, who, according to Sokolovich, has "noosiform" ears? Not only degenerates, but also artists and geniuses. In certain of his miniature stories, such as "The Idol," "The Calf's Head," and "The Elephant," Bunin dwells upon human animality. But even such a beast as the man putting on a display in the zoo ("The Idol") has slender, beautiful hands that are "completely out of keeping with everything else," and the last word in the story, describing his "flat yellow face" is *lik,* the lofty Old Church Slavic word for face, suggesting a description of a saint in an icon. Perhaps this is irony, but perhaps something more.

Bunin admires, as does Nietzsche, "all those happy, soundly constituted mortals who are far from regarding their precarious balance between beast and angel as an argument against existence." [4] But he himself, like characters such as Mitya, with his upbringing in Western religion and thought, is sometimes unable to accept this precarious balance with equanimity. In his "On the Night Sea" Bunin seems to have annihilated all of his justifications for living. With its leitmotifs "nothing" and "absolutely nothing" the story recalls the "lost generation" of American writers who were in Paris at the same time Bunin lived there. One is reminded of the Lord's Prayer full of *nada* in Hemingway's "A Clean Well-Lighted Place." Bunin seems to be suggesting that, like the collocutors of the story, we are all journeying on a "sea of night," surrounded by senseless emptiness and bound only for an absurd nothingness. Here one finds none of the marvelling joy and ecstatic horror that are the hallmarks of the Bunin story. Fortunately, "On the Night Sea" is an exception to the general tenor of Bunin's work, but the kind of pessimism it manifests explains his lifelong search to find some way to transcend the contradictions of life.

The desire to find exhaltation in the sensuous and sensual is complementary to the desire so clearly expressed in one side of Mitya—to give up the ego, resign oneself to the universal rhythms, and commune with Mother Earth. In a number of stories that reflect his reading of Ecclesiastes and Eastern religions and his knowledge of Russian folk beliefs, Bunin meditates on life's ephemerality and the ultimate dissolution of the flesh. Confronted by the fact of death and the transience of everything material, Gavril ("Transfiguration") follows the path suggested by the Preacher, rejecting earthly striving for advancement and taking joy in the simple pleasures of nature. Bunin is able to allow one of his characters to find such serenity in rejection of the ego, but the semi-autobiographical "Night," another story full of Ecclesiastes, reveals that he himself is always divided between the rejection of the senses and a joyous revelling in the sensual joys of the earth. Probably better than any other work "Night" reveals what Zinaida Gippius called Bunin's "simultaneous acceptance and rejection of life." Characteristic of Bunin's exaltation of the sensual is the ending, where the narrator compares his thirst for life to his lust for the female and cries out to God to be left with the flesh and earth. But even the ending is contradictory since, as discussed above, Bunin's revelling in sensuality and nature reveals his desire to embrace simultaneously the joys of life and the serene consolations of death. The same dichotomy is there in "Night of Denial," in which the message of man's eternal striving for both sensual ecstasy and dissolution of ego is told within a Buddhist context. Once again the message of Ecclesiastes and the East pervades the story titled "Temir-Aksak-Khan," but this story also illustrates a paradox applicable to Ecclesiastes and to much of Bunin's art. As Anthony Burgess has written in a different context, "Here is the old paradox of art. The denial of human joy is made through language which is itself a joy." [5] The whole story is a song like that of the beggar, and the effect on the reader (at least this reader) is the same as the effect of the beggar's song on the young woman: "the despairing grief . . . that lacerates the whole tale is sweeter than the most lofty and passionate joy." While Bunin may sometimes feel despair in the face of art's inadequacies and may even disparage the artistic consciousness (in a story such as "On the Night Sea"), he frequently is able to demonstrate the redeeming qualities of artistic form.

In his refusal to face the inadequacies of life, Bunin found one other refuge—the past. He was a nostalgic writer almost from the start (see, e. g., one of his best early stories, "Antonov Apples"). Born into a family of the declining landed nobility, he idealized the past of his class and complained that he had been born one hundred years too late. Of course, the Revolution and his subsequent emigration to France intensified his feelings of nostalgia. But the traditional life of the gentry was already long gone by 1917, and even had the Revolution never occurred, Bunin would have produced a good many works bemoaning the passing of the old way of life. Two of the stories presented in translation here are, in part, nostalgic evocations of pre-Revolutionary life in Moscow ("Remote," "Indulgent Participation"). Many others, set on the moribund landed estates, concentrate on other themes but have an undertone of longing for the past glory of the gentry. Like "Antonov Apples," "A Passing" is an elegy to the dying landed nobility (actually defunct by the time this story was published in France), one of Bunin's last stories expressing a farewell to his class. "Sempiternal Spring" combines the yearning for return to an idealized bucolic world of the early nineteenth (or even eighteenth) century with absolute revulsion for the twentieth century as embodied in the new Soviet state.

Revulsion and malice are quite characteristic of Bunin. His hatred was directed in particular at the Soviets, who deprived him of his homeland and destroyed the Russia of his past, and at the Modernists in art and literature, who were in vogue in Russia from the 1890's on and who looked upon the "anachronistic" Bunin with contemptuous disdain. His polemics with modernist art often are expressed in his fiction (e. g., in "The Consecration of Love" and "Sempiternal Spring"), and his abhorrence of Dostoevsky, whom he considered the precursor of perverse modernist literary tendencies, underlies the parody of *Crime and Punishment* in "Noosiform Ears." In this story Bunin takes on the whole of the "Petersburg spirit" of Russian literature, including, most prominently, Gogol and Dostoevsky. But his attack on Raskolnikov is rather unconvincing, especially if one takes into account that Dostoevsky had already presented a Sokolovich type (Svidrigailov) in his novel. Bunin is less successful in works where he expresses his personal animosities too forcefully (see also "Sempiternal Spring" and other works excoriating the Soviet regime). In his best stories he has managed to restrain his own strong feelings or to temper them with lyricism. Nor is parody his strong point. But this is not to say that he is unable to create interesting variations on the settings and themes of his predecessors in Russian and world literature. "The Consecration of Love," a polemic with Tolstoy's later works on concupiscence, has strong ties with Goethe's *Faust* and *Werther.* "The Grammar of Love" is one of Turgenev's *Hunter's Sketches* (in a number of details it recalls "Living Relics," in which a different Lushka or Lukerya appears) taken in a different direction, and another of these Turgenev sketches, "The Singers," is the basis for the situation portrayed in "Temir-Aksak-Khan." Even Gogol and Dostoevsky, about whom Bunin once stated that he could not decide which he hated most, find reflection in certain situations and themes of his stories.

Despite his roots in Russian Realism (he revered, above all, Tolstoy and Chekhov), Bunin's prose style is strongly influenced by the Romantic movement. His lavishness may sometimes seem excessive to the modern Western reader since ornate, rhythmic prose is not much in vogue at present. Even before the Revolution sympathetic readers such as Chekhov and Gorky commented unfavorably upon the "density" of Bunin's prose style, his tendency to overload sentences with descriptive detail and his fondness for a profusion of adjectives. Bunin's younger émigré colleague Vladimir Nabokov later described his prose (in *Speak, Memory*) as *"parchovaja proza"* (brocaded prose). The problem of lavishness is compounded by Bunin's fondness for old-fashioned literary devices. He overuses exclamation points, ellipses, romantic catchwords (such as *strashno* and *uzhasno*, 'terrible, awesome, horrible'), and oxymorons ('blissfully horrible,' 'grievously happy,' etc.). Twice in "The Consecration of Love" Mitya's face takes on a "deathly pallor" (*smertel'naja blednost'*). Of course, in this story, as in others, such as "Sempiternal Spring," Bunin has deliberately employed an old-fashioned style. His Mitya, who idealizes the life of his dying class and prefers romantic poets of the early nineteenth century, is himself an anachronism, and the style is in concord with the character. But such archaic stylistic effects can cause problems since an expression like "deathly pallor" may now appear to be ironic. Although Bunin uses irony subtly and effectively in some works (e. g., "Indulgent Participation" and "Light Breathing"), one sometimes has the disturbing feeling that the irony perceived by the reader in certain characters or situations was not intended by the author. In the best of his fiction Bunin is able to overcome or avoid stylistic excesses. Sensing the problem or taking to heart long-standing critical commentary, he tried to temper the lavishness and rhythmic ornateness of his prose in his émigré years. His miniatures (written primarily in 1930 and represented in this collection by "The Hare," "The Cranes," "The Calf's Head," "The Idol," and "The Elephant") exemplify a striving for economy of means; the search for an economical prose continues in the forties with *Dark Avenues*. The style of "The Cold Fall" (from this final collection) is probably as simple as that of any story he wrote. It is modelled on the starkness of the Fet poem from which the story's title is taken, almost as if in his last years Bunin were attempting to utilize the laconic simplicity of much of his own poetry (strongly influenced by Fet) in his prose style.

Throughout his literary career Bunin's themes never really change much, and one aspect of his style also remains predominant even after his attempts to tone down his prose. For want of a better word one must term this aspect his music. A certain musical structure is all-important in Bunin, who once remarked that the essential step for him in writing a story was finding the proper *sound*. He is most successful in works that are quite short since he tends to lose control of the musical tonality as a work becomes longer (although in the long *Dry Valley ((Sukhodol))* and in at least the first four books of *The Life of Arsen'ev* this control is effectively maintained). Perhaps one problem with "The Consecration of Love" is not that it is too long but that it has a lush over-ornate quality similar to what bothers the modern music lover about some nineteenth century Russian Romantic music. Judging by statements he made late in life, Bunin seemed to think that in *Dark Avenues* he had found a musical structure that was in harmony with the complexity and chaos of twentieth century life. But he was mistaken in his assertion that in the late thirties and the forties he made his music do something that exceeded the effect of anything he had previously done. It could be argued that he achieved the ultimate in musical structure much earlier, in the highly productive years between 1910 and the Revolution, when such masterpieces as *Dry Valley* and "Light Breathing" were written. Perhaps a brief analysis of the latter story, which is the epitome of Bunin's best prose, will make clearer what I have in mind when using the terms "music" and "musical structure."

"Light Breathing" treats Bunin's favorite love-death theme in a form that breathes art. Considering its length (only five pages) the story is extremely complex both in theme, tone, and structure. As usual in Bunin, romantic overtones are strong. The story starts out looking like a melodrama, and much of it is indeed melodramatic. There is the jealous Cossack officer, a stock figure in Russian Romantic literature. There is the young man, so "madly in love" with the heroine Olya that he attempts suicide. But, especially, there is the fifteen-year-old Olya herself in her role of *femme fatale.* She mocks the officer and invites him to kill her, just as she has instinctively invited the seduction by Malyutin. But Bunin at his best, like Chekhov, is able to take absurdity or melodrama and mix it with his own subtle ironic effects to produce lyricism and pathos.

The slow and mournful tempo of the early paragraphs, describing the graveyard, ends with a sudden temporal switch. As James Woodward has written, there are "six abrupt changes of temporal perspective" in this brief story,[6] and each of them is associated with a change in the rhythm and tempo. With the return to Olya's early years and description of her blossoming out into young womanhood, the tempo quickens for a time; then comes the description of the beautiful winter, "the strolls along Sobornaya Street" and the skating ("masses of people glissading about that rink in all possible directions"), the kind of long graceful rhythmic passage so typical of Bunin's nostalgic evocations of pre-Revolutionary days (see also, e. g., "Remote"). The leitmotif of utter vitality, which is associated with Olya at various points, is especially vivid in the description of her dashing across the assembly hall, pursued by those "blithefully shrieking first-form girls," only to come to a sudden stop—which prepares for a change of tempo and tone in the next scene, where the style is in harmony with the conventional respectability of the headmistress. After a shocking revelation that ends the scene, Olya's calm admission that she had been seduced, the following paragraphs are full of melodrama. The Cossack officer describes the murder and the diary entry presents the scene of the seduction in Olya's own words. But even in the diary description the absurdity of certain melodramatic details (the silk handkerchief covering her face, the words "Now there's only one way out...") cannot suppress the leitmotif of joyous vivacity so characteristic of Olya.

Another measured and mournful passage signals the return of time to the present, to the cemetery and Olya's form mistress, who visits her grave. Bunin is quite daring to introduce what appears to be an extraneous character near the end of the story, but the form mistress, like the headmistress, proves to be important as a foil for Olya. Each of the three women who appear in the story represents what a woman can make of her life. Perhaps Bunin is suggesting that despite her short life Olya has spent more time actually living than either of the other two, one of whom is steeped in safe conventionality, the other of whom exists in her own imaginary dreamworld. The penultimate temporal switch in the story is the flashback to the living Olya in the conversation that the form mistress has overheard, and, once again, there is a reversion to the rapid tempo full of joyous life. This last long paragraph, Olya's description of "what a woman must have to be truly beautiful," is also one of the most ludicrously romantic in the whole story. But in reading the lively account of sloping shoulders and calves that are "rounded just so" one comes to the final poignant realization that the form mistress has emphasized earlier on: it simply is impossible that someone whose eyes have shone that immortally and whose voice has rung out with such joyous life could be dead. The end of the vitality and of Olya's life is expressed in the coda, a final temporal switch and a final change in the rhythm, one brief sentence that returns to the stately gloom of the beginning.

An attempt at discussing "Light Breathing" in terms of musical movements, transitions, leitmotifs and tempo does not have any scientific exactitude. But there is no doubt that the work, which cries out to be read aloud in the original Russian, has its own peculiar music and derives its artistic power primarily from its musical structure. Even the sounds of certain words have significance. The breath of lovely Olya wafts through the whole story and is still there breathing with the wind at the end. The very title in Russian has a soft respiration in the "kh" sound of each word: "Lyo*kh*oe dy*kh*anie," and this "kh" sound is used effectively at several other points in the story. The name, Olya Mesherskaya, is repeated so often for its sound effects, for the lovely palatalized shushing consonant in the middle of the surname and the soft "l" in "Olya." A certain Soviet critic once made use of a special apparatus for measuring the respiration of those engaged in reading "Light Breathing." The pneumatographic tape of the machine revealed that while reading about murder, torment, death and "all of the horrible things associated with the name of Olya Mesherskaya," the reader was breathing *lightly*, as if respiring in harmony with the respiration of the story. "Light Breathing," of course, is sad, as is much of Bunin's art. But its music makes it somehow *beautifully* sad and recalls the paradox mentioned above: "The denial of human joy is made through language which is itself a joy."

Nearly fifty years after Bunin received the Nobel Prize for literature and nearly thirty years after his death, it is perhaps time for a re-evaluation of his place in Russian literature. Some of the stories presented in this collection may now seem less significant and vibrant than when they were first published. Others still have the artistic force that will make them worth reading for years to come. In my opinion, Bunin stands at a level just below that of the great Russian short story writers of the nineteenth and twentieth centuries (e. g., Chekhov, Babel). But had he been able consistently to create that perfect blend of content and form that one finds in a story such as "Light Breathing," he would certainly rank right beside them.

Robert Bowie
Oxford, Ohio
July, 1981

NOTES

1.   Quoted in *Ivan Bunin. Literaturnoe nasledstvo.* 2 vols. Ed. by V. R. Shcherbina, et al. (M.: Nauka, 1973), I, 41.

2.   Bunin diary note, dated Feb. 3, 1941. *Novyj zhurnal,* No. 113 (1973), 135.

3.   Cited in A. Baboreko, *I. A. Bunin. Materialy dlja biografii* (M.: Khudozhestvennaja literatura, 1967), p. 49.

4.   F. Nietzsche, *The Birth of Tragedy and The Genealogy of Morals,* trans. by Francis Golffing (N. Y.: Doubleday Anchor Books, 1956), pp. 232-33.

5.   *Harper's,* August, 1976, p. 80.

6.   James Woodward, *Ivan Bunin. A Study of His Fiction* (Univ. of North Carolina, 1980), p. 154.

A NOTE ON THE TRANSLATIONS

My choice of stories to be translated is predicated upon theme. I have chosen stories primarily concerned with the "eternal questions" (love, death, art, eternity) and have de-emphasized the socio-political side of Bunin's work. If there is a paucity of the "folk" (narodnyj) aspects here it is not because Bunin's works emphasizing Russian folk psychology are necessarily inferior to his more cosmopolitan works, but because the difficulties of translation are compounded to an incredible degree when the translator is forced to deal with extensive passages of substandard speech or dialect. Certain famous Bunin works ("Sunstroke," Dry Valley, "The Gentleman from San Francisco" and many others) have not been included because they have been frequently and adequately translated in the past or because space prohibits inclusion of all worthy stories in one volume. But "Light Breathing," which has also been translated many times, is included since no Bunin collection, especially a collection emphasizing his love-death theme, should be without a version of this story.

Eleven of the stories in this collection, including all of the miniatures, have never appeared previously in English translation. Many of the others were translated into English during Bunin's lifetime and before he himself made revisions of these same stories. I have taken as the definitive Russian version his final revision of each story. In one instance Bunin also changed the title of a story that had already appeared in English ("Night," formerly titled "Cicadas"). Therefore, many of the stories appear here in their final revised form for the first time in English. Only in one case does my title in English differ significantly from Bunin's Russian title. The Consecration of Love is a translation of Mitina ljubov', literally Mitya's Love, a title that is too pedestrian in English for such an ornate romantic work. I have based my title on the French Le sacrement de l'amour, which Bunin once said he preferred to his own Russian title.

In my translations I have attempted to remain as faithful to the original as possible within the bounds of English style and syntax. I have resisted the urge to tone down Bunin's lavish prose, even in instances where the ornateness of lexicon or the long intricate flow may seem excessive in English. I have also attempted to find suitable English equivalents for certain archaic Russian locutions that are such an important part of Bunin's style. Although I have made desperate efforts to retain the sentence structure, I have been obliged to break up some of the longer passages with semicolons or periods in instances where the English syntax simply could not bear to continue without a rest. In dealing with the insoluble problem of translating peasant or substandard locutions, I have chosen a language close to that spoken in the rural areas of the Southern United States. Although this may jar the aesthetic sensibilities of my readers in Yorkshire, Sydney, Toronto, Omsk, Atomsk, and Brooklyn, I would prefer to have Russian peasants speak a language that somehow suggests they have spent time in the American South than a neutral language that suggests they live in a bland world that really does not exist anywhere. After all, reading a translation always involves a certain "suspension of disbelief" since the Russians in a Russian story are not only incapable of speaking Southern American dialect—they are incapable of speaking any sort of English.

The Russian source for all translations is Ivan Bunin, Sobranie sochinenij v devjati tomakh (M., 1965-67). In case of certain inconsistencies, omissions, or misprints in this source, I have checked other sources and incorporated the necessary changes in the translations.

FIRST LOVE

Summer. An estate in a forested western province.

Torrents of fresh rain all day long, its unremitting din on the plank roof. Murk, dreariness in the hushed manor house; flies asleep on the ceiling. Beneath a flowing acqueous mesh the wet trees in the garden droop submissively, and the red flowerbeds by the terrace are uncommonly vivid. Conspicuous in the hazy sky above the garden, a stork bustles about apprehensively. Now grown dark and thin, his tail tucked under, rectricial plume sagging, he stands on the edge of his nest in the crown of a centenarian birch, in a fork between its bare white boughs, indignant, agitated, fluttering up and down, and periodically he gives the trunk a solid clatter with his bill, making a dull sound that seems to say: "What on earth is going on? It's a deluge, an utter deluge!"

But then, at about four, the sky becomes brighter, the rain sparser. A samovar is set in the passageway leading to the veranda; the balsamic odor of smoke creeps over all the estate.

And before sunset the skies have cleared. Silence, tranquility. The masters and those who have come for a visit go out into the pine forest for a stroll.

By now the blue of twilight is glowing.

In corridors cut through the forest, spread with yellow conifer needles, the paths are moist and resilient. The forest is fragrant, damp and resonant. Someone's distant voice, someone's long-protracted call or response reverberates marvelously in the far distant thickets. These corridors seem narrow, the vistas where they end are shapely, infinite, captivating in their twilight remoteness. The pine timberland surrounding them is majestically vast, dark, cramped; the mast-like boles of trees are bare and smooth, red at their crowns; down below they are grey, scabrous, mossy, intermingled one with another: mosses, lichens, boughs covered with rot and with something else that hangs down like the greenish frowzy manes of woodland ogres in fairy tales, all of this forms a labyrinth, creates a vague aura of savage Russian antiquity. When emerging into a glade, one delights in the young pine shoots. They have a lovely pallid hue, a verdure delicate and marshy, slender but vigorous, with many branchings; still covered with tiny drops of rain and fine acqueous dust, they seem to be draped in a silvery Indian muslin laced with sequins...

Two figures dashed out ahead of the strollers that evening, a small schoolboy-cadet and a big amiable dog; they kept frolicking about, romping after one another. And amidst the strollers sedately, gracefully promenaded a girl who was not quite adolescent, with long arms and legs, wearing a lightweight, cheap plaid coat that for some reason was very endearing. Everyone was grinning—they knew why he was doing all that dashing about, frolicking

1

so incessantly and feigning joy, the young cadet, who was on the verge of bursting into tears of despair. The girl also knew, and she felt proud, contented. But the look on her face was cool and fastidious.

1930

THE GRAMMAR OF LOVE

One day in early June a certain Ivlev was travelling to a distant region of his province.

He had borrowed a tarantass with a dusty skewed hood from his brother-in-law, at whose estate he was spending the summer. In the village he had hired a troika of small but sedulous horses with thick matted manes from a wealthy muzhik. His driver was that muzhik's son, a lad of about eighteen, vacant, pragmatical; he kept pondering something morosely, seemed somehow offended, had no sense of humor. Convinced that talking with him was impossible, Ivlev began observing his surroundings in that placid and aimless state of mind that goes so well with the beat of hooves and the hollow jangle of harness bells.

The drive was pleasant at first. The day was warm, dingy, the road quite smooth, the meadowlands profuse with flowers and skylarks; from the grain, from the low dove-blue rye stretching as far as the eye could see, a pleasant breeze was blowing over the sloping land, bearing pollen dust that occasionally clouded the air, so that from a distance everything looked hazy. The lad sat erect in his new cap and ill-fitting lustrine jacket. Because the horses had been entrusted entirely to him and because he was so smartly dressed, his mien was especially grave. The horses snorted, trotted along leisurely; the whiffletree of the outrunner on the left would scrape against the wheel, then stretch back out, while beneath it the white steel of a worn shoe kept flashing.

"Stopping off at the count's?" asked the lad without turning around as a village came into view up ahead of them, ringing the horizon with its willow trees and garden.

"What for?" said Ivlev.

The lad was silent for a moment; with his whip he flicked off a large gadfly clinging to one of the horses, then answered somberly:

"To have some tea."

"Tea's not what's on your mind," said Ivlev. "You're always trying to spare the horses."

"It ain't travelling ruins a horse—it's feed," the lad answered in a preceptoral tone.

Ivlev looked around. The weather had turned bleaker, discolored clouds had gathered on all sides, and now it was sprinkling; these unpretentious days always wind up with a violent downpour... An old man ploughing near the village said that the young countess was the only one at home, but they stopped off all the same. Content that the horses were resting, the lad pulled a cloth coat over his shoulders and sat placidly soaking on the driver's seat of the tarantass, which stood in the middle of the muddy yard near a stone trough that was sunk into ground studded with cattle hooves. He examined his boots, adjusted the breeching of the shaft horse with his whipstock. Meanwhile, in a drawing room that was murky from the rain outside, Ivlev sat chatting with the countess and waiting for tea. From the veranda came a scent of burning shavings, and past the open windows floated thick green smoke from the samovar, into which a barefoot wench had poured kerosene over bundles of wood chips, which now burned with bright-red flames. The countess was wearing a capacious pink dressing gown cut low over her powdered bosom; she smoked, inhaling deeply; she patted her hair frequently, baring her firm, rotund arms to the shoulders. Inhaling the smoke and laughing, she kept leading the conversation around to love, and apropos of this she mentioned her neighbor, the landowner Khvoshinsky, who, as Ivlev had known since childhood, had been mad with love for his chambermaid Lushka throughout his entire life, although she had died in early youth. "Ah, the legendary Lushka!" Ivlev remarked facetiously, slightly disconcerted by what he was about to confess. "Because of the way that eccentric worshipped her and dedicated all his life to insane dreams of her, I myself was almost in love with her as a boy; God only knows what fancies came into my head when I thought about her, although they say she was certainly no beauty."

"Indeed?" said the countess, not listening. "He died this very winter. And Pisarev—the only one he allowed to visit him, because they were old friends—affirms that in every other way he was not the least bit mad; and I'm convinced of it—he simply wasn't one to be compared with today's lot..." Finally, the barefoot wench came in; scrupulously careful of her every movement, she served him a glass of strong gray tea and a small basket of fly-specked tea bisquits on an old silver tray.

When they started off again, the rain came down in torrents. The hood had to be raised, and Ivlev had to sit in a hunched position, covered with the corneous, shriveled apron. Bells on the horses' necks were clinking, emitting a hollow din; little streams ran over their dark and glistening haunches. With grass rustling under the wheels, they passed some sort of boundary amidst the grain, through which the lad had driven in hopes of shortening the way; warm, rye-scented air gathered beneath the hood, blending with the smell of the old tarantass... So that's how things are—Khvoshinsky has died, thought Ivlev. I absolutely must stop in, at least for a look at that deserted shrine of the mysterious Lushka... But what sort of man was this Khvoshinsky? Was he insane or was he simply overwhelmed, completely absorbed by a single fixation? According to the stories of old landowners, the contemporaries of Khvoshinsky, at one time people in the province had considered him a man of rare intelligence. But all at once he was stricken with this love, this Lushka; then came her sudden death, and everything went to pieces. He secluded himself in the house, in the room where Lushka had lived and died, and spent more than twenty years sitting on her bed; not only did he never go out anywhere, but even on his own estate no one ever saw him. He sat on Lushka's mattress till it wore right through, he ascribed literally all phenomena in the world to Lushka's influence. If there was a thunderstorm, it was Lushka who had

4

visited this affliction upon them; if war was declared, it meant Lushka had so decided; in the event of a crop failure—the peasants had incurred the displeasure of Lushka...

"You're driving to Khvoshinskoe, are you?" called Ivlev, putting his head out in the rain.

"Yes," responded the boy, from whose drooping cap the water was streaming; his answer was indistinct through the din of the rain. "Up along Pisarev Hill..."

Ivlev knew of no such road. Provincial hamlets were becoming ever more impoverished and more remote. The boundary came to an end; going at a walk, the horses drew the tilting tarantass down by way of an eroded furrow to the bottom of the hill—into some still unmown meadows whose green slopes stood out dolefully against the low clouds. Then the road, which kept fading away and reappearing, began to wind back and forth across the bottoms of ravines, through gullies full of alder bushes and osiers... Someone's little apiary came into view, several logs standing on a slope in the tall grass, through which wild red strawberries gleamed... They detoured around an old dam, immersed in nettles, and a pond that had dried up long ago—a deep hollow grown over with weeds taller than a man... A pair of black snipe darted out of these weeds screeching and flew up into the rainy sky... Upon the dam, among the nettles, a massive old bush blossomed with little pale-pink flowers—that charming shrub called "God's tree"—and suddenly Ivlev recalled the locality and remembered that as a youth he had often ridden in this area on horseback...

"They say right here is where she drownded herself," remarked the lad abruptly.

"You're talking about Khvoshinsky's mistress, aren't you?" asked Ivlev. "That's not true; she did nothing of the kind."

"No, she did, she drownded herself," said the lad. "Only they think he most likely went crazy from being so poor, not on account of her..."

After a brief silence he added brusquely: "We'll have to stop off again... at this here Khvoshino... Just look how them horses is wore out!"

"So we must," agreed Ivlev.

Tin-colored with rain water, the road led to a knoll, to a spot where the trees had been cleared; a solitary hut stood there, amidst sodden, rotting wood chips and leaves, amidst stumps and vernal aspen shoots smelling bitter and crisp. There was not a soul around, only the birds sitting in the rain on tall flowers, yellow buntings, whose song rang throughout the sparse forest that rose beyond the hut; but when the troika, slushing through the mud, came even with the threshold, a whole pack of gigantic hounds, black, chocolate, smoke-grey, tore out from somewhere barking ferociously and began seething around the horses, soaring right up to their muzzles, somersaulting in the air, even gyrating under the very hood of the tarantass. Just as abruptly the sky above them was split at that very moment by a deafening peal of thunder; in a frenzy the lad began flailing the dogs with his whip, and the horses rushed off at a full gallop amidst aspen trunks, which went flashing past Ivlev's eyes...

5

Now the Khvoshinskoe estate could be seen beyond the forest. The dogs dropped behind and immediately fell silent, loping back earnestly; the forest parted and once again open fields stretched before them. As evening began to set in, the storm clouds seemed to be now dispersing, now gathering from three sides: on the left they were nearly black, with light blue apertures; on the right they were gray, rumbling with unremitting thunder; and to the west, beyond the Khvoshinsky manor, beyond the slopes above the river vale, they were turbid-blue, with dusty bands of rain through which distant mounds of other clouds showed pink. But the rain on the tarantass was slackening, and Ivlev rose, all spattered with mud; with a feeling of pleasure he threw back the cumbersome hood and drew in a long deep breath of air, redolent with the dampness of the fields.

He gazed at the approaching estate, seeing at last what he had heard so much about, and, just as before, it seemed that Lushka had lived and died not twenty years ago, but almost in times immemorial. All trace of the shallow little river that ran through the vale was lost in cattails, above which a white gull was gliding. Farther along, on a sloping hillock, there were rows of hay, soaked dark by the rain; old silver poplars were scattered among them, standing far apart one from another. On an absolutely bare spot stood the house with its glistening wet roof, a rather large house, which had once been white. There were neither gardens nor outbuildings—only two brick columns where the gates had been and burdocks growing in the ditches. When the horses had forded the stream and climbed the hill, a woman in a man's summer jacket with drooping pockets appeared, driving some turkey hens through the bur-docks. The facadè of the house was uncommonly bleak: there were not many windows, and all of them were undersized, set within the thick walls. By con-trast, the dismal verandas were enormous. From one of them a young man in a gray *gymnasium* blouse girded with a wide belt was peering down at the visitors in astonishment; he was dark, with beautiful eyes, very handsome, although his face was pale and freckled, mottled like a bird's egg.

The visit had to be explained somehow. Having ascended the steps of the veranda and introduced himself, Ivlev said that he wanted to examine and perhaps to buy the library, which, according to the countess, Khvoshinsky had owned; the young man blushed deeply and immediately led him into the house. So this is the son of illustrious Lushka! thought Ivlev, drinking in everything with his eyes as he walked, often glancing back, saying whatever came to mind just to have another look at the master of the house, who appeared too youthful for his years. The latter answered hurriedly but laco-nically, nonplussed, it seemed, both by his bashfulness and greed. He was terribly happy at the prospect of selling the books and assumed they would bring a fine price; this was evident from his very first words, from his quick awkward declaration that it was impossible to acquire such books as these for any amount of money. He led Ivlev through a half-dark passage, spread with straw that was rust-red from the dampness, into a large anteroom.

"So is this where your father lived?" asked Ivlev, entering and taking off his hat.

"Yes, yes, here," the young man answered hurriedly. "That is, of course, not here... Father sat in the bedroom most of the time... but, of course, he came in here too..."

"Yes, I know; he was ill," said Ivlev.

The young man flushed.

"How do you mean, ill?" he said, and his voice acquired a more resolute tone. "That's all gossip; father was certainly not mentally ill in any way... He just read all the time and didn't go out anywhere, that's all... No, please don't take off your hat; it's cold in here; we no longer use this part of the house..."

Indeed, it was much colder in the house than outside. In the dreary anteroom, papered with old gazettes, a quail cage made of bast stood on the sill of the window, to which the storm clouds gave a sombre cast. A little gray bag was hopping along the floor all by itself. Stooping over, the young man caught it and put it on a bench, and Ivlev realized that there was a quail in the bag. Then they went into the parlour. This room, which had windows facing west and north, occupied nearly half of the entire house. Through one window a centenarian weeping birch was visible, all black, standing out against the gold of the ever clearer evening glow beyond the storm clouds. The whole front corner was occupied by an icon case without glass, full of icons that were hung or set within it. Prominent among them, both for size and antiquity, was an icon in a silver mounting; on top of it, all waxy yellow like dead flesh, lay some wedding candles tied with pale-green bows.

"Excuse me, please," began Ivlev, overcoming his sense of impropriety. "Did your father really..."

"No, that's right," the young man mumbled, understanding him immediately. "It was only after her death that father bought those candles... He even wore a wedding band all the time..."

The furniture in the parlour was roughhewn. But along the wall there were beautiful cabinets, packed with tea china and tall, slender, gold-rimmed goblets. The entire floor was incrusted with dead withered bees that crackled underfoot. Bees were also strewn about over the drawing room, which was absolutely empty. When they had crossed this and yet another gloomy room with stove and sleeping ledge, the young man stopped beside a low door and took a huge key from his trousers pocket. Turning it with great effort in the rusty keyhole, he thrust open the door and muttered something. Ivlev saw a tiny cell with two windows. By one wall stood a bare iron cot, by the other two small bookcases of Karelian birch.

"So is this the library?" asked Ivlev, walking up to one of them. Hastening to answer affirmatively, the young man helped him open the bookcase, then began avidly observing every movement of his hands.

That library contained the most bizarre of books! Ivlev opened the thick covers, turned the rough gray pages, and read: *The Accursed Demesne...*

The Morning Star and Nocturnal Daemons... Meditations Upon the Mysteries of the Universe... A Wondrous Peregrination into an Enchanted Realm... The Latest Dream Book... But his hands, nonetheless, were trembling. So this is what he had lived on, the lonely creature who had secluded himself forever from the world in this cell and only so recently had left it... But perhaps he, this creature, had not been entirely insane? "There is a state..." Ivlev recalled the lines of Baratynsky: "There is a state, but by what name shall it be called? Nor dream is it, nor wake, it lies somewhere between. Through it, the mind's dementia may verge upon the truth..."

It had cleared in the west; gold peered from behind the beautiful lilac-tinged clouds and strangely illumined this humble asylum of love, incomprehensible love, which had transmuted a whole human life into some rapturous state of existence, a life perhaps destined to be most commonplace, if not for a certain fascinating, enigmatic Lushka...

Taking a bench from beneath the cot, Ivlev sat down in front of the bookcase and took out his cigarettes, imperceptibly examining the room and committing it to memory.

"Do you smoke?" he asked the young man standing over him.

The latter blushed again.

"Yes," he mumbled and attempted to smile. "That is, I don't really smoke; rather, I sometimes indulge myself... But then, if I may, much obliged to you..."

When he had taken a cigarette clumsily and lit it with trembling hands, he stepped over to the window and sat down on the sill, obstructing the yellow light of the evening glow.

"And what is this?" asked Ivlev, bending down to the middle shelf, which contained only one slender volume, resembling a prayer book, and a jewelry case, its corners finished in silver that was tarnished with time.

"It's just... The necklace of my late mother is in that case," answered the young man, stammering but trying to speak casually.

"May I take a look?"

"Certainly... although it really is quite plain... it couldn't be of interest to you..."

Opening the jewelry case, Ivlev saw a frayed bit of cord, a chaplet of cheap, pale-blue beads, made of some material resembling stone. And when he looked at those beads, which once had lain on the neck of the woman who was fated to be so loved, whose nebulous image now could be nothing less than beautiful, he was overwhelmed by such emotional agitation that his heart beat uncontrollably and everything went black before his eyes. After a long, long look, Ivlev carefully put the jewelry case back in its place; then he picked up the book. Tiny, beautifully printed almost one hundred years before, it was entitled *The Grammar of Love, or The Art of Loving and of Being Loved in Return.*

"That book, unfortunately, I cannot sell," uttered the young man with an effort. "It's very dear... Father even used to sleep with it under his pillow..."

"But perhaps you'll at least allow me to glance through it?" said Ivlev.

"Certainly," he whispered.

Overcoming his constraint, vaguely tormented by the young man's fixed gaze, Ivlev began leafing slowly through *The Grammar of Love*. It was divided into short chapters: "Of Beauty, Of the Heart, Of the Mind, Of Amorous Signs, Of Fervent Wooing and Resistance, Of Disunion and Reconciliation, Of Platonic Love..." Each chapter consisted of brief, elegant, at times very subtle maxims; some of them were delicately marked in pen, with red ink. "Love is no mere Episode in our Lives," Ivlev read. "Our Reason gainsays the Heart, but the Latter is not persuaded." "Never is Woman so strong as when She arms Herself with Debility." "We worship Woman because She holds Sovereignty over our Ideal Dream." "Vainglory chooses, True Love never chooses." "The Woman of Beauty is relegated to a secondary Station; first belongs to the Woman of Grace. She becomes the Sovereign of our Hearts; ere we ourselves take Cognizance, our Hearts have become Thralls of Love for All Time..." Then came "An Explication of the Language of Flowers"; once again some passages were marked: "Wild Poppy—Sorrow; Spindle Shrub—Thy Charm is engraved in my Heart; Periwinkle—Sweet Reminiscences; Sombre Geranium—Spleen; Wormwood—Bitterness Eternal..." In small, minute script on a blank page at the very end there was a four-line stanza in the same red ink. Craning his neck to look into *The Grammar of Love,* the young man said with a forced sneer:

"Father composed that himself..."

A half-hour later Ivlev said good-bye to him with a sense of relief. Of all the books, he had bought, at a very high price, only this one slender volume. In clouds beyond the fields the turbid-golden evening glow grew faint, its gleam mirrored in puddles; the fields were wet and green. The lad was in no hurry, but Ivlev did not urge him on. The lad was saying that the woman driving turkey hens through the burdocks was the deacon's wife and that young Khvoshinsky was living with her. Ivlev was not listening. He thought only of Lushka, of her necklace, which had left him with a complex feeling, like the feeling he once had experienced in an Italian village as he gazed at the relics of a female saint. She has come into my life forever! he thought. And taking *The Grammar of Love* from his pocket, he slowly reread by the light of the evening glow the poem written on its last page:

> Lovers' hearts will say unto Thee:
> "Live in sweet dream-realms above!"
> And to the grandchild of years yet to be
> They will show this selfsame *Grammar of Love.*

Moscow. February, 1915.

THE MAD ARTIST

The sun glittered golden in the east, beyond the hazy blue of remote forests, beyond the white snowy flatland upon which an ancient Russian city gazed from a low bank of mountains. It was Christmas Eve, a robust morning with temperature just below freezing and a mantle of rime frost.

The Petrograd train had just arrived. Up the hill from the railway station, along the smoothly packed snow, stretched a queue of cabmen, with passengers and without.

The large old hotel on that spacious square opposite the old outdoor bazaar was quiet and empty, tidied up for the holiday. Guests were not expected. But a gentleman in a pince-nez rode up to the veranda, a man with startled eyes, in a black velvet beret with greenish curls falling from beneath it, in a long paletot of sparkling chestnut fur.

The red-beard on the coachbox let out an affected wheeze, wishing to demonstrate that he was frozen through, that he deserved a bit extra. The passenger paid no attention, leaving it up to the hotel to settle with him.

"Take me to your very brightest room," he said loudly as he walked with magisterial stride down the wide corridor, following the young bellboy who carried his expensive foreign valise. "I'm an artist," he said, "but this time I do not want a room facing north. By no means!"

The boy threw open the door to number one, the luxury suite, which included a vestibule and two capacious rooms but had windows that were small and very deep, because of the thick walls. It was warm, cozy and tranquil in those rooms, amber with the sunlight that was tempered by rime frost on the lower windowpanes. Gingerly setting down the valise on a carpet in the middle of the front room, the bellboy, a young lad with merry intelligent eyes, stood waiting for the passport and for further instructions. The artist, small of stature, youthfully nimble in spite of his age, in beret and velvet jacket, paced from corner to corner; letting the pince-nez fall with a movement of his brows, he rubbed his pale harrowed face with white, seemingly alabaster hands. Then he cast a strange glance at the hotel employee with the unseeing eyes of a very nearsighted and absentminded man.

"The twenty-fourth of December, nineteen hundred sixteen!" he said. "You must remember that date!"

"Yes sir," answered the boy.

From the side pocket of his jacket the artist removed a gold watch, and screwing up one eye, he took a quick look at it.

"Exactly half past nine," he continued, once more adjusting the lenses on his nose. "I've nearly reached the goal of my pilgrimage. Glory to God on high and on earth peace, goodwill toward men! I'll give you the passport, don't worry; right now I can't concern myself with passports. I haven't one single moment to spare. I must complete the crowning work of all my life. My young friend," he said, stretching out a hand toward the boy and showing him two wedding rings, of which one, on the little finger, was a woman's. "That ring represents a deathbed injunction!"

"As you say, sir," answered the bellboy.

"And I will obey that injunction!" said the artist in a menacing tone. "I will paint an immortal work! And I will give it—unto thee."

"We thank you most humbly," answered the boy.

"But, my dear fellow, the fact is I've brought with me neither canvas nor paints—because of that monstrous war it was utterly impossible to get them through. I hope to acquire them here. At last I shall incarnate everything that drove me out of my mind for all of two years and that later was so marvelously transfigured in Stockholm!"

Continuing to speak, rapping out the words, the artist glared through his pince-nez straight at his collocutor.

"The whole world must know and understand that revelation, those joyous tidings!" he exclaimed with a theatrical wave of his hand. "Do you hear? The whole world! Everyone!"

"All right, sir," answered the boy. "I'll report it to the manager."

The artist put on his paletot once again and made for the door. At breakneck speed the boy dashed to open it. The artist nodded to him pompously and strode off down the corridor. On the landing of the stairwell he paused and added:

"In all the world, my friend, there's no holiday more lofty than Christmas. There's no sacrament that can equal the birth of a child. The final gasp of an old, bloody world! A new man is born!"

The dawnlight outside had dissipated, the streets were full of sunshine. Already beginning to crumble, granulate, the rime frost on telegraph lines stood out against the pale-blue sky with a delicate, dove-grey hue. Clustered together on the square was a whole forest of thick, dark-green Christmas firs. At butcher shops stood frozen white carcasses of naked pigs with deep slits on their stout napes; grey hazel-grouse were hanging there, plucked geese, turkeys plump and stiffened. Conversing one with another, pedestrians hurried along, cabmen whipped up their shaggy nags, sleigh runners squealed.

"I know thee, *Rus!*" said the artist loudly, striding through the square and looking at the tightly girded, stoutly attired, robust hucksters and market women, who were shouting out beside stands that held homemade wooden toys and large white gingerbread cakes in the form of steeds, roosters, and fish.

He hailed an empty cab and asked to be driven to the main street.

"And make it fast; by eleven I must be back home working," he said, seating himself in the cold sleigh and placing the heavy, indurated rug across his knees.

The cabman's cap gave a nod, and the small well-fed gelding set off at a rapid pace along the sparkling, smooth-pressed road.

"Faster, faster!" repeated the artist. "At twelve o'clock the sunlight will be at its brightest. Yes," he said, looking around, "familiar places, but thoroughly forgotten! What's that piazza called?"

"How's that, sir?" asked the cabman.

"I'm asking you what's the name of that square!" shouted the artist in a sudden frenzy. "Stop, you scoundrel! Why have you brought me to a chapel? I'm afraid of churches and chapels! Stop! You know, when a certain Finn once drove me to a cemetery, I immediately wrote letters to the king and the Pope and he was sentenced to death! Take me back!"

The cabman reined in the careering horse and cast a bewildered glance at his passenger.

"But where is it you want? You said Main Street..."

"I told you—to a store that has art supplies!"

"You might better hire you another cab, your honor; you got me all confounded."

"Well go straight to hell then! Here, take your pieces of silver!"

And the artist climbed awkwardly out of the sleigh, tossed a three-rouble note at the cabman and walked off in the opposite direction, down the middle of the street. His paletot had come open and was trailing through the snow, his eyes, full of suffering and dismay, wandered from side to side. When he noticed some strips of gilded trimming in a shop window, he hastily entered the store. But he had scarcely begun asking about paints when the rubicund young lady, who sat at the cashier's booth in a short fur coat, interrupted him:

"No, no, we don't handle any paints. We have only window frames, decorative trimmings, and wallpaper. But then, you're hardly likely to find a canvas and oil paints anywhere in our city."

In genuine desperation the artist clasped his temples with both hands.

"My God, is that true? Ah, how horrible! Now and precisely now the paints are a question of life and death! As early as Stockholm my idea had ripened completely, and when it becomes incarnate it will surely make an unparalleled impression. I must depict the grotto in Bethlehem, the Birth of Christ, and must imbue the whole painting—the manger, and the Child, and the Madonna, and the lion and lamb reclining together—side by side!—with such exultation of angels, with such light, so that verily this shall be the birth of a new man. Only I shall have it set in Spain, the land of our first trip, our wedding journey. In the distance—blue mountains, blossoming trees on hills, against broad celestial expanses..."

"Excuse me, sir," said the young lady in a frightened tone—"there may be customers coming in. We have only frames, trimmings, and wallpapering..."

The artist flinched, then raised his beret with exaggerated politeness:

"Ah, for the love of God forgive me! You're right, a thousand times right!"

And he walked out hastily.

A few buildings down the street, in the store called "Educational Aids," he bought a very large sheet of rough pasteboard, colored pencils, and water colors on a palette made of paper. Then he leaped into another cab and urged the driver on, back to the hotel. In the hotel he immediately rang the callbell; the same boy appeared. The artist was holding his passport in both hands.

"Here!" he said, extending it toward the boy. "Render what is Caesar's unto Caesar. And after that, my dear fellow, you must bring me a glass of water for my aquarelles. Oil paints, alas, are nowhere to be found. The war! The Iron Age! The Age of the Troglodyte!"

After thinking for a moment, he suddenly beamed with rapture:

"But what a day! Lord, what a day! At exactly midnight the Saviour is born! The Saviour of the world! That's how I'll title the picture: Birth of the New Man! I'll base the Madonna on her whose name from this day forth shall be sanctified. I shall resurrect her, she who was murdered by the evil spirit together with the new life she bore beneath her heart!"

Once again the bellboy expressed his earnest readiness to be of service and departed. But a few minutes later, when he came back with a glass and a carafe of fresh water, the artist was sleeping soundly. His pale and thin face resembled an alabastrine mask. He lay supine on a bed in the second room, high atop the pillows, his head cast back, his long grey-green hair in disarray, and even his breathing was inaudible. The boy withdrew on tiptoe; outside the door he encountered the manager, a squat man with sharp eyes and short hair brushed up on the crown of his head.

"Well, what's going on?" asked the manager in a hasty whisper.

"Asleep," answered the boy.

"Will wonders never cease!" said the manager. "And his passport's in order. There's just one notation to the effect that his wife passed on. Ivan Matveich phoned from the police, ordered us to keep an eye on him. You be on your guard now, look sharp. It's wartime, brother."

"He said, 'I'll present it to you; just let me get the thing done,' " said the boy. "He doesn't ask for a samovar..."

"There, there you see!" took up the manager and stuck his ear against the door.

But on the other side of the door all was quiet; there was only the aura of melancholy that always pervades the room of a sleeping person.

The sun slowly receded from the hotel suite. Then it was gone completely. The rime on the windows had turned grey, had become dreary. The artist suddenly awoke in twilight and rushed at once to the callbell.

"This is horrible!" he screamed as soon as the boy appeared. "You did not awaken me! Whereas precisely for this very day did we undertake our terrible Odyssey. Just imagine what it was like for her, in her eighth month of pregnancy! We passed through a thousand obstacles of all sorts, didn't sleep, didn't eat for nearly six weeks. And the sea! And the berserk pitching of the boat! And that incessant fear that at any moment you may be blown to pieces. 'Everyone up on deck! Ready the life preservers! First man to run for the lifeboat against orders gets his skull smashed!' "

13

"As you say, sir," said the boy, who was nonplussed by those strident cries.

"But what joyous light there was!" continued the artist, calming down. "With the frame of mind I was in just now, I'd have finished my work in two or three hours. But what's to be done! I'll work through the night. Just help me get a few things ready. That table, now, might do..."

He walked up to the table in front of the divan, pulled the velvet covering away, and gave it a shake:

"It stands quite steady. But listen now—you have only two candles here. You must bring eight more; otherwise I cannot paint. I need light in great profusion!"

The boy left again and returned after a long absence with seven candles in a variety of candlesticks.

"We're one short; they're all being used in the rooms," he said.

Once again the artist became agitated, started screaming again.

"Ah, how vexing that is! I needed ten, ten of them! Obstructions at every step, base treachery! At least help me to move this table, into the very middle of the room. We'll augment the light with reflections from the mirror..."

The bellboy dragged the table to the designated spot and set it firmly in place.

"Now it must be spread with something of a white color, which won't assimilate the light," muttered the artist, awkwardly helping out, dropping his pince-nez and putting it back on. "What could we use? I'm afraid of white tablecloths... That's it, my stack of newspapers; I had the foresight not to discard them!"

He opened the valise lying on the floor, removed several issues of a newspaper, covered the table, fastened the paper down with tacks, laid out his pencils and palette, set the nine candles in a row and lit them all. With that plethora of flames the room took on a strange, festive, but also ominous aura. The windows had gone black. Candlelight was reflected in the mirror above the divan, casting a bright golden glow on the grave white face of the artist and the young, perplexed face of the boy. When everything was finally in order, the bellboy withdrew deferentially to the threshold and asked:

"Will you be dining with us or elsewhere?"

The artist smiled bitterly and theatrically:

"The child! He fancies that I could eat at such a moment! Go in peace, my friend. You will not be required again until morning."

And the bellboy made a discreet departure.

Hours flowed by. The artist paced from corner to corner. He said to himself, "I must get prepared." Outside his windows was the blackness of the frosty winter night. He lowered the blinds. All was silent in the hotel. Out in the corridor, on the other side of the door, cautious, furtive steps could be heard; they were spying on the artist through the keyhole, eavesdropping. Then even the sounds of footsteps dwindled away. The candles blazed, their flames quavering, reflected in the mirror. The artist's face was becoming more and more haggard.

"No!" he suddenly shouted, coming to an abrupt stop. "First I must reconstitute her features in my memory. Away with this childish fear!"

He leaned over to the valise, long hair drooping down. Thrusting a hand beneath his linens, he pulled out a large white velvet album, then took a seat in an armchair by the table. Opening the album, he threw back his head resolutely and proudly and froze in contemplation.

In the album there was a large photographic print: the interior of some empty chapel, with arches and sparkling walls of smooth stone. In the middle of the room, on a bier covered by the funereal pall, stretched a long coffin, containing a thin woman with eyelids closed and protuberant. Her narrow and beautiful head was encircled by a garland of flowers; her crossed arms rested high upon her breast. At the head of the coffin stood three ecclesiastical candle-holders, at the foot—another, tiny coffin holding an infant, who resembled a doll.

The artist peered intently at the sharp features of the dead woman. Suddenly his face was distorted with horror. He threw the album on the rug, jumped up and rushed over to his valise. He dug everything out of it, to the very bottom, scattered his shirts, stockings and ties on the floor... No, what he was seeking was not to be found! He looked all about in desperation, rubbed his forehead...

"Half my life for a brush!" he exclaimed hoarsely, stamping his foot. "I forgot, forgot, miserable wretch! Find one! Work a miracle!"

But there was no brush. He fumbled in his pockets, found a penknife, and went running to his paletot... Would he be able to cut off a piece of the fur and tie it to a pen or to a sliver of wood? But where could he get some thread? Middle of the night, everyone's sleeping... they'd take him for a madman! And in a frenzy he snatched the pasteboard from the divan, hurled it on the table, ran into the bedroom for some pillows, placed them on the armchair to make a higher sitting position, and seizing first one colored pencil, then another, he became utterly engrossed in his task.

He worked without respite. He removed his pince-nez and bent low over the table, set down forceful and confident strokes, flung himself back, fixing his eyes on the mirror, whose bright haze was full of quavering, parti-colored flames. The hair on the artist's temples was soaked from the heat of the candles, the veins in his neck were swollen with nervous tension. His eyes were watery and glittering, his facial features sharpened.

At last he saw that the sheet of pasteboard was hopelessly ruined—crammed with absurd and garish drawings that were completely contrary one to another in both inner substance and meaning. The feverish inspiration of the artist was completely out of control, was doing exactly what he did not want done. He turned the pasteboard over, grabbed a blue pencil, and stood motionless for a short time. The open album lay beside his armchair. The long coffin and dead visage in that album persistently diverted his attention. With vehement force he slammed the album shut. Sticking out from beneath the linen in his valise was a flask of cologne in a plaitwork covering. He jumped up, quickly unscrewed its top, and began drinking, burning himself with the liquid. Having emptied almost all of the flask, panting from the effects of that aromatic flame, his throat on fire, he began striding about the room once more.

Soon a youthful energy took possession of him—bold resoluteness, confidence in his every thought, in his every feeling, an awareness that he was capable of anything, dared to do anything, that there were no more doubts for him, no obstacles. He was suffused with hope and joy. It seemed to him that the sombre, satanic delusions of life, which had flooded his imagination in black waves, were receding. Hossana! Blessed is He who cometh in the name of the Lord!

Now with astounding, hitherto unprecedented clarity, he could see in his mind's eye what his heart was craving, a heart belonging not to life's slave, but to a creator of life, so he said to himself. He had an image of the heavens plethoric with eternal light, languishing in an Edenlike azure and wreathed with wondrous, though vaguely disquieting clouds; the coruscating visages and wings of innumerable exulting seraphim stood out amidst the eerie, liturgical beauty of the heavens; God the Father, menacing and joyous, beatific and triumphant, as in the days of the Creation, towered among them like a mammoth, iridescent vision; the Maid of Ineffable Grace, Her sacred eyes filled with the bliss of the jubilant mother, standing in wreaths of clouds translucent with the blue of distant earthly realms that extended beneath Her, displayed to the world, raised high in Her divine arms the Child, radiant as the sun, and the savage, mighty John the Baptist, girded with the pelt of a beast, knelt at Her feet, kissing the hem of Her raiment in a frenzy of love, tenderness and gratitude...

And the artist rushed back to his work. He kept breaking pencils, and in feverish haste, his hands trembling, sharpened them again with the knife. The dying candles, guttering, flowing down the scorching-hot candlesticks, flamed even more torridly beside his face, which was curtained along its cheeks by his wet hair.

At six o'clock he was madly jabbing the button to the callbell: he had finished, finished! Then he ran up to the table and stood, his heart pounding, waiting for the boy. The pallidness of his face was of such a hue that his lips seemed black. His jacket was covered all over with flecks of varicolored dust from the pencils. The dark eyes burned with inhuman suffering and, at the same time, with a frenetic rapture.

No one came. A sepulchral quiet surrounded him. But he stood, he waited, transformed into sheer listening and anticipation. Just now, at any moment, the boy would come running in, and he, the creator, having consummated his labor, having poured out his soul at the bidding of the Deity Himself, would quickly say to him the words prepared in advance, awesome and victorious words:

"Take. I give this *unto thee.*"

On the verge of blacking out from the furious throbbing of his heart, he held the pasteboard firmly in his hand. But that pasteboard, covered throughout in variegated hues, contained monstrous heaps of images that had

16

overwhelmed his imagination in absolute contrast to his passionate reveries. The savage black-blue sky was blazing to its very zenith with conflagrations, with the bloody flames of smoking, crumbling temples, palaces and dwellings. Torture racks, scaffolds and gibbets with garrotted men hanging from them were black against that fiery background. Towering over all the painting, over all the sea of fire and smoke, majestic, demoniacal, stood a huge cross with a crucified man upon it, the ensanguined Martyr, His sacrosanct arms widespread, extended submissively along the crossbeam. Death, dressed in armor and serrated crown, its macabre bared teeth grinning, had taken a running start and thrust an iron trident deep in below the heart of the Crucified. The bottom of the painting depicted an amorphous pile of the dead—and the melee, the gnarring biting clash of the living, a tangle of naked bodies, arms and faces. And those faces, snarling, fanged, with eyes protruding from sockets, were so base and obscene, so distorted with hatred, spite, with the voluptuousness of fratricide, that one could readily have taken them for the faces of cattle, wild beasts, devils, but in no way whatsoever for the faces of human beings.

Paris. 1921

IN A FAR DISTANT LAND

Paper ribbon spurts from the machine beside the frozen window of the telegraph office—and Ivlev reads letter by letter the words full of wondrous meaning:

"Ivan Sergeevich marries niece at Yuletide horses sent..."

The telegrapher, over whose shoulder he reads, shouts oddly that this is officially secret, that this is Pushkin's Pskov exposé, but now Ivlev sees himself out on the road, in abysmal winter, in the depths of Russia.

He sees that evening is coming, that with evening comes the frost; he tells himself that no one can recall such a snowy winter since the time of Boris Godunov. And to this wintry Russian evening, to the snowy fields and forests Godunov lends something barbarous and gloomy, menacing. But in the sledge, among other items acquired for the wedding and the holidays, lies a pair of magnificent Swedish skis, purchased by the niece in Moscow. And their presence brings a surge of joy, a promise of something that makes the heartbeat catch. Briskly, assuredly the troika moves along.

The sledge is carpeted, plush. In imitation beaver cap and peasant greatcoat, girded by a belt with silver studs, the coachman stands in the box. Immobile behind him sit two women who are corpulent with fur coats and shawls: a hale old lady and her black-eyed rubicund niece. Like everything in the sledge, they are powdered with snow spray. Both gaze intently ahead, at the coachman's back, at the bobbing croups of the outrunners, at the horseshoes glistening through clods of snow.

Now they have come out onto the highway; the outrunners move along with less effort, no longer stretching the traces. Their home is already visible in the distance, their village, the doleful, dense, frost-bitten pine forests.

Suddenly the old lady speaks in a loud steady voice:

"Well now, thank God we're home. I thought I'd never get out of your Moscow. But here it's just like twenty years off my shoulders; can't get enough of looking around and feeling happy. Tomorrow I'm letting Ivan Sergeevich know—we won't put off your wedding any longer. Do you hear?"

"As you please, auntie; anything is agreeable to me," answers the niece distinctly, with simulated gay ingenuousness.

The troika is already dashing smartly through the village, where above peasant huts and snowdrifts stand dark pines grown grey with frost. And beyond the village, in the midst of the forest itself the manor appears: a large snowy yard, a large low wooden house. Dusk, desolation, the lights are not yet lit. Restraining the horses, the coachman drives in a wide semicircle up to the porch.

White with snow spray, they struggle from the sledge, mount the steps, and enter the warm spacious anteroom, covered cozily with horsecloths, almost pitch dark. From the back chambers a bustling old granny in woolen stockings comes running; she bows, exults, helps them unbundle. They unwrap the shawls, liberate themselves from the snowy, aromatic fur coats. The more the niece unbundles, the more gay and vivacious she becomes, and she suddenly turns out to be slender, lissome; nimbly she takes a seat on the antiquated coffer beside the window and quickly removes her grey city overshoes, revealing one leg to the knee, to the lace of her pantalettes, her black eyes gazing expectantly at her aunt, who divests herself with vigorous but slow movements, breathing laboriously.

Then suddenly it draws near, that terrible something long since foreboding. Auntie drops her raised arms, gives a weak, sweet cry—and slowly, slowly sinks toward the floor. The granny seizes her under the arms but cannot cope with her weight and cries fiercely:

"Miss!"

And through the window one sees the snowy yard, beyond it, amidst the forest, the glittering snowy fields; past the fields the low bald moon looks on, glowing. And now the granny and the aunt are no more; there is only that landscape painting in the window, only the dark anteroom; there is only the joyous horror of that darkness and the absence now of any obstacle between Ivlev and the girl who was supposed to be the bride of some Ivan Sergeevich; there is that one marvelous gleam in the black eyes that suddenly drew so very near to him; there is the quick spark of dread that came when she removed her overshoe on the coffer and the very rapture that followed immediately in the weak, sweet cry of her aunt, sinking in death-deep languor onto the floor...

For the entire next day Ivlev is filled with the importunate sensations of passionate love. The secret of what occurred in some pristine country estate underlies all he does, thinks, says and reads. This love is one hundred times more intense than even what he once had experienced in his early, most callow youth. And in the depths of his soul he knows no reason will ever convince him that this black-eyed niece does not nor ever did exist in the world, or that, therefore, she does not know what agonizing and joyous memories—their *mutual* memories—have possessed him all day.

Maritime Alps. 12 July 1923

AN UNKNOWN FRIEND

7 October

On this *carte-illustrée* with such a mournful and sublime view of a moon-lit night by the shores of the Atlantic Ocean, I hasten to send you my fervent gratitude for your latest book. These shores are my second home, Ireland—you can see from what a distance one of your unknown friends has sent regards. Be happy and may God keep you.

8 October

Here is yet another view of that lonesome country, where fate has cast me forever.

Yesterday, in a dreadful rainstorm—the rain here never ends—I went to the city on some errands, happened to buy your book, and couldn't tear my-self from it all the way back to the villa, where my husband and I live year round because of my poor health. The rain and the storm clouds made the countryside almost dark, flowers and greenery in the gardens were uncommonly vivid, the empty streetcar sped along, discharging violet flashes, but I kept reading and reading, and without knowing why I felt almost tormented with happiness.

Farewell, once more I thank you. There is something else I want to say to you, but what? I don't know, I can't put it in words.

10 October

I cannot refrain from writing you again. I suspect you receive too many of these letters. But they are all responses from the very human beings you create for. So why should I be silent? It was you who first established contact with me when you published your book; that is, it was published for me too...

The rain has been pouring down all day on our unnaturally green garden; my room is bleak, and the fire in the hearth has been lit since morning. I would like to tell you many things, but you know better than others how difficult it is, almost impossible—to express all of oneself. I am still under the effect of something elusive and equivocal, but beautiful, for which I am obliged to you. Explain it to me, just what is it, that feeling? And what is it people experience when they come under the influence of art? Fascination with human skills and powers? A sharpened desire for personal happiness, which desire ever and always lives within us but is aroused in particular by anything that functions sensuously—music, verses, some graphic recollection, some smell? Or is it a joyous sense of the divine splendor of the human soul, which only those few artists, such as you, can reveal to us, you who remind us that it does exist nonetheless, that divine splendor? For example, I may read something—at times

20

even something dreadful—and suddenly I say: God, how beautiful this is! What does that mean? Perhaps it means: how beautiful life is nonetheless!

Good-bye, soon I shall write you again. I don't think there is anything improper about that; I think it's acceptable—writing to writers. Besides, you do not even have to read my letters... although that, of course, would make me very sad.

Night

Forgive me, this may sound ugly, but I cannot help saying it: I am not young, I have a daughter fifteen years old, quite a young lady already, but at one time I was not so bad looking and I've not changed too considerably since... Nonetheless, I don't want you to imagine me as different from the way I really am.

11 October

I have written you by virtue of my need to share with you the emotion stirred within me by your talent, which has the effect of mournful but lofty music. Why is it necessary—this sharing? I don't know, and you don't know either, but we both know full well that this need of the human heart is ineradicable, that without it life does not exist, and that herein lies some great mystery. For you too write only by virtue of that need; what's more—you devote utterly all of your being to it.

I had always read a lot—and kept many diaries, as do all people dissatisfied with life—I still read a lot even now; I had also read you, but only a few of your works, I knew you mostly by name alone. But then this new book of yours... How strange it is! A person's hand writes something somewhere, a person's soul conveys a minute fragment of his innermost life through the most minute of allusions—the word can convey so much, even in a style such as yours!—and suddenly space, time, differences in people's fate and circumstances disappear, and your thoughts and feelings become my own, ours in common. Indeed, there is only one soul in the world, a universal soul. Doesn't that explain my impulse to write you, to express something, to share something with you, to complain of something? Aren't your works really the same thing as my letters to you? For you also have something to express to somebody; you project your lines out somewhere into space, toward a person who is a stranger to you. For you also complain, most often you simply complain, because complaining, in other words pleading for compassion, is utterly inseparable from the human spirit; how much of it there is in songs, prayers, verses, protestations of love!

Perhaps you will answer me, won't you, even if only a word or two? Do answer me!

13 October

Once again I'm writing you at night, already in bed, tormented by an elusive desire to say something that very easily could be called naive, that in any case cannot be expressed the way one feels it. Actually I want to say very little: only that I'm sad, that I feel very sorry for myself—and that, nonetheless, this sadness and this feeling sorry for myself make me happy. It's sad for me to think that I'm in some foreign country on the westernmost shores of Europe, in some villa outside the city, amidst the autumn darkness of the night and fog from the sea, which stretches all the way to America. It's sad that I'm alone, not only in this cozy and splendid room, but in all the world. Yet the saddest thing of all is that you, whom I have invented and from whom I am now expecting something, are so infinitely far from me, such a stranger to me, and of course, despite everything I've said, you are alien to me and justifiably so...

Really, everything in the world has its charm, even this lampshade and the golden glow of the lamp, and the glistening linen on my uncovered bed, and my robe, my foot in the slipper, my thin arm in the wide sleeve. And everything is infinitely pathetic—what's the use of it all? Everything passes, will pass, and everything is futile, just as my endless anticipation, which takes the place of life for me...

I beg of you—write. Of course only two or three words, just enough so that I know you hear me. Excuse my importunity.

15 October

This is our city, our cathedral. The desolate, rocky shores—those on my first *carte-postale* to you—are further up the coast, to the north. But even the city, the cathedral—everything here is doleful and sombre. Granite, slate, asphalt and rain, rain...

Do write me a brief note; I understand very well that you have no more than two or three words to say to me, but, believe me, I shall not be the least bit offended. Just write, write!

21 October

Much to my distress, I've received no letter from you. And fifteen days have passed since I wrote you for the first time...

But perhaps your publisher has not yet sent my letters on to you. Perhaps you are distracted by urgent matters or society life. That's very sad: even so, it's better than thinking you have simply scorned my request. Such a thought is very offensive and painful. You may say that I have no right whatsoever to your attention and that, consequently, anything I say about offense or pain is beside the point. But is it true that I do not have that right? Perhaps that right becomes mine once I've experienced certain feelings for you? Wasn't there, for example, a certain Romeo, who demanded requital for his love without any grounds whatsoever for that demand, or Othello, who insisted he had the right to be jealous? Each of them said: if I love, how can I not be loved, how can someone betray me? Mine is not the simple desire to be loved; it's more than that, much more complex. Once I love someone or something, that person or thing is already mine, a part of me... But I cannot explain it to

22

you properly; I only know that it seems and always has seemed that way to people...

But be that as it may, I have no answer from you, and I'm writing you once again. I suddenly conceived the fancy that you were somehow close to me—but then again, was it merely a fancy?—I came to believe in the fiction I myself had concocted and began writing you persistently, and now I know that the more I write you, the more indispensable will it be for me to do so because some kind of bond between you and me will grow stronger and stronger. I cannot imagine what you are like; I have absolutely no conception of even your physical features. To whom, then, am I writing? To myself? But it makes no difference. After all, I am you.

22 October

Today is a marvelous day, my soul is at ease, the windows are open and the sun and warm air remind me of spring. How strange this land is! Rainy and cold in summer, rainy and warm in autumn and winter, but from time to time we have such beautiful days that it makes you wonder: is this winter or Italian spring? Oh, Italy, Italy, and my eighteen years, my hopes, my joyous credulity, my expectations on the threshold of life, all of which lay before me and all in a sunlit fog, like the mountains, the vales, and the blossoming gardens surrounding Vesuvius! Forgive me, I know there is nothing at all novel in any of this, but what do I care?

Night

Perhaps you have not written me because I am too abstract for you. Then here are a few more details about my life. I have been married now for sixteen years. My husband is a Frenchman; I met him one winter on the French Riviera, we were married in Rome, and after a wedding trip through Italy we settled here for good. I have three children, a boy and two girls. Do I love them? Yes, I do; even so, my love for them is not like that of most mothers, who cannot conceive of life apart from the family, the children. When my children were small, I looked after them incessantly, sharing in all their play and preoccupations, but now that they are no longer in need of me I have a good deal of free time, which I spend reading. My relatives are far away, our lives have diverged, and our mutual interests are so few that we seldom even write one another. Due to my husband's position I am often obliged to go out in society, to receive guests and return their visits, to attend evening parties and dinners. But I have no friends, male or female. I have nothing in common with the local ladies, and I don't believe in friendship between men and women...

But that's enough about me. If you reply, tell me at least something about yourself. What are you like? Where do you make your home? Do you prefer Shakespeare or Shelly, Goethe or Dante, Balzac or Flaubert? Do you like music and what kind? Are you married? Are you bound up in some dreary alliance, or perhaps you and your bride are in that tender and beautiful phase when everything is new and joyous, when there still are no memories, which are only wearisome, which give you the illusion of some former happiness, an inscrutable happiness once taken for granted?

1 November

No letter from you. What torment! Such torment that I sometimes curse the day and the hour when I made my decision to write you...

And worst of all, there's no way out of this. Despite the many times I have assured myself that no letter will come, that there's nothing to wait for, I keep waiting nonetheless: who can say for sure that a letter won't arrive? Oh, if only I could be certain that you wouldn't write! Just knowing would make me happy. But no, no, hoping is better nonetheless. I'm hoping, I'm waiting!

3 November

No letter, and my torments continue... But the only time it is really oppressive is in the morning hours, when after dressing myself with unnaturally calm, deliberate movements but with hands cold from suppressed emotion, I go down for coffee, then give a music lesson to my daughter, who works through the piece with such touching diligence and sits at the piano so straight, so charmingly straight, as only a girl of fifteen can sit. Finally, at midday, the post arrives; I run to check it, find nothing—and I feel almost calm until the next morning...

But today is another splendid day. The low sun is limpid and meek. Autumn flowers bloom amidst the many bare, black trees of the garden. Beyond the garden's branches, in the vales, there is something delicate, pale-blue, uncommonly beautiful. And in my heart I feel grateful to someone and for something. For what? After all, one really has nothing and never will have anything... But is that so, does one indeed have nothing if it exists, that gratitude that moves the soul?

I am grateful also to you for giving me the opportunity to invent you. You will never know me, never meet me, but in this too there is a good deal of mournful charm. And perhaps it's best that you don't write me, that you have not written me a single word and that I never see you at all as a living person. Could I possibly talk with you like this and perceive you as I do now if I knew you, even if I had but one letter from you? Certainly you would not be the same, certainly a bit worse, and I would be less open about writing you...

It's getting cooler, but I've yet to close the window; I keep looking at tha pale-blue haze of the lowlands and hills beyond the garden. And that blue is tormenting in its beauty, tormenting because one certainly must do something with it. But what should be done? I don't know. We know nothing!

5 November

This resembles a diary, but it's not a diary, nonetheless, because now I have a reader, even if he is only hypothetical...

What prompts you to write? The desire to tell about something or to express (even if only allegorically) the whole of yourself? The latter, of course. Nine of every ten writers, even the most renowned, are just storytellers; that is, they actually have nothing in common with what is worthy of being called art. But what is art? Music, a prayer, a song of the human soul... Oh, if only I could leave behind even a few lines about how I too once lived, loved, and took joy in my life, how I too had my youth, spring, Italy... about the existence of a faraway land on the shores of the Atlantic Ocean, where I live, love, and still keep on waiting for something even now... about some poor and savage islands on this ocean and some people who live a poor and savage life, a people alien to all the world, whose origin, obscure language and reason for being no one knows nor ever will know...

Nonetheless, I keep waiting and waiting for a letter. Now this has become something like an obsession, a kind of mental disorder.

7 November

Yes, everything is marvelous. No letter has arrived, of course, not one single letter. And just imagine: because that letter has not arrived, because I have no answer from a person I have never seen nor ever will see, no response to my voice cast out somewhere into the distance, into my own dream, I feel a horrible loneliness, the horrible emptiness of the world! Emptiness, emptiness!

Rain, fog, humdrum existence once again. But there's even something good about this; that is, it's normal, just as it should be. That thought calms me.

Good-bye, may God forgive you for your cruelty. Yes, it is cruel nonetheless.

8 November

It's only three o'clock, but the fog and the rain make it seem just like twilight.

At five we're having guests for tea.

They'll drive up in the rain, in their automobiles, from the dismal city, which is even more black when rain is falling, with its black wet asphalt, black wet rooftops and black granite cathedral, whose spire fades away in the rain and murk...

I'm dressed already and seem to be awaiting my entrance onto the stage. I'm awaiting that moment when I will say all the proper things, be gracious, animated, solicitous and just a bit pale, but that can easily be attributed to the dreadful weather. Now that I'm dressed I seem to have grown younger, I feel like my daughter's elder sister, and I'm ready to burst into tears at any moment. I have experienced, nonetheless, something strange, something like love. For whom? On what account?

Farewell, I no longer expect anything—I say that with complete sincerity.

Farewell, my unknown friend. I break off this unrequited correspondence in the same way I began it—with gratitude. Thank you for not replying. It would have been worse had it been otherwise. What could you have said to me? At what point could we have stopped writing one another without a feeling of constraint? And what else could I have found to tell you besides what has already been said? I have nothing more to say—I've said everything. Actually, only two or three lines can be written about any human life. Oh yes. Only two or three lines.

Once again I'm alone in my house, with the foggy ocean nearby, with humdrum autumn and winter days, and with a strange feeling—as if I had lost someone. And I return once again to my diary, for which I have a strange need, though God only knows why this diary, and your writings, are so necessary.

A few days ago I dreamed of you. You were somehow strange, taciturn, sitting in the corner of a dark room, and you were not visible. But I could see you nonetheless. Even in my sleep I felt: how can someone you've never seen in your life appear visible in your dreams? For isn't it true that only God creates from a void? And I felt terrified and awoke full of fear, with a sense of oppression.

In fifteen or twenty years, possibly, neither you nor I will be on this earth. Till we meet again in the other world! Who can be sure that it does not exist? After all, we don't understand even our own dreams, the creative work of our own imaginations. Is it ours, the imagination, that is, to be more precise, what we call our imagination, our fancies, our reveries? Is it our own will we obey when we yearn for communion with this or that human soul, as I yearn for communion with yours?

Farewell. But no, I'll say *au revoir* nonetheless.

Maritime Alps. 1923

NOOSIFORM EARS

On that dark and cold day a number of people came across an unusually tall man who was hanging about near the Nikolaev Station and at various points along Nevsky Prospect, a man who called himself a former seaman, Adam Sokolovich. With an air of elusive gravity he stood on the sidewalk by Ligovka, gazing at the statue of Alexander III, at a chain of streetcars that formed a circle around the square, at the shadowy figures of people, at cab drivers and draymen moving toward the station, at a huge mail car emerging from under the station arch, at a hearse, which bore away amidst all this bustle a squalid, bright-yellow coffin unaccompanied by mourners; he stood on the Anichkov Bridge, staring gloomily at the dark water, at barges grey with dirty snow; he rambled along Nevsky, carefully scrutinizing goods in the store windows. Not to notice and not to remember him was impossible, and anyone who happened to cross his path experienced a feeling of vague unpleasantness, a kind of malaise, and turned away thinking:

"What a horrible man!"

His clothing—boots, tight trousers, heavy woolen overcoat spattered in back with mud, British leather cap—appeared to have been worn indefinitely, continuously, in all kinds of weather. Unusually tall, thin and ungainly, with long legs and big feet, his face freshly shaven except for a yellowish, rather sparse, American-style trimming of hair beneath his powerfully developed jaw, his sombre visage intense and malevolent, he stood for hours in front of showcase windows, steadily gnawing at the mouthpiece of his cigarette, his long arms thrust in his pockets. Was he really so interested in all those neckties, watches, valises and stationer's wares? It was immediately obvious that he was not, that he was one of those strange people who rove about the city from morning till night solely because they can think only while in motion, out on the street, or who, having no home to go back to, prowl around in expectation of something.

He spent the evening in a cheap restaurant not far from Razyezhaya, accompanied by two nondescript sailors.

The three sat wearing their coats in that cold and dingy room, at a little table placed awkwardly by the wall, and Sokolovich's seat was particularly uncomfortable. Directly facing his back, a small Tatar with a rotund head stood at a snack counter in the interior of the room; on the wall in front of him hung a placard advertising a certain beer, depicting three happy men-about-town with top hats pushed back on their heads and frothing beakers in their hands; to the right an icy dampness kept blowing in from the street with the incoming patrons, and to the left the waiters, running back and forth to the counter, kept stirring up the air. Near that counter a stairway of three steps led up—to a narrow corridor filled with cooking odors and the pungent smell of gas—and through an open door a billiards room was visible, dark in its upper half, bright below, where balls were meeting with a brisk clatter and men were walking about in waistcoats with cuesticks on their shoulders; their heads were lost in the murk. Seating himself in that awkward position at the table, Sokolovich took a pipe from his coat pocket; knitting his brow, he stared intently at the beer placard. The sailors conversed with the waiter who had just come over to them, while Sokolovich, packing his pipe with tobacco, said languidly in his hollow voice, addressing no one in particular:

"Why is it people collect all kinds of nonsense, but they don't collect advertising matter, that is, the historical documents that portray human ideals most precisely. For example, don't those dandies there really express the aspirations of nine-tenths of all mankind?"

"You're nothing but a son of a Polack," hostilely responded one of the sailors, Levchenko.

"I'm a son of humanity," said Sokolovich with a kind of strange solemnity, which also could be taken for irony. "My being Polish hasn't kept me from seeing the world and all its divinities. It hasn't kept me from working as a driver either... There's really no pleasure comparable to that, you know—watching the street rushing toward you, and some lady beautiful in a dither up ahead, not knowing which way to fling herself."

When he had spoken, he lit the tobacco and propped an elbow on the table, cradling his pipe in his massive left hand; there was no shirt beneath the cuff of his coat, and there was a bluish tattoo on that flat, elongated hand—a sinuous Japanese dragon.

All evening they drank Caucasian brandy from cups, pretending it was tea, munched on pink peppermint sweets and smoked to excess. Like all working-class people, perpetually affronted by life, the sailors talked on and on, each trying to speak only of himself, searched their memories for the basest deeds of their enemies and oppressors, boasted—one of them supposedly had poked a cantankerous first mate "right in the snout," the other had tossed a boatswain overboard—and they kept up a steady argument, screaming incessantly:

"All right, do you want to make a bet?"

Sokolovich sucked on his pipe, worked his jaw, and maintained a morose silence. Although he had frequented every sort of dive from Kronstadt to Montevideo, he never drank heavily, preferring only ginger beer or absinthe. On that evening he kept pace with his drinking companions, but the brandy had no apparent effect on him. This also provoked the sailors, the more so because, as they later acknowledged, they were always irritated by Sokolovich's strong repulsive face, by his tendency to be enigmatic and pensive, and by their lack of any real information about or understanding of either his character, his past, or his present homeless and idle life. At one point Levchenko, who had become drunk rather quickly, screamed at him:

"You're a funny bird, you are! It's us who's treating you, so why don't you be sociable instead of just dragging off your stinking pipe?"

Rudely and dispassionately Sokolovich cut him off:

"Do me a favor, stop that bellowing. It makes me angry. Time and again I've told you that alcohol has little effect on me and doesn't afford me any particular pleasure. My sense of taste is blunted. I'm what they call a degenerate. Understood?"

Levchenko lost his composure and answered with unnatural flippancy:

"Well now, don't you go putting on airs neither! What is it I'm supposed to understand? If you was degenerate you'd be sick, you'd have a weakness for drink, but you're telling me just the opposite. You could kill a man with one hand, but you say..."

"What I say is true," interrupted Sokolovich, raising his voice. "All degenerates have some perceptions and faculties that are sharpened, heightened, and others that, on the contrary, are dulled. Understood? And strength has nothing at all to do with it."

"But how do I recognize this here degenerate if he's healthy as an ox?" Levchenko asked mockingly.

"By the ears, for example," answered Sokolovich, half serious, half mocking. "Degenerates, geniuses, tramps and murderers all have noosiform ears, that is, ears shaped like a noose—the very thing used to choke the life out of them."

"Well, you know, anybody can kill if they fly off the handle," the other sailor, Pilnyak, put in casually. "Once in Nikolaev I was..."

Sokolovich waited until he had finished, then said:

"Indeed, I too suspect, Pilnyak, that ears of this sort are characteristic not only of so-called degenerates. As you know, a craving to kill, and, for that matter, to indulge in all sorts of cruelty, is latent within everyone's soul. And there are even some who, for any number of reasons, feel an utterly overpowering urge to commit murder—due, for example, to atavism or to some hatred for mankind that has mysteriously developed within them—they kill with complete impassivity, and after they have killed someone, not only are they not tormented, as people like to think, but, on the contrary, they return to normal, feel a sense of relief—even if their wrath, hatred, and secret craving for blood have had loathsome and pitiful consequences. And it's altogether high time to throw out this fairy tale about the torments of conscience, the horrible agonies that murderers are said to experience. People have done enough lying about how blood supposedly makes them shudder. We've had enough novels contrived about crimes with punishment; it's time to write about crime without any punishment whatsoever. The killer's attitude depends on his point of view toward murder and on what he expects subsequent to his action, the gallows or decorations and praises. For example, do those who condone family vendettas, duels, war, revolution and public executions really feel so tormented and horrified?"

"I read Dostoevsky's *Crime and Punishment*," remarked Levchenko with a certain pomposity.

"Did you now?" said Sokolovich, casting a ponderous glance at him. "And did you read about the headsman Deblair? He recently died at his villa in the environs of Paris at the age of eighty, after having lopped off exactly five hundred heads in his day, by order of his highly civilized government. Penal records are also crammed full of entries about the cruelest tranquility, about the cynicism and morally edifying expatiations of the most bloody criminals. But it's not a matter of degenerates, headsmen, or convicts. All the books of humanity—all those myths, sagas, folk epics, stories, dramas, novels— they're all filled with the very same entries, and do they ever make anyone shudder? Every little boy is enthralled by Cooper, where all they do is take scalps, every *gymnasium* student learns that the Assyrian rulers covered the walls of their cities with the skin of prisoners, every pastor knows that in the Bible the word "killed" is used more than a thousand times and, for the most part, used with the greatest boasting and giving of thanks to the Creator for everything brought to pass."

"That's why it's called the Old Testament; it's ancient history," objected Levchenko.

"And the New Testament is such," replied Sokolovich, "that it would make the hair of a gorilla stand on end if he knew how to read... No," he said, knitting his brow and looking off to one side, "there's no comparison between Cain and our biped gorillas! They've left him far behind; they've long since lost their naivety—probably ever since they built Babylon at the site of their so-called paradise. Real gorillas haven't yet had any Assyrian rulers, or Caesars, or inquisitions, or any colonization of America, or kings who sign death sentences with cigars in their mouths, or inventors of submarines that in one fell swoop send several thousand men to the bottom of the sea, or Robespierres or Jack the Rippers... What do you think, Levchenko?" he asked, once again fixing his stern gaze on the sailors: "Did all those gentlemen suffer the agonies of Cain or Raskolnikov? Did all the murderers of tyrants and oppressors suffer torments, murderers who have their names inscribed in golden letters in the so-called annals of history? Do you suffer torments when you read that the Turks have slaughtered another hundred thousand Armenians, that the Germans are poisoning wells with pestilential bacilli, that the trenches are heaped up with putrefying corpses, that army aviators are dropping bombs on Nazareth? Do people feel tormented in some Paris or other, or in London, cities built on human bones and flourishing on the most ferocious and most commonplace cruelty toward one's so-called fellow man? It turns out that only Raskolnikov was tormented and even then only because of his own anemic debility and because that was the way it was planned by his malicious creator, who had to shove Christ into all his trashy novels."

"Weigh them anchors! Cast off!" screamed Levchenko, hoping to make a joke of a conversation that had begun to depress him.

Sokolovich was silent for a moment; then he spat between his knees and added dispassionately:

"At present tens of millions of people are participating in warfare. Soon the whole of Europe will be crawling with murderers. But we all know perfectly well that this won't drive the world out of its mind one iota. They used to say that a trip to Sakhalin Island was a dreadful undertaking. But I'd like to know who would dream of being afraid to travel through Europe in a year or two, after this war has ended."

Pilnyak began telling about an uncle who had murdered his wife in a fit of jealousy. After listening for a moment, Sokolovich remarked with an air of gloomy reflection:

"People are altogether much more prone to murder a woman than a man. Our sensory perceptions are never so acutely responsive to the body of a man as they are to the body of a woman, that base creature who gives birth to us all, and who revels in true voluptuousness only when she yields herself to the coarsest and strongest males of the species..."

And placing his elbows on his knees, he fell silent once more and seemed to have completely forgotten his collocutors.

At some time between eleven and twelve he parted with the sailors in a casual, condescending manner; they remained in the restaurant, while he made his way once again toward Nevsky.

The resplendence of illuminations on Nevsky Prospect was smothered by the dense haze, which was so penetrating and cold that a policeman's mustache had acquired a whitish tint, seemed to have gone gray as he stood on the corner of Vladimirskaya, directing the maelstrom of carriages, sleighs and goggle-eyed automobiles whirling toward one another. Near Palkin a sloe-black stallion who had fallen on his side, onto the shaft, desperately thrashed about, flailing his hoofs against the slippery roadway, struggling to right himself and get back up; hastily and frantically bustling about, looking very strange in his monstrous overskirt, a foppish cabman was attempting to help him, and a red-faced giant of a constable, who had difficulty moving his cold benumbed lips, was screaming, waving a hand in its cotton glove, driving away the crowds. Sokolovich heard some muffled voice telling how an old white-bearded man in a long raccoon coat, said to be a famous writer, had been run down and crushed while crossing the street, but he did not even pause to listen. He turned onto Nevsky Prospect.

A few pedestrians overtook him, peering up in astonishment at his face; he himself overtook others. His hands stuffed into his pockets, his shoulders slightly raised, hiding his scraggly fog-moist chin in his collar and looking askance at the feckless dark mass of people flowing along in front of him, almost unnaturally conspicuous in that mass because of his stature, he sauntered along the sidewalk on his big feet, always stepping out first with the left foot, and taking longer strides with the left than with the right. From the poles of street lamps carbonic-black shadows fell into the smoky haze. With a monotonous tramping of hooves compact droves of rime-frosted cab horses clattered along in that smoke; trotters were flying amidst them, their strength and impertinence conspicuous, their nostrils blowing vapor, which blended with the misty waves that rolled along on the wind. A man and woman flashed by and rushed away in a mad whirl—a budding young officer, firmly clasping the waist of the lady, who was nestling against him and hiding her face in an astrakhan muff... Sokolovich slackened his pace and gazed at that couple for a long time, stared after them into the distance, where, amidst what looked like periodic flarings of greenish heat lightning, the endless chain of wine-red streetcar lights evanesced in the icy murk of that enormous torrent Nevsky seemed to be. His large face was ferocious with intense concentration.

He walked diagonally across Anichkov Bridge and set off along the other side of the street. The wind and fog bore down with still more vehemence; far away, high in the darkness and mist, loomed the reddish eye of the clock in the tower of the municipal *duma.* Sokolovich stopped and stood for quite a long time, lighting a cigarette and louring at the prostitutes who had appeared on the sidewalk, who kept meandering by in a slow, endless stream. Behind him was the huge translucent showcase window of a closed store with its mournful, nocturnal illumination; waxen, blonde-haired dandies with large but sparse eyelashes peered out inertly from behind the window, dressed in expensive overcoats and fur mantles, wooden legs lifelessly protruding from their fashionable, splendidly pressed pantaloons... Then he plodded on, reached the Kazan Cathedral, now decapitated by the foggy darkness, and climbed the steps to the veranda of Dominick's.

Inside, amidst the cramped masses of people who ate and drank standing up and in their coats, as if they were still out on the street, he took a seat in a dark corner—the only lighted spot was the snack counter, which was besieged by the mob—and ordered black coffee. With extraordinary abruptness a puny man in a derby, his small face frozen stiff, appeared at his table and hastily asked permission to take a sulphur fusee from the matchbox; striking it hastily, he asked in a quick patter of words:

"Excuse me, please, but you look an awful lot like a Vilnius acquaintance of mine, Yanovsky."

Sokolovich stared him straight in the eye and answered with a ponderous gravity:

"You're mistaken, mister plainclothes man."

He stayed at Dominick's until one in the morning. Finally, the deserted restaurant resounded with the banging of chairs, which the flunkies, who had suddenly become boorish and coarse, were turning upside down and tossing onto the tables. He glanced at his big silver watch and arose from his seat.

Nevsky Prospect in the dead of night and the fog is dreadful. Desolate, lifeless, it is covered by a murky brume that mists it in obscurity, that seems linked to the arctic murk that drifts in from the end of the world, from the land called the North Pole, where something beyond human comprehension lies concealed. The center of this misty torrent is still illumined from above by the off-white glow of electrical orbs. But on the sidewalks, beside black shop windows and locked gates, it is darker. Humming, leisurely sauntering along these sidewalks, their cheap finery clashing with the surroundings, stroll the women, in the guise of insouciance but chilled to the marrow by that icy dampness, and some of their faces are so striking for the nullity they express that an uncanny fear arises, as if one had stumbled upon a creature of some other species, not a human being, but some unknown breed.

After Sokolovich had left Dominick's and had walked roughly two hundred paces, he selected one of these prostitutes, later found to be a certain Korolkova, who called herself simply 'kinglet,' a small, meager woman whose tawdry and modish attire made her appear more ample, wearing a hat that was also of ample dimensions and made in a very peculiar style, of black velvet adorned with a cluster of glass cherries. Her small broad-cheeked face with black, deeply sunken, beady eyes had something about it reminiscent of a bat. Letting her head sway slightly with affected flippance, even, so it seemed, with a certain awareness of the irresistible charm of her sex, one hand holding up her skirt, the other, in a large flat muff made of glittering black fur, covering her mouth, she had suddenly blocked the path of the round-shouldered, shuffling Sokolovich. He cast a sharp glance at her and immediately shouted in his hollow voice for a night-duty cabman, who was parked at the corner. Then, seating themselves in the tacky four-wheeler, this couple rolled away, first along Nevsky, then through the square, past the gleaming clock on the Nikolaev Station, which now was totally dark, having dispatched all its trains into the depths of snowy Russia, past the horrible stout horse that eternally bows its large head, in sleet or in fog, begging its portly rider for free rein, then along Goncharnaya—and still further, through foggy streets and alleyways, into that mysterious, mute remoteness of the capital's nocturnal outskirts.

As they rode Sokolovich smoked in silence. Korolkova, who apparently was oppressed by this silence, remarked that in her opinion the "Golenishev-Kutuzov" brand of cigarettes was better than the one called "Lilac." This attempt to strike up a simple conversation, even what could be taken as a friendly conversation, as yet unrelated to the aim of their journey, was pathetic and touching; but Sokolovich remained silent. Then she started asking to be paid in advance and added with unnatural audacity that she would agree to stay the whole night, but only for a very good price. Without replying he took out two silver rubles and handed them to her. She accepted them, checked one of them with her teeth, discovered it was counterfeit, and put it in her muff, stating that this one didn't count, that she would keep it for no special reason, as a souvenir, since there was a war going on and silver was rare and illegal; after that she started asking for more. Sokolovich did not respond for a moment, then gave her one more ruble. Next she tried a different approach—being a woman; she suddenly gave a shudder and made a movement as if to nestle up to him. The shudder was affected but the feeling that had suddenly gripped her was, most likely, not; she felt a strong attraction toward him, so large, powerful, categorical in his ugliness and his merciless, sombre sobriety. But he made no response to her movement.

They rode far out of the city. Korolkova ordered the cabman to stop beside a two-storied brick building with the sign: "Rooms for Travelers. Belgrade." By now it was a quarter to two; the area was deserted.

After having ascended the battered stair-carpeting to the second floor of the Belgrade, the guests were met in a semi-dark corridor by the concierge Nyanchuk, who had been sleeping on a narrow wooden settee beneath a sleazy winter coat with threadbare lambskin collar. In his drowsy stupor he was dazed by the stature, the somberly intense countenance and the scanty, fog-moist, American-style beard of Sokolovich. He arose and asked in a hostile tone:

"What is it you need?"

"As if you didn't know, blockhead," said Sokolovich through his teeth, walking presumptuously by him and putting a silver half-ruble in his hand as he passed.

Nyanchuk was on the verge of being offended and saying, "Takes one to know one," but he felt the money in his hand and recognized Korolkova, who proclaimed as she walked by: "You didn't know me; that means I'll get rich!"—so he only scowled. Maundering discontentedly about how they already had problems with the police every day, he led the way for Sokolovich; striking a match, he flung open the door to a very warm, stuffy room imbued with a peculiar cloying odor, half its window obstructed diagonally by the roof of some outbuilding. Beyond the window, beyond the dark glass pane, there was a dull sound of resonant voices, the rumble of some machine, and what seemed a vision of hell, the blazing crimson flame of a huge torch.

"What's that?" Sokolovich stopped and asked harshly, even anxiously.

"Night work, cleaning sewers," muttered Nyanchuk, still feeling offended; when he had lit two candles sitting on the windowsill in red rosettes, he lowered the puffy white blinds made of calico cloth and made inquiries as to what the guests would like.

Sokolovich ordered some kvass for himself and added with an odd smirk:

"And let's have some fruit for the lady."

"We haven't got no fruit," Nyanchuk replied. "Except grapes. Ruble and a half a bunch."

"Lovely," said Sokolovich, "Bring on the grapes."

Korolkova was obviously flattered by such treatment. Making a real attempt to act the part of a noble-born lady who is treated to grapes in the middle of winter, glancing about the room, stamping her frozen feet and blowing into her muff, she said archly:

"Oh my, they're probably cold!"

A moment later Nyanchuk brought in a big iron tray, containing the grapes and two uncorked bottles frothing over with foam, and when he had gone Sokolovich immediately locked the door. As Nyanchuk left the room, Korolkova was standing beside the table, still breathing into her muff, nibbling on the firm green grapes mottled with sawdust, and her dreadful companion with that yellow necklace of beard below his freshly shaven face was removing his coat in the corner, unwinding a long scarf of coarse violet wool. After that the room, with the ominous flame still blazing and the cryptic night work still dully rumbling on outside its window, became shrouded in mystery.

At four o'clock a bell in the corridor began jangling. Nyanchuk awoke and jumped up from the settee, wearing long drawers with foot straps and felt slippers. When he reached the switchboard he found the third button pushed forward. Behind the door of room number three a woman's voice asked for a ten-pack of "Zephyr" cigarettes. Returning from the snack bar with the cigarettes, the drowsy Nyanchuk forgot exactly which room had wanted them and rapped on number eight, the room he had given Sokolovich. Behind the door a coarse low bass asked in a slow drawl:

"What is it?"

"Your little miss asked for some cigarettes," said Nyanchuk.

"My 'little miss' did not ask for cigarettes, and there's no possibility whatsoever that she could have," the bass voice answered peremptorily.

Recalling at once who had wanted the pack, Nyanchuk placed it in the plump female hand thrust through the crack in the door of number three, lay down once more in the quiet semi-dark hotel, and fell fast asleep to the measured ticking of the clock at the end of the corridor.

It was already past six when he awoke again; towering high above him, in his coat and peaked cap, the lodger from number eight was poking at his shoulder.

"Here's for the room and for your trouble," he said. "Let me out. It's time I was at the factory, and the lady said she'd like to be awakened at nine."

"But what about the grapes?" Nyanchuk asked quickly, in an anxious tone.

"I've accounted for everything," said Sokolovich. "According to my figures it comes to four rubles seventy. And I'm giving you five and a half. Understood?"

And he started walking calmly toward the stairway.

Eyes half closed with craving for sleep, squirming about to adjust the coat he had thrown over his shoulders, Nyanchuk once more led the way, tramping along down the steps of the staircase. Sokolovich waited patiently as he struggled with the key, which he had great difficulty turning in the keyhole. Finally the door swung open. He walked past Nyanchuk, raised the gate slightly, and covering his throat with his hand, like an opera singer afraid of catching cold, he mumbled a hollow "Good-bye" into his beard and stepped out on the street, into the damp and fresh air. It was still utterly dark and quiet, but in that darkness and hush the proximity of morning could already be sensed. Above all the distant surrounding expanses, above the whole enormous nest of the still mute metropolis hung the muffled, faraway moan of the mills and factories, summoning the countless working masses from all their squalid shelters, from all their hovels and miserable dives. Standing with its black shadow opposite the hotel, a floodlight illumined part of the carriage-way and street. The fog had dissipated, a light snow had fallen in the night; soaring high in the air from behind the fence adjacent to the floodlight, a massive bulk of lumber exuded a funereal white glow against the blackness of night. Sokolovich turned to the right and vanished in the distance. Chilled to the bone, Nyanchuk slammed the door and ran back up the stairs.

There was no point in lying down again. He began to search under the settee for his boots—and suddenly he noticed that the door of number eight was ajar and light was spilling from within. He jumped up and rushed to the room; inside there was a dreadful hush, the kind of hush that a room with some-one in it never has, even a room occupied by only a sleeping person. The guttering candles crackled in their split rosettes, shadows were darting in the gloom, and on the bed, protruding from beneath a blanket, were the short bare legs of a woman lying flat on her back. The head was hidden beneath two pillows that were pressed down upon it.

1916

REMOTE

Once upon a time, long, long ago, a thousand years ago, there lived in the Arbat, at the hotel North Pole where I lived as well, a certain inaudible, inconspicuous, most humble of the humble Ivan Ivanich, a man already rather old and quite threadbare.

From year to year Moscow lived on, doing her prodigious deeds. He too did something or other and for some reason lived on in the world. He would leave about nine and return before five. Musing quietly, though not at all sadly, he would take his key from the nail in the lobby, climb to the second floor, and walk down the zigzagging corridor. This corridor had a very complex, very foul odor, dominated by that pungent and stifling substance that they use to polish the floors of sleazy hotels. The corridor was dark and ominous (the rooms had windows facing the courtyard, and very little light came through the transom glass above the doors), and all day long a small lamp with a reflector burned at the end of each of its articulations. But it seemed that Ivan Ivanich experienced utterly none of those burdensome sensations that the corridor aroused in people unaccustomed to the North Pole. He would walk down the corridor calmly and simply. And he would encounter his fellow lodgers: a university student with youthful beard and shining eyes, dashing briskly along and putting his arms through the sleeves of his coat on the run; a stenographer with an independent air, tall and alluring despite her resemblance to a white Negro; a small, elderly lady in high heels, always dressed up and rouged, with brown hair, with phlegm gurgling incessantly in her chest—an encounter with this lady was always presaged by the muffled jingle of the bells that were dashing along the corridor on her snub-nosed pug dog, who had a protruding lower jaw and fiercely, senselessly goggling pop-eyes... Ivan Ivanich, who would bow politely to everyone he encountered, was not at all offended when he received barely a nod in reply. He would pass one articulation, turn into another still longer and blacker, where the red wall lamp was glittering still farther in the distance; he would put the key into his door, and then seclude himself behind it until the next morning.

How did Ivan Ivanich occupy himself in his room, how did he while away his leisure time? God knows. His domestic life, in no way manifested outwardly, of no use to anyone, was a complete mystery to us all—even to the chambermaid and floor boy, who disturbed his cloistered existence only when serving the samovar, making the bed, or cleaning the vile washstand, from which the water always spurted unexpectedly, not into the face, not on the hands, but very high and to the side, obliquely. Ivan Ivanich, I repeat, led a life of rare inconspicuousness, of rare monotony. Winter was passing, spring arriving. Horse-drawn trams sped, rumbled, jangled along Arbat Street, people were continuously streaming by one another, rushing somewhere; light four-wheeler cabs went crackling and clattering along, hucksters with trays on their heads screamed out; towards evening a golden-luminous sunset gleamed in the remote aperture at the end of the street, and over all the noise and din a low bass peal from an ancient pyramidical belfry spread melodiously. Ivan Ivanich apparently neither saw nor heard any of this. Neither winter nor spring, neither summer nor fall had the slightest apparent influence either upon him or upon his way of life. But then one spring there came from somewhere a certain nobleman with the title of prince, and he took a room in the North Pole and became Ivan's nextdoor neighbor. And then some utterly unexpected, unanticipated change came over Ivan Ivanich.

How could the prince have overwhelmed him? Certainly not by his title. After all, that aged fellow lodger of Ivan Ivanich, the little lady with the pug dog, was also a titled personage, but he felt absolutely nothing for her. How could the prince have captivated him? Certainly not by his wealth or appearance. The prince had squandered all his means, he was slovenly, huge and ungainly, with bags under his eyes and loud labored respiration. Ivan Ivanich, nonetheless, was both overwhelmed and captivated, and above all, he was completely knocked out of his perennial rut. His whole existence was transformed; he was in a state of incessant agitation. He became absorbed in anxious, petty and ignominious mimicry.

The prince arrived, settled down, began going out and coming back, meeting certain people, fussing about over certain matters—exactly in the same way, of course, as did everyone who lodged at the North Pole. Of these a great many had come and gone in the memory of Ivan Ivanich, although the idea of intruding upon their privacy and becoming acquainted with them had never even entered his head. But for some reason he singled out the prince. Upon meeting the prince the second or third time in the corridor, for some reason he scraped and bowed, introduced himself, and, with all sorts of the most complaisant of apologies, asked to be told as precisely as possible what time it was. And having got acquainted in such a clever manner, he simply became infatuated with the prince, made an utter shambles of his usual pattern of life, and slavishly began imitating the prince's every movement.

The prince, for example, went to bed late. He would return home about two in the morning (always by cab). Ivan Ivanich's lamp also began to burn until two. For some reason he would await the prince's return, his ponderous footsteps in the corridor, his whistling snuffle. He waited with joy, almost with trepidation, and at times he even leaned out of his cramped little room to catch sight of the approaching prince and have a word with him. Walking along leisurely, as if he did not see him, the prince would always ask exactly the same question in a profoundly apathetic tone:

"Well, then, you're not in bed yet?"

And paralyzed with delight, but without the least timidity, without the least subservience, Ivan Ivanich would answer:

"No, prince, not yet. The night is young; it's only ten past two... So you've been out making merry, having a good time?"

"Yes," the prince would say, snuffling and puffing as he tried unsuccessfully to get his key in the door; "I met an old acquaintance; we stopped in at a tavern for a while... Good night..."

With that the whole matter would end, so coldly, yet politely, would the prince cut short his late night conversation with Ivan Ivanich; but even this was enough for Ivan. He would return on tiptoe to his room, routinely dispose of all that had to be done before sleeping, cross himself a bit and nod toward the icon corner, climb inaudibly into his bed behind a partition, and fall asleep at once, absolutely happy and with absolutely no intention of deriving any selfish benefit from his relations with the prince, if one may discount a most innocent prevarication to the floor boy in the morning:

"Well, I was up too late again last night... The prince and me got to talking again and sat up till the cocks crowed..."

In the evening the prince would set a pair of big downtrodden shoes outside the door and hang out the most capacious of silvery pantaloons. Ivan Ivanich, too, started setting out his wrinkled little boots, which previously had been shined only once in a blue moon, and hanging out his tiny britches with their missing buttons, which had never been hung out previously, not even for Christmas or Easter.

The prince would awaken early, let out a terrible cough, take an avid draw on a thickly rolled cigarette, then open his door and shout into the corridor, loudly enough for all the building to hear: "Hey, boy! Bring the tea!" And in his dressing gown, flapping his slippers, he would go off to answer nature's call and stay for long periods of time. And Ivan Ivanich started doing the same; he shouted into the corridor for a samovar, and, in galoshes on bare feet, in a wretched summer coat over soiled drawers, he too ran off to nature's call, although previously he had always done so in the evening.

The prince once mentioned that he was very fond of the circus, that he attended it frequently. And Ivan Ivanich, who had never been fond of the circus, who had last been to the circus not less than forty years ago, decided to see one performance all the same, and that night he gave the prince an ecstatic account of the enormous delight he had experienced...

Ah, spring, spring! The crux of the whole matter, it seems, is that all this nonsense took place in the spring.

Every spring seems like the end of something overcome and the beginning of something new. This deception was especially sweet and cogent during that long remote Moscow spring—for me because of my youth and because my student days were ending, but for numerous others simply because it was spring, an unusually marvelous spring. Every spring is a festival, but that spring was especially festive.

Moscow had lived through her intricate, wearisome winter. Then she had lived through Lent and Easter, and once again she felt as if she were finished with something, as if she had cast some burden from her shoulders, as if she had finally attained something genuine. And multitudes of Muscovites already were changing or preparing to change their lives, to live them somehow all over from the beginning, this time in a different way than previously, to start living more sensibly, properly, more youthfully; they hurried to clean their apartments, to order summer suits, to go out shopping—for shopping, of course (even for mothballs), is joyous! They were preparing, in a word, for departure from Moscow, for vacations at summer houses, in the Caucasus, in the Crimea, abroad, that is to say for the summer, which, so it always seems, must be inevitably happy and long, oh so long.

How many splendid, soul-exhilarating suitcases and new creaking clothes hampers were bought on Leontevsky Lane and at Muir-Merrilees! How many haircuts and shaves were dispensed at Basile's and Théodore's! Sunny, stimulating days followed one after another, days with new aromas, with a new cleanliness about on the streets, with a new gleam of church cupolas against the bright sky, with a new Strastnoy and a new Petrovka, with new radiant attire on foppish beauties and stylish damsels, dashing along Kuznetsky in the lightweight cabs of daredevil hackneys, with the new light-grey derby of a celebrated actor who was also dashing away somewhere on "pneumatics." Everyone was concluding some phase of his previous life, which had not been lived as it should have been, and for nearly all of Moscow it was the eve of a new, inevitably happy life; so it was for me too, even especially so for me, far more than for others, so it seemed to me then. And ever nearer and nearer came the time of my parting with the North Pole, with all by which I had lived my student life there; from morning to night I was bustling, riding about Moscow, absorbed in all sorts of joyous concerns. But what was my neighbor next door doing, that most modest of the hotel's inhabitants? Well, approximately the same things that we were doing. The same thing, ultimately, had happened to him as to all the rest of us.

The April and May days flowed on, horse-drawn trams sped jangling by, people were rushing continuously, light four-wheeler cabs went crackling and clattering along, hucksters with trays on their heads screamed tenderly, sorrowfully (although the matter at hand was only asparagus), a sweet, warm redolence was wafting from Skachkov's pastry shop, vats of bay leaves stood at the entrance of the Prague, where fine gentlemen dined on young potatoes in sour cream, inconspicuously day approached evening, and now the golden-luminous sky before sunset was gleaming in the west, and over the happy, teeming streets a low bass peal from a pyramidical belfry spread melodiously... Day after day the spring city lived her enormous, multifarious life, and I was one of the happiest participants in that life; I lived in all her smells, sounds, all her bustling vanity, her encounters, business affairs, purchases; I rode along in cabs, went to the cafe Tremblay with my friends, ordered iced fish soup with beet tops and onions at the Prague, and tossed off a shot of cold vodka with a bite of fresh cuke... But what about Ivan Ivanich? Well, Ivan Ivanich also went off somewhere, also dropped in a few places, attended to personal matters, small matters, inordinately small, and acquired in return the right to continued existence among us, that is, to a room at the North Pole and a thirty-kopeck dinner in a chophouse dive across from it. Only this modest right was he earning himself somewhere, somehow, and it seemed that he was absolutely alien to all our hopes for some new life, for a new suit, a new hat, a new haircut, for competing on a level with someone in something, making an acquaintance, forming a friendship... But then the prince arrived.

How could he have enchanted, overwhelmed Ivan Ivanich? But of course the object of enchantment is not important; what is important is the craving to be enchanted. The prince, moreover, was a man with remnants of the grand manner, a man who had squandered nearly everything, but who, as a consequence, had lived the good life in his time. So poor Ivan Ivanich, too, started dreaming of living in a new way, in a spring way, with a certain ostentation and even certain diversions. Well, is that really so bad—to turn in not right at ten, to hang out your trousers to be cleaned, to answer nature's call before washing? Doesn't that really rejuvenate you—to stop in for a haircut, to have your beard trimmed and shortened, to buy a greyish hat that makes you look years younger, and to return home with a piddling little purchase, even if it is just a quarter pound of some trifle, prettily tied by the hands of a bonny shop girl? Gradually but ever increasingly yielding to temptation, Ivan Ivanich did all of this in his own way; that is, he performed, within the limitations of his powers and means, almost everything the others were performing: he made an acquaintance and began mimicking—true, no more than anyone else!—and he amassed spring hopes and brought a certain measure of vernal profligacy into his life, and took part in the ostentation, and clipped his beard, and began returning to the North Pole just before evening with some piddling parcels in his arms. And what's even more: he bought himself a greyish hat and something in the way of luggage—a little suitcase all studded with glistening tin tacks, for a ruble seventy-five—since he dreamed of going without fail that summer to the Trinity Monastery or the New Jerusalem...

Whether this dream was ever realized and how Ivan Ivanich's sudden surge toward a new life eventually ended I really don't know. I think that it ended, as do most of our surges, rather poorly, but, I repeat, I cannot say anything definite. I cannot say because shortly after that all of us, that is the prince, Ivan Ivanich and I, parted one fine day, and we parted not for the summer, not for a year, not for two, but forever. Yes, no more, no less than forever; that is, never to meet again, not ever, till the end of the world, which thought, despite all its apparent bizarreness, simply horrifies me now: just think of it— never! In fact, all of us who live on earth together during a particular time and who experience together all the earthly joys and sorrows, seeing one and the same sky, loving and hating, ultimately, the same things, and every one, down to the last man, doomed to one and the same execution, to one and the same disappearance from the face of the earth, all of us should harbor for each other a feeling of utmost tenderness, of poignant intimacy that moves us to tears, and we should simply cry out with fear and pain when fate separates us, since there is always a possibility that any separation, even for ten minutes, may become eternal. But, as everyone knows, such feelings are usually located in the most remote extremities of our being, and we often part from even those most dear to us in a way that could not possibly be more frivolous. In just this way, of course, did we too part—the prince, Ivan Ivanich and I. One day near evening a cab arrived to take the prince to the Smolensk station—a rather sorry little cab, which cost him maybe sixty kopecks, while mine, to the Kursk station, ran a ruble and a half and had a frisky grey mare. And we parted, without even saying good-bye. Ivan Ivanich remained in his gloomy corridor, in his cage with the dingy glass above the door, and the prince and I drove off in opposite directions, each of us having seated himself in his light four-wheeler after shoving tips into everyone's hands; the prince was apparently rather indifferent, but I was brisk and lively, all decked out in new clothes, vaguely anticipating some marvelous encounter during the trip, on the train... And I remember as if it were now: I was riding towards the Kremlin, and the Kremlin was illumined by the evening sun; I rode through the Kremlin, past the cathedrals—how beautiful they were, my God!—then along Ilinka, redolent of all sorts of ironmongery, candle waxes and oils, where evening shadows already had fallen, then along Pokrovka, now enveloped in pealing, booming bells, blessing the happily ended bustle and vanity of the day. As I rode along I not only rejoiced in myself and in the whole world, but I was truly drowning in the joy of being, having somehow instantly forgotten the North Pole, and the prince, and Ivan Ivanich by the time I had reached Arbat Square; and most likely I would have been amazed had I been told that even they would be preserved forever in that sweet and bitter dream of the past by which my soul will live to the grave, and that there would come a day when I would call out in vain even to them:

"Dear prince, dear Ivan Ivanich, where do your bones lie rotting today? And where are they, our common, foolish hopes and joys, our long remote Moscow spring?"

Amboise. 1922

INDULGENT PARTICIPATION

In Moscow—let us say on Molchánovka—lives "a former artiste of the Imperial Theatres." Alone, very elderly, broad-cheeked, spare. She gives singing lessons. And this is what happens to her every year in December.

One Sunday—let us imagine a very frosty, sunlit morning—the bell in her vestibule rings.

"Annushka! Someone's ringing!" she cries anxiously to the cook from her bedroom.

The cook runs to the door—and steps back in astonishment: so dazzling, so smartly arrayed are the guests—two young ladies in furs and white gloves and their escort, a coxcomb of a student from the university, frozen through in his light uniform coat and thin boots.

The guests wait for quite some time in the cold sitting room, which admits an amber glow through the frosty mosaic of the windows; then they hear the brisk footsteps of their hostess and hurriedly arise to greet her. She is agitated—knowing why they have come; she has heavily powdered her face and perfumed her large, bony hands...

"For goodness' sake, forgive me, ladies and gentlemen, it seems I've made you wait," she says with a captivating smile and the most worldly nonchalance; as she makes her swift entry, she has difficulty controlling the beating of her heart.

"But no, you must forgive us the intrusion," the student interrupts with refined deference, bowing and kissing her hand. "We come to you with an assiduous and most humble request. The organization committee for the traditional literary-vocal-musical evening in aid of impecunious matriculants of the Fifth Moscow *Gymnasium* has bestowed upon us the honor of petitioning you in regard to your indulgent participation in that evening, which is to transpire on the third day of the Christmas holidays."

"Ladies and gentlemen, if possible, spare me!" she begins captivatingly. "The fact is..."

But the young ladies pounce upon her with such cordiality, with such ardor and flattery that she cannot manage even this feeble attempt to refuse or evade...

After this three whole weeks go by.

For three whole weeks Moscow works, does business, makes merry, but among all its most diverse occupations, interests, and distractions, it secretly harbors only one feeling—anticipation of the portentous evening performance on the twenty-seventh of December. A great many placards of all colors and sizes mingle in motley assemblage on all its streets and crossings: *The Lower Depths, The Blue Bird, The Three Sisters,* Chaliapin in *Water-Nymph,* Sobinov

43

in *Snow-Maiden,* Shor, Krein, and Erlich, Zimin's opera, an evening with Igor Severianin... But now what catches all eyes? Only the small placard printed in large letters with the given name, patronymic, and surname of that indulgent participant in the literary-vocal-musical evening in aid of impecunious pupils of the Fifth Moscow *Gymnasium.* All this time the participant herself never goes out, sits at home working without respite so as not to disappoint the expectations of Moscow; endlessly she contemplates her repertoire, testing her voice from morning to evening, preparing first one selection, then another... Now the days go by with extraordinary rapidity, and this rapidity horrifies her: before you have time to blink your eyes that terrible December twenty-seventh will be here!

She has stopped giving lessons, receives no one, never leaves the house for fear of catching bronchitis or a head cold. What, exactly, should she perform? The audience has no inkling of the difficulty this question presents to even the most experienced artiste! After long, agonizing doubts and waverings, however, she settles the matter by retaining her old, unchanged repertoire. Once again she rehearses three pieces. The first is French, tender and sad, bewitching like a lullaby, but concealing the enormous passion, strength and pain of an enamored feminine soul, which madly thirsts for happiness but sacrificially abnegates this happiness; the second is full of scintillating coloratura and Russian impetuosity; and then—the *pièce de résistance:* "I would kiss you, but I fear the moon would see," in which, as always, she will display extraordinary resplendence, will perform "with fervor," wantonly, youthfully, and will break off on such a desperately high and exultant note that the entire concert hall will shudder with applause. Besides these, she prepares twelve other pieces for encores... The days keep flashing by, and now a certain foreboding grows in her soul, as if the hour of her execution were approaching. She works, however, and works still more. And then, at last, that final fateful day arrives!

On the morning of December twenty-seventh all her faculties are strained to the limits of intensity. In the morning still one more rehearsal, but this is the final, the dress rehearsal. Now she sings as if on stage, in full voice, with all the expressiveness of high art; she and her accompanist review her entire program—and she has that feeling: all the work was not in vain! But who knows, for all that, what awaits her in the evening? Triumph or perdition? Her face is aflame, her hands like ice... After the rehearsal she goes into her bedroom, undresses, and lies down. Annushka brings her something singularly exceptional —impressed granular caviar, cold pullet and port: on the day of a performance this is the lunch of all great artistes. Having eaten, she orders the cook to pull the shutters, to leave her, and to maintain absolute silence in the house; she closes her eyes and lies in the darkness completely quiescent, trying to think of nothing, to let nothing agitate her—an hour, two, three, right up to six o'clock in the evening. At six she jumps up: a strident ring in the vestibule—the hairdresser!

Heart beating, ears and cheeks blazing, hands icy, she measures out forty whole drops of an etheric-valerian mixture, and in her robe, with hair let down, like a virgin they have come to adorn, to prepare for immolation, she takes her seat before the mirror. Having first warmed his hands over the stove in the kitchen, the hairdresser comes in and says encouragingly:

"Marvelous weather! A little nippy, but marvelous!"

He works slowly, with refinement, feeling that he too is a participant in the forthcoming event, understanding completely and sharing her artiste's agitation since he himself is an artist at heart. With his casually light conversation, his jokes, and, in general, all his proficiency in these matters—together with his implicit faith in her forthcoming success—he calms her little by little, restores her vigor, fortitude and hopes... But when he has completed his work, when he has examined it from all sides and is convinced that nothing better can possibly be made of these magnificent waves and coifs, he leaves, and the clock in the dining room slowly strikes seven. Once again her heart begins to founder: they are coming for her at half past eight!

Eight strikes and still she is not ready. She has taken drops again—this time Hoffmann's; she puts on her best linen, rouges and powders herself... Then at half past eight the bell rings once more, jolting her like thunder: they've come! Annushka runs clumsily into the vestibule; she too is beside herself, so agitated that at first she cannot get the door open...

They—this time two university students—have arrived in a huge antediluvian hired coach with two mammoth nags in harness. They too are men-about-town and they too wear no galoshes, and their feet too are rigid from the frost. The sitting room, as usual, is cold; lamps smelling of kerosene burn drearily. In only their dress coats they patiently sit, their mirror-smooth heads glistening, wafting the sweet scent of brilliantine and pomade, with large, white satin bows on their chests, like groomsmen at a wedding. They sit in silence, wait politely, steadfastly, look at the doors closed on all sides around them, at the frozen window panes, flickering with fiery dots of blue and red, at the grand piano, at the portraits of great male and female singers on the walls; they listen to the numb knell and the din of trams beyond the windows, to the apprehensive steps of Annushka and the artiste herself behind the doors... Time passes, a quarter hour, a half hour, forty minutes... Then, all at once, one of the doors unexpectedly opens wide. As if on cue they jump from their seats, and with a captivating-insouciant smile the artiste rushes to greet them:

"For goodness' sake, forgive me, gentlemen, it seems I've made you wait... What now, could it really be time? Well, all right then, we'll go if you wish; I'm ready..."

Even through the rouge and powder on her cheeks crimson blotches burn; her breath is redolent of drops, lilies-of-the-valley, her hands of cream, her airy, smoke-colored, gossamer dress of fragrances. She looks like Death, setting off for a ball. She has thrown something silky-black, Spanish over her intricate elevated coiffure, over the grey hair waved and fluffed on all sides, and has draped a coat of white curly goat's hair over the bare shoulders with the enormous clavicles... The students rush headlong after her into the anteroom. The slimmer and taller one seizes her overshoes, hastily drops on one knee and fits them adroitly over her black satin slippers with the diamond buckles; when she bends to help him and to make a modest attempt at straightening the hem on the white lace tips of her pantalettes, he smells how her armpits reek with the rankness of mice...

She sang of the storm cloud that met the thunder and of some kind of sanctuary—"the Lord has sent us to a sink-tuary here"—and with special resplendence, "I would kiss you..." A carping old gaffer sitting in the first row snickered sarcastically at this point, twisted his head with unequivocal insinuation: my humble thanks, but please, no kisses... For all that he only made a fool of himself. The success of the artiste was colossal; incessantly they called her back and forced encores upon her— especially the sensitive young people, who stood in the aisles shouting even with menace and beating together their cupped palms with an awesome, booming resonance.

1929

A PASSING

I

The prince died just before evening on August twenty-ninth. He died as he had lived—taciturn, estranged from everyone.

Glowing with twilight gold, the sun dropped periodically behind swarthy delicate storm clouds that were spread like islands above distant fields to the west. It was a calm plain evening. The spacious yard of the manor was empty; the house, which seemed to have become even more decrepit over the summer, was hushed.

First to learn of the prince's death were the mendicants, who were always roving about the village. They appeared beside the ruins of stone columns at the entrance to his estate and in clashing, discordant voices began singing the ancient folk canticle "On the Passing of Soul from Body." There were three of them: a pockmarked lad in a sky-blue shirt with the sleeves cut off, an old man standing very straight and tall, and a suntanned girl, about fifteen years old but already a mother. Holding in her arms a drowsy child, the nipple of her small breast in its mouth, she sang loudly, impassively. Both muzhiks were blind, their eyes covered by whitish cataracts; but her eyes were clear and dark.

Doors were slamming in the manor house. Natasha dashed out onto the front veranda and tore like a whirlwind across the yard to the workers' annex; through the open door of the house a clock on the wall could be heard, languidly striking six. Only a moment later a farm hand ran through the yard, putting his arms into the sleeves of his coat on the run; he would saddle a horse and gallop off to the village for the old women. A visitor at the estate, the pilgrim-woman Anyuta, whose short-clipped hair made her look like a boy, stuck her head out the window of the annex, clapped her hands, and screamed something after him—her voice doltish, maundering and ecstatic.

When young Bestuzhev went into the room, the dead man lay supine on the antique walnut bed beneath an old blanket made of red satin, the collar of his nightshirt undone, his immobile, somehow drunken eyes half closed, his dark face thrown back, now paler, long unshaven, with big graying moustaches. The shutters in this room had been closed, as he had wished, all summer—now they were being opened. On the chiffonier by the bed the yellow flame of a candle burned. Tilting his head to one side, his heart pounding, Bestuzhev avidly scrutinized that strange, now almost cold object that was immersed in the bedding.

One after another the shutters were opened. As it burned out with an orange tint amidst the storm clouds, the remote sun peeped in the windows, through the dark branches of old coniferous trees in the front garden. Bestuzhev stepped back from the dead man and flung open one of these windows. He felt the flow of pure air that was drawn into the room, into that stagnant, variegated medicinal smell. Natasha, who had been crying, entered and began taking out everything that the prince, suddenly gripped by some apprehensive avidity a week before, had ordered dragged into his room and laid out before him on tables and armchairs: a shabby Cossack saddle, bridles, a brass hunting horn, coupling straps for coursers, a cartridge belt. No longer constrained by the knocking and jangling of bits and stirrups, going about her business with a firm severe expression on her face, she blew out the candle with a forceful puff as she walked past the chiffonier... The prince was immobile; his half-open eyes, which appeared to be gazing somewhat askance, were also immobile. A dry evening warmth, blending with crisp air from the river, filled the room. The sun had expired, everything had faded. The coniferous needles of the front garden were dry and dark against that transparent sea of the sky, greenish above and saffron below, off in the distance to the west. Some kind of bird was chirping outside the window, and the noise it made seemed extremely shrill.

"No need to mourn," said Natasha gravely as she came in again; pulling out a drawer of the chiffonier, she removed some clean underlinen, some sheets, and a pillowcase. "The master died easy, God grant us all such a death. And there ain't nobody to mourn for him; he didn't leave nobody behind," she added, and went out again.

As he sat against the windowsill, Bestuzhev kept gazing into the dark corner, at the bedding where the dead man lay. He kept trying to understand something, to gather his thoughts, to be horrified. But he felt no horror. He felt only astonishment, the impossibility of grasping, of comprehending what had happened... Was it all really over, and could one speak so freely in this bedroom now, as Natasha had just spoken? But then, thought Bestuzhev, she had been just as unconstrained earlier when she spoke of the prince—for the whole past month—as one speaks of a man who has already left the realm of the living.

From the yard, from the dusk, came a faint, uncommonly pleasant redolence of smoke. It was soothing, it bespoke the earth, the constancy of simple human life. In the darkened meadows, by the river, the gristmill hummed on steadily... A week ago the prince had been sitting on an old mill-stone by its gates—in a cap, in a waisted coat of fox fur, thin and bent, his face sombre, his arms propping him up on the grey porous rock. An old man who had brought several *chetveriks* of newly reaped grain to be ground cast a squinting, sullen glance at him as he undid the sacking that held his grain. "Ain't you got skinny now!" he said coldly and scornfully, although he had always spoken to the prince with deference before. "You don't amount to nothing! No, there ain't much of living left in you. What'll you be, about seventy?" "Almost fifty-one," said the prince. "Fifty-one!" repeated the old man mockingly as he busied himself with the sacking. "That just can't be," he said firmly; "you're a far sight older than I am." "You idiot," said the prince, smirking. "Don't you know we grew up together?" "Well, whether we did or whether we didn't, there ain't much living left in you now," said the old man, and exerting all his strength, he raised the heavy bag full of rye, pressed it to his chest, then hastily, half squatting, he carried it off into the humming, mealy white mill...

"You go on out now, young master," said Natasha impassively but pointedly as she entered the room with a bucket of hot water.

And with that bucket, with those words Bestuzhev suddenly felt frightened. He arose from the windowsill, and, without looking at Natasha, went out through the vestibule adjacent to the dead prince's room, onto the back veranda. In the dusk beside the veranda Evgenia and Agafya, two old peasant women who had arrived from the village, were washing their hands. One of them was pouring water from a jug, the other was bent over, firmly wringing out the hem of her dark dress, which she held between her knees, shaking her fingers. That was even more frightening—those peasant hags. Hurrying past them, Bestuzhev entered the dry garden, its foliage already sparser as autumn approached, mysteriously illumined in its bottomlands by the round, huge, translucent moon, which had just appeared amidst the distant boles of trees.

II

Everything in the room where the prince had died was in order before ten; everything was tidy, the bed was gone, there was a warm redolence of scrubbed floors. The body, towering beneath a sheet, looking very large, lay on tables placed diagonally across the front corner, beneath antique icons next to the window, whose upper pane sparkled silver with moonlight. Three thick candles in tall, ecclesiastical candlesticks burned transparently at its head, their crystalline fumes quavering. Freshly washed and combed, wearing a new waisted coat, Tishka, the son of the church custodian Semyon, read the Psalter plaintively and hurriedly. "Praise ye the Lord from the heavens," he read, imitating the monastic sisters—"Praise ye him, all his angels: praise ye him, all his hosts..." Transparent spears of flame, golden, with bright-blue foundations, quavered and darkly fumed on the candles.

The only light in the house was in the domestics' chamber. A table stood beneath the window there, and on this table a samovar was boiling. They were drinking tea: Natasha, in a black kerchief, pallid and grave, Evgenia, looking the very image of death, the sorrowfully meek Agafya, the carpenter Grigory, who already had begun making a coffin in the barn, and the church custodian Semyon, an old man with lacklustre, leaden eyes that had been ruined by perpetual reading over the dead by the light of a quavering candle. Semyon, who was to replace his son as reader, had brought his own book, covered by some rough, grayish-brown material that appeared to be wooden, spotted with wax, the corners of its pages scorched here and there.

"Don't matter how bad you live, it's still hard parting with this good earth," said Agafya sorrowfully as she poured tea from her cup into her saucer.

"Surely is hard," said Grigory. "Had he known, now, he'd of lived different, he'd of forsook all that he owned. But then, we're afraid to have done with earthly lands and chattels; you keep thinking there won't be nowhere to go in your old age... Then one fine day it turns out you ain't even lived to no old age!"

"Our life runs back like a wave from the shore," said Semyon. "Death, now, they say, must be received with joy and a-trembling."

"Passing, not death, my dear," Evgenia corrected him in a dry didactic tone.

"Whether it's with trembling or not, ain't nobody wants to die," said Grigory. "Take just any little gnat, even he's afraid of death. That means even they've got souls too."

"Not only souls, dear friend, but souls immortal," said Evgenia still more didactically.

When he had finished his last cup of tea, Semyon jerked back his head to shake the sweaty, dark-grey hair off his brow, arose, crossed himself, took his psalter and walked on tiptoe through the dark drawing room and dark guest room to the body.

"On your way now, dearie," said Evgenia as he left. "And do a right and proper reading for him. When somebody reads good, the sins drop away from a sinner like leaves off a dry tree."

Semyon replaced Tishka, put on his spectacles, and gazing severely through them, he gently picked away the wax from the guttering candles, then slowly crossed himself, spread his book open on the lectern and began reading softly, with tender and sad conviction, only occasionally raising his voice in admonishment.

The door leading into the vestibule beside the back veranda was open. As he read Semyon heard someone's feet tramping on the veranda. Two peasant girls, both in their very best clothing, in new, sturdy shoes, had come to view the dead body. They stepped into the room shyly and joyfully, whispering back and forth to each other. Crossing herself and trying to step gingerly, one of them approached the table, her breasts quivering beneath her new pink blouse, and drew back the sheet from the prince's face. The gleam of the candles fell on the girl's blouse, her frightened face was pallid and comely in that gleam, and the dead face of the prince shone like ivory. The large graying moustaches, which had grown thick during his illness, were diaphanous now, the eyes, not completely closed, glistened with some dark fluid...

Tishka smoked avidly in the entrance hall, waiting for the girls to come out. They slipped past, pretending not to notice him. One of them ran down off the veranda, but he managed to catch the other, the one in the pink blouse. Struggling to break free, she said in a whisper:

"Have you gone crazy? Let go! I'll tell your papa..."

Tishka let her go. She ran out toward the garden. The moon, now smaller, white, clear, hung high above the dark garden, and the dry iron on the bathhouse roof glittered golden in its light. In the garden shadows the girl turned around, glanced at the sky, and exclaimed:

"What a night—Lord have mercy!"

And her charming, happy voice rang out with joyous tenderness, resounded in the silent night air.

III

Bestuzhev paced from one end of the yard to the other. From that yard, empty, spacious, illumined by the moon, he gazed at the lights in the village beyond the river, at the bright windows of the annex, where he could hear the voices of people having supper. The barn gates were thrown wide open, a broken lantern burned on the tarantass coach box. Standing in a bent position with one leg thrust out obliquely, Grigory slid his plane along a board that was stuck into an old joiner's bench. A red-hazy flame quavered in the lantern, shadows quavered in the dusky barn... When Bestuzhev paused for a moment by the barn gates, Grigory raised his exhilarated face and said with tender pride:

"Near about got the lid done..."

Later Bestuzhev stood for a short time, leaning his elbows on the wide-open window of the annex. The cook was clearing remnants of supper from the table and wiping it with a tattered cloth. Two young boys, the herdsmen, were preparing for sleep: barefoot Mitka was praying on the plank bunk spread with fresh straw; Vanka prayed in the middle of the room. The tousled, ginger-haired stovemaker, broad-shouldered and very small of stature, in a black shirt covered with flecks of slaked lime, sat on a bench rolling a cigarette; he had come from the village beyond the river to begin work the following day, repairing the walls in the dilapidated ancestral crypt.

From her place on the stove Anyuta spoke, her voice doltish, ecstatic and maundering:

"Now you done passed away, your honor, you never got nothing through your head... And you never did give me nothing... 'We ain't got it, we ain't got it, just you wait a spell...' So now *you* can wait... Go on and wait... Just go on and wait now! You had enough waiting, dearie? You got anything through that head? You know now what you ever got through your head, stupid? What would it hurt you, giving out a ruble or two, to cover my body! I'm miserable, I'm a freak. I ain't got nobody. Look here at this!"

And she tore open her blouse and showed her naked bosom:

"Naked all over. That's right, stupid! And back in the old days I loved you, I pined for you, you was handsome then, you was merry and tender, just like a little miss! All through your young years you was a-wasting and grieving over your Ludmilochka, while she just racked and tormented you, stupid, then she upped and went to the altar with somebody else, and I was the onliest one that truly loved you, but I kept still and told it to my pillow! I might be miserable, I might be a freak, but maybe my soul, now, is like the angels and archangels; I was the onliest one that loved you, and it's only me sitting here rejoicing in your mortal end..."

Then she burst into wild, joyful laughter and weeping.

"Come on, Anyuta, let's us go read the Psalter," remarked the stovemaker loudly, in the tone one uses with children to amuse someone. "Come on, you ain't scared?"

"Idiot! If my legs was right I'd go for sure; ain't that what you ought to do?" screamed Anyuta through her tears. "It's a sin, being scared of the dead. They're holy and immaculate."

"I ain't scared neither," said the stovemaker casually, lighting his cigarette, which flared up with a green flame. "Why if you like, I'll lay with you all night down in the family crypt..."

Anyuta sobbed ecstatically, wiping her eyes with her blouse.

Without disturbing the bright and lovely regnancy of the night, making it even more lovely, airy shadows from the white storm clouds passing over the moon fell on the yard, and the moon, gleaming, rode upon those clouds in the depths of the pure sky, above the glittering roof of the dark old manor house where only one window was lit, the last window—by the head of the quiescent prince.

1918

NIGHT

The dacha is dark, the hour late; a ceaseless murmur streams all around me. After a long walk by the precipice over the sea I lie in a reed chair on the balcony. I am thinking—and listening, listening: a crystalline murmur, an obsessive witching spell!

The abysmal night sky is replete with multicolored stars suspended within it, and there is the fragile grey Milky Way, transparent and also full of stars, inclining in two uneven wisps of smoke toward the southern horizon, which is starless, consequently almost black. The balcony faces the garden, strewn with shingle and with sparse dwarfish trees. From the balcony the night sea unfolds. Pale, milky, mirror-smooth, it lies lethargically quiescent, silent. The stars too seem disposed to keep silent. And, as in some jangling dream, the monotonous crystalline din, never ceasing even for a second, pervades all this mute night world.

What am I thinking?

"And I decided to seek and search out by wisdom concerning all things that are done under the sun; but this sore travail hath God given to the sons of man that they may torment themselves... God hath made men reasonable, but alas, they have sought out many inventions." And the Preacher counsels paternally: "Be not righteous over much, and burden not thy mind with philosophy." But I am forever "philosophizing." I am "righteous over much."

What am I thinking? When I asked myself this, I wanted to recall precisely what I was thinking, and immediately I began thinking about my thought, about how this thought seems the most marvelous, the most incomprehensible—and the most pernicious—thing in my life. What was I thinking, what was within me? Reflections (or a semblance of reflections) about my surroundings, and for some reason a desire to remember, to preserve, to retain those surroundings within me... And what else? A feeling of great happiness because of the great serenity, the great harmony of the night, but also a nebulous anguish and some sort of cupidity. Why the anguish? Because of the dim sensation that in me alone there is no serenity—a perpetual dim torment—and there is no mindlessness. Why the cupidity? Because of the craving to make use somehow of this happiness and even of this anguish and craving, to create something from them... But this too, O Preacher, is anguish: "In days to come all will be forgotten. There is no remembrance of former lives. Also their love, and their hatred and their envy is now long perished; neither have they any more a portion in any thing that is done under the sun."

What was I thinking? But the precise subject of my thought is not important—what is important is my thinking, a process that is an absolute mystery to me, and still more important and more of a mystery is my thinking about this thinking and about the fact that "I understand nothing, neither of myself nor of the world," and at the same time I *understand my non-understanding,* I understand that I am lost amidst this night and this incantatory murmur, which seems now living, now dead, now senseless, yet sometimes revealing the most vital, most imperative truths.

This reflection about my own reflections, this understanding of my own non-understanding is the most irrefutable proof of my involvement in something a hundredfold larger than me; it is, therefore, proof of my immortality. Apart from all that is my private self, there is obviously within me a certain something that is fundamental, indecomposable—truly a particle of God.

Yes, but a particle of that which has neither form, nor time, nor space, of that which means my ruin. Eat thereof and ye shall be as God. But "God is in heaven, and we upon earth." In eating thereof, we are passing from the earth, from earthly forms and laws. God is infinite, boundless, ubiquitous, innominate. But these very divine properties are horrible to me. And if they grow continually within me, then my earthly "being" and "doing," my life as a man expires...

The small trees stand immobile and dark in the garden.

Grey shingle gleams between them, flowers glow white in the flower-bed, and beyond that is the precipice—and the sea ascends into the sky like a milk-white Shroud of Christ.

This milkiness has a mirror-smoothness; but the horizon is gloomy and baleful—because of Jupiter and because there are almost no stars in the southern sky above the skyline.

Golden enormous Jupiter burns so regally at the end of the Milky Way that barely visible shadows from the table and chairs are cast onto the balcony. It seems like a minute satellite of some other world; in a misty-golden column its radiance falls from the immense heights of the heavens into the mirror-smooth milkiness of the sea, while on the horizon, clashing with the light, what seems like a dark knoll stands in dismal silhouette.

And the incessant din never ceases even for an instant, suffusing the silence of the sky, the earth and the sea with what seems a diaphanous murmur, like millions of streaming, merging rivulets or some wondrous flowers that seem ever growing in crystalline spirals...

Only man marvels at his own existence and meditates upon it. This is what most distinguishes him from other creatures, who are still in paradise, mindless of themselves. But men also differ one from another—by the degree, the extent of this marvelling. Why is it God has so deeply marked me with the fatal brand of the marveller, the reflecter, the "philosophizer," why does all this keep growing and growing in me? Do they philosophize, these myriads of nocturnal steppeland cicadas, who seem to suffuse the whole universe around me with their song of love? They are in paradise, in the beatific sleep of life, but I have awoken and sit awake keeping my vigil. The world is within them and they within it, but I seem to be gazing at it from aside. "The fool sitteth idly and devoureth his own heart. He that observeth the wind shall not sow..."

I listen and think. As a result I am infinitely alone in this midnight hush, jangling bewitchingly with myriads of crystalline wells, which flow inexhaustibly, with utmost submissiveness and mindlessness, into some abysmal Womb. The sublime light of Jupiter eerily illuminates the vast expanse between heaven and sea, the great temple of night above whose Royal Portals it is raised as a sign of the Holy Spirit. And I am alone in that temple; I sit within it keeping my vigil.

Day is the hour of deeds, the hour of bondage. Day exists in time and space. Day is fulfillment of earthly duty, service to earthly being. And the law of day decrees: be thou active in toil; interrupt it not for consciousness of thine own self, of thy place and thy goal, for thou art a slave of earthly being, and a certain task has been allotted unto thee, a calling, a name. But what is night? And is it befitting for man to sit before it keeping vigil, in that inscrutable state that we call "philosophizing"? We were enjoined to eat not of the forbidden fruit; listen, just listen to them, those selflessly ecstatic singers: they have not eaten, they do not eat! And what but exaltation of them did the Preachers derive from all their wisdom? It was they who said: "All is vanity of vanities, and man reapeth no profit from all his endeavors!" But it was they too who added—with bitter envy: "The sleep of a labouring man is sweet! And there is nothing better for a man than that he take delight in his labour, and merrily eat his bread, and drink his wine in the joy of his heart!" What is night? That which makes free for a certain interval the slave of time and space, takes from him his earthly task, his earthly name and calling—and makes ready for him, if he sits keeping vigil, a great temptation: sterile "philosophizing," sterile striving for understanding, that is, redoubled nonunderstanding: understanding neither the world, nor one's very self enveloped in it, nor one's beginning, nor one's end.

Neither of them exists for me, neither beginning nor end.

I know I am so many years old. But I was told this, that I was born in such a year, on such a day and at such an hour; otherwise I would not have known not only the day of my birth and, consequently, the sum of my years, but even the fact that I exist by reason of birth.

Birth! Just what is that? Birth! By no means is my birth my beginning. My beginning lies both in the (absolutely inscrutable) murk, where I was conceived before birth, and in my father, mother, in grandfathers and great-grandfathers, for they too are I, only in somewhat different form, of which a great deal has been repeated almost identically in me. "I remember that once, myriads of years ago, I was a goat yeanling." I myself had a similar experience (in the very land of the one who made this statement, in the tropics of India); I experienced the awesome sensation that I had been there before, in that paradisal warmth.

Self delusion? Auto-suggestion?

But it is quite probable that my forebears dwelt precisely in the tropics of India. How could they, in passing on so many times to their descendants and, finally, in passing on even to me almost the exact form of ear, chin, brow, how could they not pass on too the more delicate and imponderable, their carnality, which was bound to India? There are those who fear snakes or spiders "irrationally," that is, in a way contrary to the reason; this is a sensation of some previous existence, the dark recollection, for example, that once an ancient forebear of the one who is now afraid was threatened constantly with death from cobra, scorpion or tarantula. My forebear dwelt in India. So why, when I see coconut palms bent back from the ocean strand, when I see naked, dark-brown people in the warm tropical water, why should I not recall what I once felt when I was my naked dark-brown ancestor?

But neither do I have an end.

Not understanding my birth, insensible to it, neither do I understand nor apprehend my death, of which, again, I would not have had the remotest conception, awareness, or perhaps even sensation had I been born and lived on some island, absolutely uninhabited, without a single living creature. All my life I have lived under the augury of death—and all my life, nonetheless, I have felt that I will never die. Death! But every seven years a man is regenerated; that is, imperceptibly he dies as imperceptibly he is reborn. Therefore, many times I too have been regenerated (that is, have died while being reborn). I was dying, yet was living, have died even repeatedly—yet in principle I am just the same, and, furthermore, I am replete with the whole of my past.

Beginning, end. But my conception of time and space is terribly shaky. Not only do I sense this more and more as years go by, but I become more conscious of it.

I have been singled out from others of my kind. Even though all my life I have been agonizingly aware of the weakness and inadequacy of all my talents, in comparison to some I am not an altogether ordinary man. But precisely because of this (that is, by virtue of a certain singularity, by virtue of my belonging to a special category of men) my conception, my sense of time, of space and of my very self is especially shaky.

What category is this, what men are these? Men who are called poets, artists. What must they possess? The ability to feel with special intensity not only their own time, but also that of others, the past, not only their own country, their own generation, but also different, other countries, generations, not only themselves, but everyone else—that is, what is usually called the ability to reincarnate, and, besides that, an especially vital and especially graphic (sensuous) Memory. To be numbered among such men one must have traversed the long path of incarnations in the chain of his ancestors, until suddenly he becomes the peculiarly consummate image of his savage forebear, with all the crispness of his sensations, all the graphicness of his thought, with his enormous subconsciousness, but one also must have been immeasurably enriched on the long path, one must have acquired enormous consciousness.

Does such a man suffer tremendous torment or is he blessed with tremendous good fortune? Both. The curse and the joy of such a man is a keenly intense ego, a craving for the uttermost confirmation of that ego and also (by virtue of enormous experience during his abode in the enormous chain of incarnations) uttermost awareness of the vanity of this craving, an acute sensation of the All. And so: Buddha, Solomon, Tolstoy...

In youth and maturity gorillas have awesome physical strength, are immeasurably sensual in disposition, merciless in pursuing satiation of their lust, characterized by extreme spontaneity; but by old age they have become indecisive, pensive, doleful and compassionate... The resemblance to the Buddhas, Solomons, and Tolstoys is striking! And, generally speaking, in the regal breed of these saints and geniuses how many there are whose external appearance even suggests a comparison to gorillas! Everyone is familiar with the eyebrow arches of Tolstoy, the gigantic stature of the Buddha and the lump on his skull (and the fits of Mohammed, when the angels revealed to him amidst lightning "the mysteries and abysses not of this earth," and "in the trice of an eyewink," that is, beyond all laws of time and space, they bore him from Medina to Jerusalem—to the Rock Moriah, which was "incessantly oscillating between heaven and earth," as if blending earth with heaven, temporal with eternal).

At first all the Solomons and Buddhas embrace the world most greedily, then they most passionately curse its temptations. At first they are all great sinners, then great foes of sin, at first great amassers, then great dissipaters. They are all insatiable slaves of Maya—there she is, the jangling, conjuring Maya, listen, just listen to her!—and each is distinguished by a feeling that becomes ever more intense with the years, a sensation of the All and of one's inevitable dissolution within It...

With a faint stir of air the smell of ocean crispness and of flowers from the flower bed suddenly drifts up to the balcony. And presently a rustle is heard, the soft sigh of a wave half-asleep, slowly rolling in somewhere down below to the shore. Happy, somnolent, mindless, submissive, dying unaware of its death! It has rolled in, splashed, illumined the sands with a pale-blue radiance—the radiance of innumerable lives—and just as slowly has receded, has returned to its source and its grave. The innumerable lives seem to sing all around still more frenziedly, and Jupiter, its golden torrent pouring into the great mirror of waters, seems to glitter in the heavens still more awesomely and regally...

Am I really not beginningless, endless, ubiquitous?

Decades now separate me from my infancy and childhood. Long, infinitely long ago! But I need only think for a moment and time begins to melt. Many times I have experienced something miraculous. Many times this has happened: I return to those fields where I was once a child and a youth, and as I look around, I suddenly feel that the many long years I have lived since then seem never to have been. This is absolutely not, by no means a recollection; no, I simply have become my former self again. Once again I have the very same relationship to these fields, to this air of the openlands, to this Russian sky, the very same apprehension of all the world that I had right here, on this country path, in the days of my childhood and adolescence!

Many times at such moments I have thought: every instant of all by which I once lived here has left, has mysteriously imprinted its vestige as if upon some innumerable, infinitely minute, inmost recording discs of my ego—and now some of them have suddenly come to life, have manifested themselves. Another second and they will fade once more in the murk of my being. But let them; I know they exist. "Nothing perishes—all things are but altered." But could there be something that is subject not even to alteration, that undergoes no modification, not only during my lifetime, but even over the course of millenia? A great multitude of imprints have been passed on to me by my ancestors, my forebears. A wealth of capabilities, genius, talent—what is all this but a wealth of these imprints (both inherited and acquired), but various kinds of sensitivity to them and the totality of their manifestations in rays of the Sun that fall intermittently from somewhere upon them?

Having chanced to awaken recently at dawn, I suddenly was staggered at the thought of my age. Once it seemed that this was some unique, almost awesome creature—a man who had lived forty or fifty years. And now, at last, I too had become such a creature. What, then, am I? I said to myself; what exactly have I now become? And by slightly exerting my will, by looking at myself as one looks at a stranger—how marvelous that we can do this!—I felt, of course, with total conviction, that even now I was absolutely the same person I had been at age ten or twenty.

I lit a lamp and looked in the mirror: yes, there was gauntness now, rigidity of the features, silvery patches on the temples; the color of the eyes was somewhat faded... But so what?

And with a particular nimbleness I arose and went into the other rooms; they were still just barely brightening, still nocturnally serene, but already receiving the new, slowly dawning day, which feebly, mysteriously divided their semi-darkness at the level of my chest.

A special pre-dawn serenity still reigned too in all that enormous nest of humanity called a city. The houses stood mutely, posing in a special, non-diurnal way, with a great many windows and a profusion of inhabitants, who all apparently were so diverse and so identically devoted to sleep, non-consciousness, helplessness. The street lay mute (and still empty, still pure) beneath me, but by now the gas lights burned green in the transparent twilight. And suddenly once again I experienced the inexpressible feeling that I have experienced all my life when I chance to awaken just at daybreak; I felt great happiness, the childishly credulous, soul-touching sweetness of life, the beginning of something altogether new, good, lovely—and my intimacy, brotherhood and unity with all others living on earth. How well I always understand at such moments the tears of the Apostle Peter, who precisely at dawn sensed so keenly, so youthfully, tenderly all the force of his love for Jesus and all the evil that he, Peter, had perpetrated the night before in his fear of the Roman soldiers! Once more I experienced, as if I myself had lived through them, all the events of that remote, evangelic morning in the Grove of Olives, the denial by Peter. Time disappeared. I felt with all my being, Ah, what an insignificant period that is—two thousand years! I have already lived half a century; I need only multiply my life by forty to reach the time of Christ, of the Apostles, "ancient" Judea, "ancient" humanity. *The very same sun* that the pale teary-eyed Peter once gazed upon after his sleepless night will rise again at any moment over me. And almost the same feelings that overwhelmed Peter at Gethsemane now overwhelm me, evoking in my eyes too the same sweet, grievous tears that Peter shed by the fire. So where is my time and where is his? Where am I and where is Peter? If we are so fused, though only for an instant, just where is it, that ego of mine, which all my life I have desired so passionately to confirm and set apart? No, that has absolutely no significance—my living on earth not in the days of Peter, Jesus, Tiberius, but in the so-called twentieth century! And I have lived so much by my imagination in others' lives, remote lives, feeling that I have existed always and everywhere! Where is the line between my reality and my imagination, my feelings, which, after all, are reality too, something indubitably existing?

All my life, consciously and unconsciously, I have been striving to surmount, to destroy space, time and form. Unappeasable, immeasurable is my craving for life; I live not only in my present, but also in all my past, not only in my own life, but also in thousands of others' lives, in everything contemporaneous with me and in something back there, in the haze of distant ages. But for what? In order to destroy myself by so doing, or, on the contrary, to confirm myself, to enrich and strengthen myself?

Men fall into two categories. One enormous category includes those of their own fixed time, mundane builders, doers, men who seem almost without past, without ancestors, faithful links in the Chain of which the wisdom of India speaks; what do they care that both beginning and end of that Chain slide away so awesomely into boundlessness? And the other category, very small in comparison, includes those who not only are not doers, not builders, but are outright devastators; who long have known the vanity of doing and building, men of dream, of contemplation, who marvel at themselves and at the world, men who "philosophize," who have responded in secret to the ancient call: "Withdraw from the Chain!"—who now crave disappearance, dissolution in the One, and who, simultaneously, suffer fierce excruciation, grieve for all the visages, the incarnations within which they have abided, and, especially, for every second of their present existence. These men are endowed with a great wealth of apprehension, received from their innumerable predecessors; they sense the infinitely remote links of the Chain, of being; marvellously (and perhaps for the last time?) they have resurrected in their person the strength and vigor of their forefather in paradise, his corporeality. These men are paradisiacally sensual in disposition but already deprived of Paradise. This accounts for the great fissure within them: the torment of leaving the Chain, of separation from it, the consciousness of its vanity—and of its redoubled, awesome charm. And each of these men is most justified to intone the ancient plaint: "O Eternal and All-Embracing All! Once Thou didst not know Desire, Craving. Thou didst conceive and lead forth the immeasurable Chain of incarnations, of which it is incumbent upon each to be ever more incorporeal, ever nearer the beatific Beginning. Now ever more loudly sounds unto me Thy call: 'Withdraw from the Chain! Withdraw and leave no trace, no legacy, no heir!' Yes, Lord, I hearken unto Thee now.

But still bitter to me is my severance from the fraudulent, bitter sweetness of Being. Still am I in awe of Thy without-beginning and Thy without-end..."

Yes, if only one could engrave this fraudulent, yet unspeakably sweet "being" at least in word, if not in flesh!

In the most ancient of my days, thousands of years ago, I spoke in measured tones of the measured sounding of the sea, sang of how I felt joy and sorrow, of how the blue of the heavens and the white of the clouds was remote and magnificent, of how the form of the female body was agonizing in its inscrutable charm. And now I am just the same. By whom and for what am I impelled to bear this burden without respite—to express incessantly my feelings, thoughts, ideas, and to express them not simply, but with exactitude, beauty and power, which must enchant, enrapture, arouse sadness or happiness in men? Who instilled in me, and why, the unappeasable need to infect them with what I myself am living, to pass on myself to them and seek in them for sympathy, for unity, fusion with them? Since infancy never do I feel anything, do I think, nor see, nor hear, nor smell without that "cupidity," without the craving for enrichment, which I need to express the utmost richness of myself. I am obsessed by the eternal desire not only to amass and then to dissipate, but also to stand out among millions of men like me, to become known to them and worthy of their envy, rapture, wonder, of eternal life. The crown of every human life is the memory of it; the best that may be promised to man over his coffin is memory eternal. There is no soul that would not pine in secret dream of that crown. And my soul? How weary it is with that dream— for what, why?—the dream of leaving myself in the world for eternity, my feelings, visions, desires, of prevailing over what is called my death, which will come for me indisputably in due time and in which, nonetheless, I do not believe, do not want to and cannot believe! Relentlessly, with all my being, I scream without words: "Sun, stand thou still!!" And all the more passionately do I scream because in truth I am destroying rather than preserving myself—and cannot do otherwise since I have been given the skill to surmount them—time, space, form—to sense my non-beginning and my without-end, that is, the All, which draws me anew into Itself, as a spider draws its web.

But on and on sing the cicadas. They too have been given to know it, this All, but their song is sweet; for me alone it is sad—a song full of paradisal mindlessness, of beatific selfless ecstasy!

Jupiter has attained its ultimate height. And the night has attained ultimate silence, ultimate quiescence before Jupiter, the ultimate hour of its beauty and grandeur. "Night unto night passeth knowledge." What kind? And when? Perhaps during this, its cryptic, most lofty hour?

The unbounded, abysmal temple of the star-glutted sky has become still more regal and menacing; many large, early morning stars have ascended into it. And now the misty-golden column of radiance falls precipitously into the milky mirror-smoothness of the sea, swathed in lethargy. In that barren southern garden strewn with pale shingle the small dark trees appear still more immobile, seem to have become still smaller. And the incessant din, never ceasing even for an instant, suffusing the silence of the sky, the earth and the sea with what seems a diaphanous murmur, now resembles still more some wondrous flowers that seem ever growing in crystalline coils... What then, at last, will it attain, this jangling silence?

But there it is again, that sigh, the sigh of life, the rustle of a wave rolling onto the shore and spilling over, and afterwards another slight stir of the air, of the ocean crispness, and the smell of flowers. I seem to awaken. I look around and stand up. I run down from the balcony, walk, crunching shingle, through the sand and sit down at the very edge of the water; ecstatically I plunge in my hands, which ignite instantaneously, blaze with myriads of glistening drops, innumerable lives... No, my time has still not come! Still there is something that outweighs all my philosophizing. Like my passion for woman it still is there, my lust for this aqueous night womb...

God, let me be!

Maritime Alps. 17 September 1925

TEMIR-AKSAK-KHAN

"A-a-a, Temir-Aksak-Khan!" savagely wails the lilting, passionately, hopelessly grievous voice in the Crimean village coffee-house.

The spring night is dark and humid, the black wall of the mountain precipice barely visible. Beside the coffee-house, which coheres to the cliff, an automobile with open top stands on the main road, in the chalky mud, and two long columns of bright smoke stretch forth into the darkness from its horrible dazzling eyes. Out of the distance, far below, the roar of the unseen ocean drifts up, and a moist restive wind wafts from the darkness on all sides.

The air in the coffee-house is thick with tobacco smoke; the interior is dimly illumined by a lamp made of tin, hung from the ceiling, and heated by a pile of incandescent embers, glowing on a hearth in the corner. The wretched mendicant, who began his tale of Temir-Aksak-Khan with that agonizing cry, is seated on the clay floor. He is a one-hundred-year-old monkey in a sheepskin jacket and a shaggy astrakhan cowl that is rust red from the rain, the sun and time. On his knees he holds something resembling a crude wooden lyre. He is bent over and his listeners cannot see his face, can see only the brown ears protruding from beneath the cowl. Periodically ripping out harsh sounds from the strings of his instrument, he wails with insufferable despairing grief.

Seated on a stool near the hearth is the proprietor of the coffee-house, an effeminately plump, handsome Tatar. At first he wore a smile that expressed in turn affection and a bit of melancholy, then condescension and mockery. But now he sits in frozen immobility with brows raised, and the smile is tinged with perplexity and misery.

On a bench beneath the small window sits a hadji, smoking; he is tall, with thin shoulder blades and grey beard, wearing a black robe and a white turban that is in perfect contrast with the dark swarthiness of his face. Neglecting his chibouk, he has thrown his head back against the wall and closed his eyes. One leg, in a striped woolen stocking, is bent at the knee and propped up on the bench, the other hangs down, its slippered foot dangling.

And beside the hadji, seated at a table, are the travellers who had taken it into their heads to stop the car and have a cup of miserable coffee in this village coffee-house: a ponderous gentleman in a bowler and weather-proof macintosh and a beautiful young lady, pale with strained attentiveness and agitation. She is from the southern regions; she understands the Tatar language, understands the words of the song... "A-a-a, Temir-Aksak-Khan!"

Nowhere in the universe was there a khan more resplendent than Temir-Aksak-Khan. All of the sublunar world was trembling at his feet, and the most lovely of women and of maidens on earth were ready to die for the pleasure of being, if only for one brief moment, his slaves. But just before his demise Temir-Aksak-Khan sat in the dust on the flagstones of the marketplace and kissed the tatters of passing cripples and beggars, saying to them:

"Tear out my soul, ye afflicted and poor, for my soul is bereft of the wish to desire!"

And soon thereafter, when the Lord God had at last taken pity upon him and released him from the vain magnificence of this earth and the vain delights of earthly existence, all of his kingdoms disintegrated, his cities and palaces crumbled into desolation, and the ashes of the sands covered their ruins beneath the eternally blue sky (blue like the glaze on fine china) and the eternally blazing sun (blazing like the flames of the inferno)... *A-a-a, Temir-Aksak-Khan! Where are thy days and thy deeds? Where thy battles and victories? Where are those young, tender, jealous ones who loved thee, where are the eyes that came into thy bedchamber shining like black suns?*

All are silent, all are captivated by the song. But the effect is strange: the despairing grief, the bitter reproach that lacerates the whole tale is sweeter than the most lofty and passionate joy.

The travelling gentleman stares intently at the table and fervently draws on his cigar. The eyes of his lady are open wide; tears are flowing down her cheeks.

Having sat there perfectly still for a short time, they go out, across the threshold of the coffee-house. The beggar has finished his song and begun gnawing and tearing at the spongy flat-cake given him by the proprietor. But it seems as if the song has not ended, as if it has no end and never will have.

Before leaving, the lady gives the beggar a large tip, a gold piece, then has the disquieting notion that this is not enough; she would like to go back and give him still another, no, two or three, or would like even to take his rough hand and kiss it right in front of everyone. Her eyes are still burning with tears, but she feels as if she has never been happier than at that very moment, after hearing the tale about how everything under the sun is vanity and sorrow, on that dark and damp night with the faraway roar of the unseen ocean, with the smell of spring rain, with the restless wind that penetrates to the very depths of the soul.

Half reclining in the motorcar, the driver hastily leaps out, bends over into the light of the headlamps, sets about doing something, looking like a wild animal in his fur coat, which seems to have been turned inside out; the automobile suddenly comes to life, drones, shudders with impatience. The gentleman helps his lady get in, then sits down beside her; she thanks him in a distracted way when he covers her knees with the lap rug... The car rushes along, following the beveled highroad downhill, ascends an incline, resting its bright columns of light on some kind of shrubbery and then whisking them off, dropping them into the darkness of another declivity... High on the summit, above the outline of barely visible peaks, which seem enormous, the stars are glistening through fragments of clouds; far up ahead there is a glimpse of the almost imperceptible whiteness of surf at the bend of the gulf; the wind blows softly and forcefully into their faces...

O, Temir-Aksak-Khan, went the song, never in the sublunary realm had there been one more courageous, more happy, more resplendent than thee, swarthy of visage, fiery of eye, as bright and beneficent as Gabriel, as wise and magnificent as King Suleiman! More radiant and green than the foliage of Paradise was the silk of thy turban, and its diamond-studded, glittering plume was lambent with the starry fire of those precious stones, and the most lovely of queens and slave girls in the world were ready to die for the happiness of lightly touching their lips to thy dark and narrow hand, refulgent with the rings of the Orient. But, having drunk to the dregs that chalice of earthly delights, in the dust, in the marketplace didst thou sit, Temir-Aksak-Khan, and thou didst clutch at and kiss the ragged vestments of the cripples passing by:

"Tear out my anguishing soul, ye afflicted!"

And the centuries have rushed past above thy forgotten grave, and the sands have covered the ruins of thy palaces and mosques beneath the eternally blue sky and the ruthlessly joyous sun, and the wild dogrose plants have grown through the remnants of the azure faiences of thy sepulchre, so that ever and ever again, with each new spring, the hearts of the nightingales might languish upon that sepulchre, bursting asunder with their grievously blitheful songs, with the misery of ineffable joy... *A-a-a, Temir-Aksak-Khan, where is it, thy bitter wisdom? Where are the torments of thy soul, which spewed out in bile and tears all the nectar of earthly delusions?*

The mountain peaks have passed, faded away; now the sea is dashing along beside the highroad, running up with its roar and its cankerous shellfish smell onto the white shingle of the shore. Far up ahead, in the dark lowlands, red and white lights are sprinkled about, a rosy glow hangs over the city, and above it all, city and gulf, the night is black and soft, like soot.

Paris. 1921

TRANSFIGURATION

The farmstead was prosperous, the family large.

Having spawned children and grandchildren in profusion, the old man passed opportunely to his reward, but the old lady outlived her time; she lived on so long that it seemed there never would be an end to her pitiful and irksome existence.

She and the old man themselves had been the builders and sovereigns of all that extensive, substantial, filthy and cozy nest, which had long since taken root in this spot, had become homey and lived in, with its barn, hollow osiers, its granaries, old-fangled hut in three wings, with its cattleyard, almost barbarously crude, mired in manure and glutted with masses of well-fattened brutes. Once she and the old man themselves had been young, handsome, clever and exacting, but later somehow they began floundering amidst the young folk, who were ever more numerous and more robust; first in one thing, then in another they began acquiescing to them, and finally they were reduced to utter nullity, grew shriveled, hunched and wizen, skulked away to rest on the sleeping shelves or on the stove, became estranged, first from the family, then even from one another, until finally they were parted forever by the grave.

After the old man's death the old lady began feeling especially uneasy about her place on this good earth; her effacement was absolute; she seemed to have forgotten completely that she, she herself was the procreator of all this young, powerful realm in which she had become so superfluous. Somehow she had turned out to be the most insignificant creature on all the farmstead, living there as if out of charity, good for nothing but huddling on the hot stove in winter and minding the chicks in summer, watching over the hut while the others were working... Could somebody such as this inspire fear? Why, no one could even be bothered to notice her!

But then she took thoroughly sick, lay huddled on the stove beyond all dissembling, eyes closed, breathing feverishly and helplessly, with such great weariness that even the hearts of her broad-shouldered daughters-in-law were squeezed with pity. "Mama, how about me fixing you up some chicken or a little milk and noodles? Wouldn't you like something? How about if I put on the samovar?" But she only breathed on in semi-oblivion, her hand only quivered in a weak gesture of gratefulness...

Finally she released them all—succumbed.

Winter, deepest hour of night. A night that is her last among the living. Raging snow and murk envelop the farm; the whole village sleeps. All of the household sleeps as well; both inhabited wings are full of sleeping people. And over all this wintry night and this squall, over the slumber and remote seclusion of farmstead and village she reigns, the Dead: yesterday's pitiful and cowed little crone has been transfigured into something menacing and mysterious, into the most lofty and portentous thing in all the world, some inscrutable and awesome deity—into a corpse. She lies in her coffin in the unheated wing; she is white, like snow, cloistered in the depths of her sepulchral world, head slightly raised by a straw pillow, chin sunk into her chest; a shadow falls from the black eyelashes that are prominent against the white face. The coffin stands behind a table, brightly illumined by a whole cluster of wax candles that are stuck to it and are blazing torridly, disquietly; it is covered by a brocade funereal pall, flimsy with decrepitude, rented from the church. It stands on a bench beside a small window, beneath the icons; the frigid squall is raging beyond this window, whose dark panes gleam and scintillate with the snow that freezes to their exterior.

The youngest son of the deceased, Gavril, who has recently been married, stands reading the Psalter. He has always been distinguished in the family for good sense and neatness, for his even temper, his love for reading and church rituals. Who, then, could be better suited to read tonight? He had entered the icy room casually, not the least bit fearful of the long night impending, alone with the dead, giving no thought to the night, with no conception of what awaited him; and now he has long had the feeling that something lethal and irremediable has come into his life. He stands and reads, bending toward the hot shuddering candles; he reads unceasingly, all at the same pitch— maintaining the high ecclesiastical intonations, the elevated tone he had begun with—he reads, understanding nothing but powerless to stop. He feels that there is no salvation for him now, that he is absolutely alone face to face with this awesome creature, all the more awesome since it is the very mother who bore him, alone not only in this icy room, but in all the world; he can sense that the night is abysmally deep and deaf, that there is no one he can turn to for protection or help.

What has happened to him? Did he overestimate his presence of mind when he took it upon himself to read over the dead woman late at night, in the hour of universal sleep? Is he stricken with horror, has he lost the capacity to move? No, something much more awesome and marvelous has happened, something miraculous; he is overwhelmed not by horror, but by this very marvel, this sacrament being consummated before his eyes. Where is she now, what has become of her, pitiful, small, squalid with old age, timidity and helplessness, for so many years almost unnoticed by anyone in their large family, which was coarse with its own strength and youth? She is no more, she has vanished; is that really she, that Something, icy, immobile, breathless, mute, but absolutely distinct from the table, the wall, the pane, the snow, absolutely not a thing, but a being, whose cryptic existence is just as inscrutable as God? Could it really be that this thing lying silently in the beautiful new coffin lined with lilac velveteen, with its white crosses and winged heads of cherubim, could this really be the one who was huddled on the stove just the day before yesterday? No, she has undergone a transfiguration—and everything in the world, all the world has been transfigured for her sake. And he is alone, all alone in that transfigured world!

He is spellbound, imprisoned, and he must stand there till dawn and read unceasingly in the extraordinary, eerie and majestic tongue that is also part of that world, its baneful Word, so ominous for the living. And he musters all his strength to read, to see, to hear his own voice and stay on his feet, as with all his being, ever more deeply, he apprehends the ineffable, bewitching something that like a liturgy is being celebrated before him and within his very self. Then suddenly the brocaded funereal pall on the chest of the corpse slowly rises a bit and still more slowly sinks back—she's faintly breathing! And still higher and brighter gleam the flames of the candles, shuddering, dazzling, and everything around him is transmuted into unremitting rapture, which numbs his head, shoulders and legs. He knows, he still can understand that this is the frigid wind blowing through the window from the storm outside, that this is what whiffs up the pall and flutters the candles. But it's all the same—that wind too is she, the demised one, from her wafts that unearthly, icy breath, pure as death, and it is she who at any moment will arise to judge the whole world, all the world of the living, so contemptible in its beastly sensuality and its transience!

Today Gavril is a youthful-looking muzhik with grey, neatly combed hair. He does not manage the farmstead; he has left the managing to his brothers and his wife. The occupation he has chosen is unnecessary for a man of his means but is the only one he loves—coachman.

He is always on the road, and the road, the distant expanses, the view of sky, fields, woods, changing with the seasons, the coach box of cart or sleigh, the swift pace of a pair of faithful, sensitive horses, the sound of the harness bell, and a long conversation with a congenial passenger—all of this affords a happiness that never betrays him.

He is casual, affable. His face is clear and gaunt, his grey eyes truthful, unclouded. He is not talkative, but to a worthy man he is willing to tell the tale, difficult to convey, resembling a yuletide story, but, in fact, truly miraculous, the tale of what he lived through by his mother's coffin, on her last night among the living.

Paris. 1921

THE HARE

The opaque murk of a snowstorm. Glass in the windowpanes is pasted over with fresh white snow, and the light in the manor house has a white, snowy hue; pounding incessantly, monotonously beyond the walls, monotonously knocking at regular intervals against the roof, a bough on the old tree in the front garden creaks and groans. As always during a snowstorm I take peculiar delight in the aura of olden times, in the cosiness of the house.

Then the door slams in the vestibule and I hear Petya, who has returned from hunting, hear him stamp his felt boots, shake himself free of snow, then walk with soft steps through the reception hall to his room. I get up and go into the vestibule. Did he have any luck?

He did.

Sprawled on a bench in the vestibule lies a hare, whitened with frost, front legs thrust forward and hind legs backward. I gaze at him and touch him with a feeling of wonder and rapture.

He has a broad forehead, with large and goggling, backward-staring glassy eyes that are golden at the pupil and still have all their lustre—still the same aimless gleam they had in life.

But now his heavy carcass is utterly rock-hard and cold.

Stretched taut and covered in coarse fur, his legs are also like rock. The grey-brown tuft of a tail has the screwed-tight appearance of a taut knot. There is clotted blood on the bristling feline whiskers and the cleft upper lip.

Marvelous, simply marvelous!

An hour ago, no more than an hour ago, twitching those whiskers, with those long ears flattened back, peering keenly, intently over his shoulder out of the glass of those eyes, golden at the pupil, he lay out in the field, in a frozen depression beneath a snowdrift, filling that hole with his intense warmth, revelling in the raging haze of the blizzard, which blew from all sides and brought snow down upon him. Suddenly discovered and roused by the dog, he fled in a headlong dash, the mind-spinning beauty of which cannot be expressed in the words of man. And how fierce and wild was the pounding of his terror-stricken heart when the shot stunned him and brought his flight to an abrupt end and Petya caught him firmly by the ears, and with what a piercing infantile scream did he respond to the last thing he felt—the quick sharp flame of a dagger, which pierced deep into his throat...

No words can convey the ineffable delight I take in that smooth fell and that stone-rigid carcass, and in my very own being, and in the cold window of the vestibule, covered over, pasted over with fresh white snow, and in all that blizzardly, pale light spilling throughout the house.

19 August, 1924

THE CRANES

A clear and cold day in late autumn; I ride at a steady jog-trot along the highroad. Gleaming low sun and empty fields; an autumnal mute anticipation in the air. Then, from behind me, in the distance, a clacking of wheels. I listen: a faint brisk clack, the clatter of a light drozhky. I turn around—someone is overtaking me. That someone comes nearer and nearer; now I can see his horse distinctly, racing at full speed, then the driver himself, glancing out occasionally from behind the horse and laying on first the whip, then the reins... What can the problem be? He keeps coming on and now he has almost reached me—I hear the furious breathing of the horse over that clacking sound, then a desperate shout: "Master, give way!" Startled and confused, I swerve sharply off the road—and they flash past in a trice, first the marvellous bay mare, her eye, her nostrils, new reins the color of sealing wax, new gleaming harness, lather below her tail on the thighs, then the man himself: a muzhik, a black-bearded gallant utterly possessed by the swift ride and by a senseless, devil-may-care frenzy. He casts his rabid gaze upon me as he flies past, and I catch several striking details: his hearty red mouth and the pitch-black of his handsome youthful beard, his new cap, his yellow silk shirt beneath black *poddyovka* thrown open. I recognize him—the rich provident miller from near Livny—and he dashes away like the wind. After barreling on for about one more verst, he suddenly leaps from the drozhky. Immediately I begin riding hard to reach him, and this is what I see as I approach: the horse stands on the road, sides heaving laboriously, the sealing-wax reins hang over the shafts, and the driver himself lies on the road nearby, face down, the skirts of his *poddyovka* spread wide.

"Master!" he shouts fiercely into the earth. "Master!"

And he waves his arms about in despair.

"Ah, it's so sa-a-a-ad! Ah, master, the cranes is done flew away!"

And shaking his head from side to side, he chokes on drunken tears.

1930

THE CONSECRATION OF LOVE

Mitya's last happy day in Moscow was the ninth of March. So, at least, it seemed to him.

Near midday he was walking with Katya up Tverskoy Boulevard. All at once winter had yielded to spring; the patches of sun were almost hot. It appeared the skylarks had indeed returned, bringing with them warmth and joy. Everything was wet, everything was melting, dripping, dribbling from buildings; yard men were clearing ice from the sidewalks, heaving down glutinous snow from the roofs; there was animation everywhere, masses of people all about. Lofty clouds drifted apart like faint white smoke, blending into the moist-blue sky. Pushkin towered, assuasively pensive, in the distance, and the Strastnoy Monastery gleamed. But best of all, Katya, who was prettier than ever that day, utterly guileless and intimate, would often take Mitya's arm with childlike trust and look up at his face, which was happy, even appeared almost arrogantly happy as he walked along with such lengthy strides that she barely managed to keep up with him.

When they had reached the Pushkin Monument she said abruptly:

"How funny you are; when you laugh you stretch open that big mouth of yours with a kind of sweet, juvenile awkwardness. Don't be offended; it's for your very smile that I love you. And, of course, for your Byzantine eyes..."

Trying not to smile, suppressing both a secret gratification and a vague resentment, Mitya answered congenially as he gazed at the monument that now rose high above them:

"As for juvenile behavior, it seems you and I have a lot in common there. And I'm about as similar to a Byzantine as you are to a Chinese empress. You're all simply mad on those Byzantiums and Renaissances... I can't understand your mother!"

"Well, what would you do in her place—lock me up in some castle tower?" asked Katya.

"No, I'd simply not allow all those professed theatrical bohemians in the house, all those future celebrities from studios and conservatories and drama schools," answered Mitya, still trying to be calm and amiably casual. "You told me yourself that Bukovetsky once asked you to have dinner at the Strelna and that Egorov suggested sculpting you naked, posing as some kind of moribund ocean wave, and of course you were terribly flattered by such an honor."

"All the same, I won't abandon my art even for your sake," said Katya. "Maybe I'm repulsive, as you so often tell me," she said, although Mitya had never told her anything of the kind. "Maybe I'm depraved, but take me for what I am. And let's not quarrel; stop being jealous for at least today, on such a marvellous day! Why can't you understand that, even so, you're better for me than any of them, you're the only one?" she asked softly, urgently, gazing into his eyes with affected seductiveness; then pensively and languidly she declaimed:

> Betwixt us there's a slumbrous secret,
> A ring has passed from soul to soul . . .

This final touch, these verses pained Mitya to the quick. On the whole, much was unpleasant and painful even on that day. The jesting remark about his juvenile awkwardness was unpleasant; it was not the first time Katya had made such remarks, and made them in earnest. Now in one respect, now in another, Katya had often proved herself more of an adult than him; often (and unwittingly, that is, quite naturally) she had demonstrated her superiority over him, and he was painfully aware of that, took it as a sign that she was versed in some secret profligacy. The "even so" was unpleasant ("even so, you're better for me than any of them") and the sudden lower tone of voice that for some reason she adopted when she said it; especially unpleasant were the verses, the mannered declamation. But Mitya could bear even the verses and the declamation, that is, what most reminded him of the set that was drawing Katya away from him, arousing his acute hatred and jealousy, he could bear all of this with comparative ease on that happy day, the ninth of March, his last happy day in Moscow, so it often later seemed to him.

As they were returning that day from Kuznetsky Avenue, where Katya had bought several Skryabin pieces at Zimmerman's, she spoke in passing about his, Mitya's, mother and said with a laugh:

"You can't imagine how frightened I am at the very thought of her!"

For some reason not once in the whole time they had been together had they touched upon the future, on what was to become of their love. Now suddenly Katya had brought up his mother and had spoken as if it were thoroughly understood that this was her future mother-in-law.

II

Then everything appeared to flow along as before. Mitya accompanied Katya to the studio of the Moscow Art Theater, to concerts, to literary evenings; he went to her house on Kislovka, overstaying himself, sitting until two in the morning, taking advantage of the strange freedom accorded Katya by her mother, a nice kindly woman with vermilion hair, always smoking, always well-rouged (long separated from her husband, who had another family now). Katya would also drop in at Mitya's student lodgings on Molchanovka, and, just as before, they spent nearly all their time in that oppressive daze that accompanied their kisses. But Mitya was troubled by a persistent feeling that something terrible had suddenly begun, that something had changed, or had begun to change, in Katya.

It had quickly flown by, that buoyant, unforgettable time when they had just met, when, barely acquainted, they suddenly felt that nothing was more interesting than talking (morning till night) only with one another—when so unexpectedly Mitya had found himself in that fairyland world of love that he had awaited secretly since childhood, boyhood. It was December—frigid, fine, day after day adorning Moscow with dense rime frost and the turbid-red sphere of the low sun. January, February began whirling Mitya's love in a vortex of unremitting happiness, which already seemed realized, or at least was just on the brink of realization. But already even then something had begun (more and more often) to aggrieve him, to poison the happiness. Already even then it often seemed, somehow, that there were two Katyas. One was she for whom Mitya had felt an urgent need, had begun desiring from the first moment of their acquaintance, and the other was the real, the common-place Katya, grievously irreconcilable with the first. At that time, nevertheless, Mitya had experienced nothing comparable to his present feelings.

Everything could be explained. Spring's feminine concerns had commenced, shopping, placing orders, interminable alterations of one thing or another, and Katya did indeed have occasion to make frequent visits to dress-makers with her mother; she also had examinations to face at the private school of dramatics where she studied. Her preoccupation, her distraction, therefore, could be entirely natural. Mitya continually tried to find consolation in such thoughts. But consolations were to no avail—his morbidly suspicious heart produced counter-arguments that were stronger, that were corroborated more and more manifestly. Katya's inner aloofness kept growing and with it grew his morbid suspiciousness and his jealousy. The director of the drama school made Katya's head whirl with praises, and, unable to restrain herself, she repeated his words to Mitya. The director had told her: "You, my dear, are the pride of our school"—he called all of his actress-pupils "my dear"—and during the Lenten season, in addition to her group lessons, he began to work with her privately, so as to make a brilliant display of her at the examinations. It was well known that he debauched his young actresses; every summer he took one or another of them with him to the Caucasus, to Finland, or abroad. And Mitya began imagining that now the director had designs on Katya, who, although not at fault, probably sensed his intentions, understood them none-theless, and therefore appeared to be in collusion with him, involved in a vile illicit relationship. This thought was all the more tormenting since it was only too apparent that Katya's interest in Mitya had diminished.

By all indications something had begun drawing her away from him. Just thinking of the director was enough to upset him. But not only the director! It seemed that some other interests had begun taking precedence over Katya's love. Interests in whom, in what? Mitya did not know; he was jealous of everyone, of everything, but primarily of the way of life, as he imagined it, that she now appeared to have adopted behind his back. It seemed that she was gravitating irresistibly away from him and toward something, perhaps toward the sort of thing that was terrible even to contemplate.

Once, in her mother's presence, Katya had remarked half in jest:

"Mitya, where women are concerned your reasoning is based altogether on the old 'Rules of the Household.' You'll turn out to be an absolute Othello. I, for one, wouldn't ever think of falling in love with you, and I'd never marry you!"

Her mother objected:

"But I can't conceive of love without jealousy. One who is not jealous, in my opinion, is not in love."

"No, mother," said Katya with her habitual penchant for repeating the views of others. "Jealousy shows a lack of respect for the person one loves. If I can't be trusted, I'm not loved," she said, deliberately looking away from Mitya.

"But in my opinion," objected her mother, "jealousy is what love is. I even read that somewhere. It was proved very conclusively, and they even gave examples from the Bible, where the Lord God Himself is called jealous and vengeful..."

As for Mitya's love, it was now manifested almost exclusively by his jealousy. This was not ordinary jealousy, but, so it seemed to him, a special kind. Although they had allowed themselves too much, he and Katya had not yet taken the final step toward intimacy. When they were alone Katya was sometimes even more passionate than before. But this had begun to seem questionable now, sometimes even horrifying. All of the feelings that contributed to his jealousy were horrible, but among them there was one that was most horrible of all, one that Mitya could not formulate, was utterly incapable even of understanding. It consisted of the idea that these manifestations of passion, the very passion that was so beatific, so blitheful, that, when applied to them, to Mitya and Katya, was more lofty, more lovely than anything in the world, became unspeakably vile, seemed even somehow grotesquely unnatural when Mitya thought of Katya with another man. At such times he would feel an acute revulsion toward her. Everything that he himself did with her in private was full of paradisal captivation and chasteness. But as soon as he imagined someone else in his place, everything changed instantaneously— everything was transformed into something shameless, which provoked a craving to strangle Katya, Katya herself, precisely her, not the fancied rival.

III

Katya's examinations, which were held at last (in the sixth week of Lent), seemed to confirm decisively that Mitya had good reason for his torments.

Katya did not even see him there, did not notice him at all, was utterly alien, promiscuous.

She was a great success. She wore all white, like a bride, and was captivating in her agitation. The audience clapped cordially and fervently, while the director, a smug thespian with impassive, sorrowful eyes, sat in the front row, and simply to make a show of his exorbitant pride, he gave her instructions from time to time, speaking softly but in such a way that the unbearable sound of his voice carried throughout the auditorium.

"Less preciosity," he said ponderously, calmly, with an imperious air that suggested Katya was every bit his own private possession. "Don't act, live the role," he said distinctly.

That too was unbearable. And even the reading was unbearable, although it prompted applause. Katya was burning with embarrassment, blushing furiously, her weak voice sometimes cracked, she had trouble catching her breath, and that was touching and charming. But she read with a vulgar singsong mellifluence, every sound full of pose and stupidity, considered the highest of declamatory art in the set so detestable to Mitya, which now absorbed Katya's every thought. She did not speak, but constantly vociferated, with a certain importunate, languorous ardor, with an excessive beseeching that had absolutely no basis for its urgency, and Mitya was so ashamed for her that he could not bear to look. But most horrible of all was the blend of angelic purity and profligacy in everything about her, in her blazing face, her white dress, which seemed shorter on stage since those sitting in the auditorium viewed Katya from below, her small white slippers, her legs, tightly encased by silk stockings. "In the church choir a young girl sang," read Katya with affected, excessive naivety about some girl who was, ostensibly, angelic in her innocence. And Mitya felt both poignantly close to Katya—as one always feels in a crowd toward the one he loves—and fiercely hostile toward her, took pride in her, realized that, even so, she belonged to him and simultaneously felt a pain that rent his heart: no, she no longer belonged to him!

After the examinations the happy days returned. But Mitya could not believe in that happiness so easily as he once had believed. Recalling the examinations, Katya remarked:

"How silly you are! Really, couldn't you sense that I was reading so well just for you and you alone!"

But he could not forget how he had felt at the examinations and could not admit that even now he was experiencing the same feelings. During one of their arguments Katya, who could sense what he was feeling and keeping from her, exclaimed:

"I don't understand why you love me if, in your opinion, everything about me is so nasty! Just what is it, after all, that you want of me?"

But he himself could not understand why he loved her, although he felt that his love not only was not diminishing, but was ever growing, together with the jealous struggle he was waging with someone, with something on account of it, this love, on account of its intensifying power, the increasing demands that it made of him.

"You love only my body, not my soul!" Katya once said bitterly.

74

Again these were someone else's words, histrionic words, but despite all their absurdity and banality, they touched upon something grievously insoluble. He did not know why he loved her, could not say exactly what he wanted... What does it mean, after all—love? Answering this question was all the more impossible since in nothing that Mitya had heard about love, in nothing that he had read was there a single precise definition of the word. In books and in life everyone apparently had agreed once and for all to speak only about love that is almost discarnate or only about what is called passion, sensuality. But his love resembled neither the one nor the other. What did he feel for her? That which is called love or that which is called passion? Was it Katya's soul or her body that produced an almost giddy sensation, a kind of death-laden beatitude when he undid her blouse and kissed her breasts, paradisally captivating and vestal, bared with a kind of soul-stunning docility, with the shamelessness of purest innocence?

IV

She was changing more and more.

Her success at the examinations was partly responsible. There were, however, certain other reasons for the change.

With the coming of spring Katya appeared somehow to have undergone an instantaneous transformation into a young society miss, smartly, elegantly dressed, always rushing somewhere. Now Mitya even felt ashamed of his dark corridor when she drove up—she never came on foot now, but always by cab—when she scurried along that corridor in her susurrous silk, veil lowered over her face. Now, invariably, she treated him with tenderness, but invariably was late and cut short their meetings, saying she had to go to the dressmaker's again with her mother.

"You know, we're decking ourselves out with mad abandon!" she said blandly, gaily, her eyes glittering wondrously, perfectly aware that Mitya did not believe her but saying it all nonetheless, since they had utterly nothing to talk about anymore.

Now she almost never removed her hat, kept her umbrella in her hand, sat on Mitya's bed as she prepared to go, her calves, tightly encased in silk stockings, driving him mad. And after telling him that in the evening she would be out again—she had to visit someone again with mother!—just before leaving, she invariably went through one and the same ritual, clearly aimed at duping him, at compensating for all his "silly," as she called them, torments: with a sham-surreptitious glance over her shoulder at the door, she slipped off the bed, brushing her hips against his legs, and said in a hasty whisper:

"Well, kiss me then!"

V

Finally, at the end of April, Mitya decided to go to the country for a rest. He had thoroughly drained, thoroughly tormented both himself and Katya, and the torment was all the more unbearable since there appeared to be no reason for it whatsoever. Had anything really happened, was Katya really guilty of anything? One day, with the firmness of desperation, Katya had told him:

"Yes, do go, go away; I simply haven't the strength! We must part temporarily, to clarify our relationship. You've got so thin that mother has convinced herself you have consumption. I simply can't take any more!"

So Mitya's departure was fixed. But, although beside himself with grief, to his great amazement Mitya was almost happy nonetheless. As soon as the departure was fixed, everything abruptly reverted to the way it had been. He had always wanted desperately to deny all the horrible suspicions that gave him no peace day or night. The slightest change in Katya, therefore, was enough to change his view of everything again. Once again Katya had become tender and passionate beyond all pretense—he sensed this with the unerring discernment of his jealous nature—and once again he began sitting with her until two in the morning, again they found something to talk about, and the closer it came to the day of his departure, the more absurd their separation appeared, the need to "clarify the relationship." One day Katya even broke into tears— she had never wept before—and those tears suddenly made her frightfully dear to him, transfixed him with a feeling of acute pity and a vague sense of guilt.

At the beginning of June her mother was leaving to spend all summer in the Crimea and was taking Katya with her. They decided to meet in Miskhor. Mitya also was to come to Miskhor.

He prepared to leave, made ready for departure, wandered around Moscow in a strange stupefaction, peculiar to one who goes briskly about his business although inflicted with some grave disease. He was steeped in morbid sadness and at the same time morbidly happy, moved by Katya's renewed intimacy, her solicitude—she had even gone with him to buy straps for his luggage, as if she were his fiancée or wife—and by the renewal of almost everything that recalled the first days of their love. All his surroundings gave rise to the same sensations as before—buildings, streets, people who were walking and riding along them, the weather, which was vernally dour each day, the smell of dust and rain, the ecclesiastical smell of poplars, flowering in the side lanes beyond the fences. Everything bespoke the bitterness of separation and the blithefulness of summer hopes, of hopes for their meeting in the Crimea, where all obstacles would disappear and everything would be realized (although he had no idea what, precisely, this everything was).

On the day of his departure Protasov dropped in to say good-bye. Among upper-form *gymnasium* pupils, among university students, one often meets youths who have adopted a cordially morose, derisive bearing, the air of being older and more experienced than anyone on earth. Such a person was Protasov, one of Mitya's closest friends, his only real friend, who, despite all of Mitya's reticence and taciturnity, knew all the secrets of his love. He watched as Mitya strapped up the suitcase, noticed how his hands trembled, then smiled with lugubrious sagacity and said:

"You're nothing but children, Lord have mercy! And besides, mein lieber young Werther from Tambov, it's high time for you to realize that Katya is, above all, a most typical feminine individuum, and that the very chief of the gendarmes himself couldn't change that. You, a masculine individuum, are climbing up the walls, presenting her your most lofty of instinctual demands for the perpetuation of the species, and, of course, all this is perfectly legitimate, even, in a certain sense, consecrated. Your body is the highest reason, as Herr Nietzsche so justly remarked. But equally legitimate is the fact that you can break your neck on that consecrated path. There are creatures in the animal world whose very prospectus of existence is based on the assumption that they pay the price of their own being for their first and last act of love. But inasmuch as that prospectus, presumably, has no absolute binding force on you, just you mind your P's and Q's and look out for yourself. Generally speaking, don't be in any hurry. 'Junker Schmidt, my word of honor, summer will return!' The world has wise ways, unbeknown to man; don't assume this is the bitter end—Katya ain't the only fish in the ocean. I see by your efforts to strangle that suitcase that you're in total disagreement, that this is a cherished fish, indeed. Well then, forgive me for the unsolicited advice—and may God's servitor St. Nikola, with all his holy henchmen, preserve thee!"

Protasov squeezed Mitya's hand and left, and as Mitya strapped his pillow and blanket tightly to the suitcase, the sound of singing reached him through a window that was open onto the courtyard; testing his voice, the boy who lived across from him, a student of vocal music who practiced from morning to night, had burst out with "The Asra." Mitya hastened his work with the straps, fastened them up perfunctorily, grabbed his peaked cap, and set off for Kislovka—to say good-bye to Katya's mother. The tune and words of the student's song were ringing in his head, repeating themselves so urgently that he wandered along even more stupefied than ever, taking no notice of either streets or pedestrians. It really did look like this was the bitter end, like "Junker Schmidt had drawn his pistol for to shoot himself!" All right, so what, the bitter end is the bitter end, he thought, and once again his mind drifted back to the song, which told how a sultan's daughter strolled in the garden, "her lustrous beauty gleaming," and how there in the garden she met a black thrall, who stood by the fountain "paler than death," how one day she asked him who he was and whence he came and how he answered, beginning ominously but humbly, with morose simplicity:

Mohamet is my name...

and ending with a rapturously tragic wail:

I'm of the unfortunate tribe of the Asra;
Once having loved, we die!

Katya, who was dressing to go to the station and see him off, called out affectionately from her room—the room where he had spent so many unforgettable hours!—that she would be there before the first bell. The gentle and kindly woman with vermilion hair sat alone, smoked, and gazed at him very sadly—most likely she had known the situation for a long time, had guessed everything. Flushed scarlet, shuddering internally, he kissed her soft flaccid hand, bowing his head in a filial gesture, and with maternal endearment she kissed him several times on the temple and made the sign of the cross over him.

"Come now, dear boy," she quoted Griboedov with a listless smile; "life is meant for laughing! Well then, Christ be with you, go on now, go..."

VI

After Mitya had disposed of everything that had to be done before checking out of his lodgings, he and the hall servant stowed his luggage in a listing horse-drawn cab, and at last he seated himself awkwardly amidst his belongings, was jerked into motion, and immediately experienced the peculiar sensations that grip the departing traveller—finished (forever), a certain portion of my life!—and at the same time a sudden buoyancy, hopes for the beginning of something new. Feeling somewhat calmer, he brightened up, had a new perspective on things around him. The end, farewell to Moscow and to everything he had experienced there! It was drizzling, dour, the sidestreets were empty, the cobblestone dark and glimmering like iron, the buildings mirthless, dirty. His cabman drove at a tormenting, plodding pace, and from time to time the odor that wafted from him forced Mitya to turn away and try not to breathe. They drove past the Kremlin, crossed Pokrovka, once again turned off onto sidestreets, where crows in the gardens were screeching hoarse greetings to the rain and to evening, where in spite of everything it was spring, spring smells were in the air. Then at last they arrived and Mitya rushed off at a run behind his porter, through the teeming station, out onto the platform, then to track number three, where the long cumbersome Kursk train already stood waiting. And instantaneously, amidst all the huge hideous mob laying siege to the train, beyond all the porters, who screamed forewarnings as they rolled their thundering baggage carts along, he caught sight of, singled out the one who stood all alone in the distance, "her lustrous beauty gleaming," who seemed an absolutely unique creature, not only in all this mob, but in all the world. The first bell already had rung—this time he, not Katya, had been late. It was touching that she had arrived before him; she was waiting for him and rushed to him once again with the solicitude of a wife or fiancée:

"Darling, quick, find a seat! It's time for the second bell!"

After the second bell she was even more touching, looking up at him from the platform as he stood in the door of the third-class coach, which was crammed full by now and reeking. Everything about her was captivating—her dear pretty face, her slender figure, her freshness, her youth, still an admixture of the womanly and the childish, her upraised gleaming eyes, her plain pale-blue hat with a certain refined panache in the way it was shaped, and even her dark-grey suit, even its material and the silk of its lining, which Mitya gazed at adoringly. He stood there, thin, ungainly; for the trip he had put on coarse high-topped boots and an old jacket with buttons copper-red, rubbed bare of their surface lacquer. Katya gazed at him, for all that, with sincere love and sadness on her face. The third bell tore through his heart so abruptly and stridently that Mitya threw himself from the coach like a madman, and just as madly Katya rushed horror-stricken to embrace him. He pressed his lips to her glove, and leaping back, onto the coach, started waving his cap in a frenetic rapture, his eyes full of tears, while she took up her skirts and floated backward with the platform, her upraised eyes still fixed upon him. She was floating more and more rapidly, the wind was blowing Mitya's hair more and more furiously as he leaned out the window, the locomotive was accelerating more and more swiftly, more and more mercilessly, its insolent, menacing bellow demanding the right of way—and suddenly both she and the end of the platform broke away as if sundered...

VII

The lengthy spring twilight had long since set in, dark with rain-glutted storm clouds; the cumbersome coach went thundering through a bare, cool field—it was still early spring in the open country—conductors walked down the corridor of the coach, requesting tickets and setting candles in the lamps, but Mitya still stood by the audibly quavering window, the smell of Katya's glove on his lips, still glowing all over with that poignant flame left by the final instant of parting. And the long, happy and grievous Moscow winter, which had transfigured his whole life, rose up before him in its entirety, in a completely new light. Katya's image too appeared now in a new light, once again seemed to have changed... Yes, who is she, what is she? And love, passion, the soul, the body? What is that? None of that exists—something different exists, completely different! That smell of the glove—isn't that also Katya, love, the soul, the body? The muzhiks, the laborers in the coach, the woman leading her hideous child off to the toilet, the dim candles set in quavering lamps, the twilight on empty spring fields—everything is love, everything the soul, and everything is torment and everything unspeakable joy.

In the morning there was the town of Orel, a transfer, a provincial train beside a distant platform. And Mitya felt, What a simple, calm and kindred world this is in comparison to the Moscow world, which already has receded somewhere, into some remote fairytale kingdom revolving around Katya, who now appears so solitary, pathetic, and so tenderly beloved! Even the sky, smeared here and there with the pallid blue of rain clouds, even the wind was simpler and calmer... The train from Orel ambled along leisurely and Mitya leisurely ate spice bisquits impressed with a Tula trademark as he sat in the almost empty coach. Then the train accelerated, began lulling him, muffling him in sleep.

He awakened only in Verkhovye. The train had stopped; there was quite a bustle, masses of people, but there was also a kind of backwoods aura. Vapors with a pleasant redolence wafted from the station kitchen. Mitya consumed a delicious bowl of cabbage soup and drank a bottle of beer, then dozed off again—a profound fatigue had come over him. When he awoke the train was tearing through a vernal birch forest, a familiar forest now, located just before his final stop. Once again darkness was gathering with the dusky hues of spring; through the open window came the redolence of rain and of what seemed like mushrooms. The forest was still utterly bare, but the thundering train, nonetheless, reverberated more distinctly here than in the fields; vernally sorrowful station lights flashed briefly in the distance. Then came the high green light of the semaphore—especially captivating in the twilight of a bare birch forest—and with a thud the train began switching over onto a different track... Lord, how rustically pathetic and dear was that farm hand who stood waiting on the platform for the young master!

The twilight and storm clouds grew denser as they left the station and rode out through a large village, also springlike, muddy. Everything was immersed in that extraordinarily soft twilight, the profoundest silence of the earth, of the warm evening, blending with the dark of amorphous, low-hanging rain clouds, and once again Mitya marveled and rejoiced. How calm, simple and squalid is a country village, these crude acrid peasant huts, long since sleeping—after Annunciation Day the good country folk stop kindling their lights—and how fine it is in this dark and warm steppeland world! The tarantass plunged along over ruts, through mud; the towering oaks beyond the farmstead of a rich muzhik were still utterly denuded, inimical, mottled with the black nests of rooks. Near a hut, peering into the dusk, stood a strange muzhik who could have emerged from antiquity: bare feet, rough torn peasant coat, sheepskin cap over long straight hair... A warm, blitheful, balmy rain began falling. Mitya thought of the girls, the young peasant wenches sleeping in those huts, of everything female, to which he had drawn so near that winter with Katya, and all was blended—Katya, the girls, the night, spring, the smell of rain, the smell of earth, upturned and prepared for fertilization, the smell of horse sweat, and the smell of a kidskin glove in his memory.

VIII

Life in the country began with lovely placid days.

Katya's image appeared to have paled in the night, evaporated into the surroundings on the way from the station. But it only seemed that way, and it went on seeming that way for a few more days, until Mitya had slept off his trip, recovered his senses, become accustomed to the novelty of impressions familiar from childhood: the home where he grew up, the country village, spring in the country, the vernal nudity and emptiness of the world, once again pure and young, prepared for burgeoning anew.

The estate was small, the manor house old and modest, household management uncomplicated, requiring few menials. A quiet life began for Mitya. His sister Anya, a second-form *gymnasium* pupil, and his brother Kostya, a young military cadet, were still in Orel attending school, due to arrive no earlier than June. His mother Olga Petrovna was concerned, as usual, with managing the estate, aided only by her steward—"the bossman" as he was called by the servants; after spending much of her day in the fields, she went to bed as soon as it was dark.

On the day after his arrival, when Mitya, who had slept twelve hours, emerged washed and dressed in clean clothing from his sunlit room—its windows faced east, towards the garden—and walked through all the other rooms, he experienced a vivid sense of their kindredness and their placid simplicity, which calmed both body and soul. All objects throughout the house were in their customary places, just where they had been for many years, and there was the same familiar and pleasant redolence; throughout the house everything had been tidied up for his arrival, floors had been washed in every room. They were finishing off washing the drawing room, which adjoined the vestibule and the "domestics' chamber," as that room was still called even now. A freckled peasant girl, a day worker from the village, stood on the windowsill beside doors that led onto the terrace, stretching to reach the upper pane, making it whistle as she rubbed it, her bluish, somehow remote image reflected in the lower panes. Having pulled a large rag from the pail full of hot water, the maid Parasha, sleeves turned up, feet bare, legs white, walked across the soaked floor on her small heels, and wiping the sweat from her flushed face with the bend of her wrist, she said in her amicable, free and easy patter:

"Go on out get you some food; your mama and the bossman went off before sunrise to the depot; most likely you never even heard her..."

And immediately, forcefully came the reminder of Katya. Mitya found himself physically drawn to the bare female arm and feminine curve of the girl who stretched upward from the windowsill, her skirt, beneath which the bare legs extended like firm columns, and he joyously sensed Katya's prepotency, his belonging to her, felt her secret presence in all the impressions of that morning.

That presence made itself felt more and more vividly with each new day and became more and more lovely as Mitya recovered his senses, calmed down, forgot that other, that commonplace Katya, who in Moscow had so often and so grievously failed to blend with the Katya his desires had created.

IX

Now, for the first time, he was living at home as an adult, whom even mother treated somehow differently than before; what's more, his first real love lived in his heart, and he was bringing to fulfillment exactly what his whole being had secretly awaited since childhood, boyhood.

Even during his infancy something beyond expression in human speech had stirred wondrously and cryptically within him. Once somewhere, on a certain day, probably also in spring, in the garden beside the lilac bushes—the piquant smell of Spanish blister flies stuck in his memory—still a very small child, he stood with some young woman—most likely his nanny—and all at once a celestial radiance appeared to flare up before his eyes—perhaps it was on her face, or perhaps on the sarafan over her full bosom—and something passed through him in a wave of heat, leapt up within him, veritably as a child moves in its mother's womb... But it all had a dreamlike air. Dreamlike too was everything that came later—in childhood, boyhood and *gymnasium* years. There were certain peculiar, utterly unique transports over first one, then another of the little girls who came with their mothers to the children's fetes held for him, a secret, avid curiosity toward every movement of the enchanting, also utterly unique little creature in a frock, in tiny shoes, with the bow of a silk ribbon on her head. There were (and this was later, in the provincial capital) much more conscious transports, lasting nearly a whole autumn, over a schoolgirl who often appeared at evening in the tree beyond the fence of the neighboring garden. Her sportiveness, derisiveness, her brown frock, the round comb in her hair, her dirty arms, laughter, ringing cries—it all had such an effect on Mitya that he thought of her from morning to night, pined, sometimes even wept, ravenously desiring something of her. Then all this ceased somehow of its own volition, was forgotten, and there were new, some longer, some shorter—but all, once again, inscrutable—transports; there was the piquant joy and bitterness of sudden infatuations at *gymnasium* balls... There was a certain bodily languor and nebulous presentiments in the heart, anticipations of something...

He was born and grew up in the country, but while in *gymnasium* he had no choice but to spend spring in the city—with the exception of one year, the year before last, when he came to the country for Shrovetide, fell ill, and stayed at home recovering for March and half of April. Those days were unforgettable. He lay in bed nearly two weeks, doing nothing each day but looking out the window, watching the skies change in harmony with the world's increasing warmth and light, watching the snow, the garden, its boles and branches. Morning, and the room so bright and warm from the sun that reinvigorated flies are crawling about the panes... After-dinner hour on the following day: sunlight from behind the house, from its other side, the pallid, nearly sky-blue vernal snow visible through the window, and large white clouds in the azure, in the crowns of trees... Then, one day later, such bright interstices in the cloudy sky and such a wet glitter on the bark of trees, and it does so drip from the roof above the window that you never get enough of looking and rejoicing in it all... Later came the warm fogs and rain; the snow was devoured, disappeared in several days, the ice on the river broke into motion, and the earth in garden and yard began laying itself bare, became newly, joyfully black... Mitya long remembered one day at the end of March, when, for the first time, he rode out on horseback into the fields. Not brightly, but so vividly, so youthfully did the sky shine in the pallid colorless trees of the garden. The breeze in the field was still crisp, the crop stubble was feral and rust-red, and in the ploughed section—they were ploughing already for oats—greasily, with primordial vigor, the upturned black clods glistened. He rode across the entire field of stubble and clods to the forest, which he could see in the pure air from afar—bare, small, visible from end to end—then he descended into its lowland hollows and let the hooves of his horse rustle through the deep overlay of last year's leaves, which in some places were utterly dry, straw-yellow, in others wet and brown; he crossed ravines strewn with these leaves, where flood water still was flowing, and from beneath the bushes, swarthy-gold woodcocks came ripping, crackling out right beneath the horse's legs... What had it meant to him, all that spring, and especially that day, when such a crisp breeze was blowing toward him in the field, when the horse, struggling to cope with the waterlogged stubble and the black ploughed earth, wheezed so loudly through his big nostrils, snorting and groaning internally with splendid, savage force? It had seemed at the time that his first real love was that spring itself, its days of sheer infatuation with someone or something, when he loved all the schoolgirls and all the peasant wenches in the world. But how remote those days seemed to him now! What an utter child he had been then, innocent, ingenuous, with his meager stock of modest sorrows, joys and reveries! His aimless, discarnate love of that time had been a dream, or rather the recollection of some marvellous dream. But now Katya was in his world, a soul who incarnated that world in her person and who hovered triumphantly over all of it.

X

A reminder of Katya seemed ominous only one time during those early days in the country.

Once, in late evening, Mitya went out onto the back veranda. It was very dark, quiet, redolent of damp fields. Beyond the night clouds, above the nebulous contour of the garden, tiny tear-moist stars were glowing. Suddenly something far away in the distance gave a savage diabolic hoot, followed by a paroxysm of yelping and shrieking. Mitya winced, froze in his tracks, then carefully descended from the veranda, entered the dark tree-lined avenue, which appeared to be surveying him with enmity on all sides, stopped once more and began waiting, listening: what could it be, where was it—that which had flooded the garden so abruptly and awesomely with its din? A barn owl or a timber screech owl consummating his love, nothing more, he thought, but he stood dead still, as if he sensed the veiled presence of the devil himself in that murk. And suddenly it resounded again, a low ululation that startled Mitya to the depths of his soul, booming and rumbling somewhere near, in the treetops of the avenue—and the devil bore himself noiselessly off to some other part of the garden. There, first of all he began yelping, began puling and weeping beseechingly, plaintively, like a child, flapping his wings and caterwauling in grievous ecstasy, then began a shrieking, a loutish cackling, as if he were being tickled or tortured. Shuddering all over, Mitya strained his eyes and ears in the darkness. But that devil suddenly broke off, made a choking sound, and after rending the dark garden with a death-laden anguished wail, he vanished as if the earth had swallowed him up. Having waited several more moments in vain for the resumption of this amatory horror, Mitya quietly returned to the house—and the whole night long he was tormented in his sleep by all those aberrant and revolting thoughts and feelings into which his love had been transformed that March in Moscow.

In the morning, in the sun, however, his nocturnal agonies quickly dissipated. He recalled how Katya had burst out weeping after they had decided that he must leave Moscow for a while; he recalled with what rapture she had welcomed the idea that he too would come to the Crimea in early June, how touchingly she had helped him as he prepared to leave, how she had seen him off at the station... He took out her photograph and spent a long, long time peering intently at her small head with the stylish coiffure, marvelling at the purity and clarity in that direct, frank gaze of her slightly rounded eyes... Then he wrote her an exceptionally long and exceptionally earnest letter, full of faith in their love, and once again he was enveloped by the ceaseless sensation of her amorous and radiant omnipresence in everything by which he lived and rejoiced.

He remembered what he had experienced when his father died, nine years before. That too was in spring. On the day after his death Mitya walked timorously, bewildered and horror-stricken, through the drawing room where his father lay on a table, elegantly, smartly arrayed in nobleman's uniform, chest raised high, large pallid hands crossed upon it, nose white, beard black and diaphanous; stepping out onto the veranda, he glanced at the huge coffin lid standing by the door, covered on top in golden brocade—and suddenly the thought seized him: death is here on earth! It pervaded everything: the sunlight, the vernal grass in the yard, the sky, the garden... He went into the garden, onto the linden avenue splotched with light, then off onto branch avenues that were still more sunny, gazing at the trees and the first white butterflies, hearing the first birds warbling blithefully—and he recognized nothing: death, that horrible table in the drawing room and that long brocaded coffin lid on the veranda, pervaded everything! The sun was shining differently somehow, not as before, the grass was a different green; inert butterflies perched in a different way on the spring grass blades that were warm, as yet, only on their tops. Nothing was the same as it had been twenty-four hours ago, everything was transfigured as if the end of the world were near, and spring's captivation, its eternal youth, had become pathetic and bleak! This lasted for a long time afterwards, for the whole of that spring, just as one long smelled—or fancied—that awesome, vile, sweetish smell in the well-scrubbed, frequently aired house...

And now Mitya was experiencing the same kind of dazed obsession— but one of an utterly different order. This spring, the spring of his first love, was also absolutely unlike all previous springs. The world once again had been transfigured, once again was full of what appeared to be some extraneous thing, but not at all something malign or horrible; on the contrary—something wondrously blending with the joy and youth of spring. That extraneous something was Katya, or, rather, it was the summit of earthly captivation that Mitya wanted and demanded of her. Now, as each spring day passed in turn, he demanded more and more of her. And now that she was not here, now that there was only her image, a nonexistent, merely desired image, it seemed that in no way had she violated the immaculacy and magnificence that he demanded of her, and with each passing day she made her presence felt more and more vividly in all of Mitya's surroundings.

XI

He became joyfully convinced of this during the very first week of his sojourn in the country. Spring seemed ready to appear at any moment now. He sat with a book beside the open window of the guest room, gazing through the fir and pine boles of the front garden at the dirty stream in the meadow, at the village on the slopes beyond the stream. In the bare age-old birches of the neighboring squire's garden, tirelessly, from morning to night, steeped in the languor of their blissful ferment, the rooks were screeching as they screech only in early spring, and the view of the village on the slopes was still feral and drab; so far only the willows were overlaid with a yellowish greenery there... He went into the garden; it was still stunted and bare, transparent— only the grassy strips were green, dappled all over with tiny turquoise flowers; acacia blooms along the avenue were like powdery rime, and in the hollow, in the southern, lower part of the garden a solitary wild cherry flowered pallidly with tiny white blossoms... He went out into the fields. It was still empty, still drab there in the openland, the stubble still thistly like a brush, the desiccate field paths still violet and scabrous with hummocks... And all of this had the bareness characteristic of youth, of the time of anticipation— and all of it was Katya. It only seemed that he was distracted by the peasant girls working as day-laborers, who did now one chore, now another around the estate, by the farm hands in the workers' annex, by reading, strolls, visits to muzhik acquaintances in the village, conversations with mother, rides out into the fields in the light drozhky with the steward (a coarse, strapping retired soldier)...

Then still another week went past. One night there was a torrential cloudburst, and then somehow the hot sun's power became ascendant, spring lost its meekness and pallidness, and right before his eyes everything around him began changing in leaps and bounds. They started ploughing, transforming the stubble into black velvet; the boundary strips around the fields turned green, the verdure in the yard was more succulent, the blue of the sky more dense and bright; the garden was rapidly dressing itself in crisp greenery that was soft even to the eye; gray panicles on the lilac began turning mauve, became redolent, and a multitude of black and metallically blue, huge glittering flies appeared on its dark green, glossy leafage and in the hot patches of light on the trails. Branches were still visible on the apple and pear trees, hardly touched by the tiny, greyish, uniquely soft leafage, but these apples and pears, which stretched out networks of skewed branches beneath other trees in all directions, had begun curling with lacteal snow, and with each passing day this bloom became more white, more dense and more fragrant. At this wondrous time Mitya was intently and joyfully observing all the spring changes taking place around him. But Katya not only did not pale, was not lost amidst them; on the contrary—she had a share in all of them and imparted to everything her presence, her beauty, which burgeoned in harmony with the burgeoning spring, with that ever more sumptuously white garden and the ever darker blue of the sky.

XII

Then one day on his way to tea, as Mitya entered the drawing room, full of the early evening sun, the mail lying beside the samovar suddenly caught his eye, the mail he had awaited in vain all morning. He dashed up to the table—Katya should have answered at least one of the letters he had sent long ago—and brightly, balefully it lay there glimmering, the small, highly elegant envelope with the superscription in that familiar pathetic hand. Seizing it, he strode out of the house, then through the garden, along the central avenue. He walked to the most distant part of the garden, where the hollow passed through it, and after having stopped and looked around, he quickly tore open the envelope. The letter was brief, only a few lines, but Mitya must have read it over nearly five times before he could grasp the words—his heart was pounding so. "My beloved, my one and only!" he read again and again—and these exclamatory phrases made the earth float beneath his feet. He raised his eyes. The sky above the garden gleamed joyously and exultantly, the snowy whiteness of the garden was also gleaming all around; in the crisp greenery of distant bushes a nightingale, already sensing the early evening chill, sang distinctly, intensely, with all the blithefulness of mindless nightingale rapture— and the blood drained from Mitya's face, tremors passed over his scalp...

He walked back slowly to the house; the chalice of his love was full to overflowing. And just as carefully did he bear his love within him on the days that followed, in quiet, happy anticipation of a new letter.

XIII

Days passed but the letter he longed for did not come.

The garden was dressing itself in a variety of colors.

A huge old maple, towering over all the southern part of the garden, prominently visible from everywhere, became still larger and still more prominent—arrayed in crisp dense greenery.

Higher and more prominent too was the central avenue, upon which Mitya constantly gazed from his windows. The crowns of its old lindens, also covered, though still transparently, in a pattern of young leafage, rose and stretched over the garden like a light-green row of hills.

And beneath the maple, along the avenue there was a sheer expanse of curly, aromatic, cream-colored blossoms.

And all of this: the huge and splendrous maple crown, the light-green hills of the avenue, the nuptial white of apple, pear, and pin cherry trees, the sun, the blue of the sky, and everything that was thriving and spreading in the bottomlands of the garden, in the hollow, along the branch avenues and trails, at the base of the manor's southern wall—lilac bushes, acacias and currants, burdocks, nettles, wormwood—everything was strikingly dense, crisp and new.

Since vegetation was encroaching from all sides, the fresh green yard appeared more cramped, the house somehow smaller and more beautiful. It appeared to be expecting guests. For days on end the doors and windows in all the rooms were open: in the white drawing room, in the blue, old-fashioned guest room, in the small divan room, also blue and hung with oval miniatures, in the sunny library, a large and empty corner room with old icons set in the front-corner shrine and low, ash bookcases along the walls. And the trees were right up against the house, gazing festively into the rooms with their variety of green colors, some light green, some dark, apertures of bright blue between their branches.

But there was no letter. Mitya knew how hard it was for Katya to write letters, realized how much trouble she had getting herself to sit down at a desk, to find pen, paper, envelope, to buy a stamp... But once again rational considerations were of little help. After several days the happy, even proud assurance he had felt as he awaited the next letter disappeared; he pined and worried even more. After such a letter as the first something still more lovely and blissful should follow immediately. But Katya was silent.

He stopped going out so often to the village, went riding in the fields less frequently. He sat in the library, leafed through journals that had been yellowing and withering on the bookshelves for decades. These journals were full of lovely verses by the old poets, marvelous lines almost always dealing with the same thing—that with which all verses and songs have been replete since the world began, the one thing that nourished his own soul now, and in one way or another he could invariably apply these verses to himself, to his love, to Katya. For hours on end he sat in the armchair beside the open bookcase and tormented himself, reading and rereading:

> The household sleeps, dear one; come out in the garden haze!
> The household sleeps, and only the stars upon us gaze...

All these enchanting words, all these adjurations seemed his own, appeared to be addressed to only one person, to the one whom he, Mitya, saw persistently everywhere and in everything, and sometimes they had an almost menacing ring:

> Over smooth and tranquil river
> Fly the swans, their wings aquiver,
> And the waters undulate.
> Oh, come back! The star belts glimmer,
> Slowly trembling, green leaves shimmer,
> And the cloud banks congregate...

Closing his eyes, shivering, he repeated this adjuration several times in a row, this call of the heart overflowing with amorous force, a heart craving exultation, beatific deliverance. After that he sat for a long time staring straight ahead, listening to the profound rustic silence surrounding the manor— and then bitterly shook his head. No, she did not respond, she was gleaming mutely somewhere out there, in that remote and alien Moscow world! And once again the tenderness streamed from his heart—once again something grew and spread, menacing, ominous, incantatory:

> Oh, come back! The star belts glimmer,
> Slowly trembling, green leaves shimmer,
> And the cloud banks congregate...

XIV

One day after Mitya had eaten dinner—they dined at noon—and dozed a bit, he left the house and walked at a leisurely pace out into the garden. The peasant girls who often worked in the garden, spading up the ground under the apple trees, were working there that day too. Mitya was going out to sit with them and have a chat; this had become a habit of late.

The day was hot and quiet. Walking in the diaphanous haze of the avenue, he saw the curls of snow-white branches stretching far into the distance all around him. Especially dense and vigorous was the bloom on the pear trees, and the mixture of that white with the vivid blue of the sky produced a violet tint. The pear and apple trees were blooming and shedding; the tilled earth beneath them was strewn with faded petals. The warm air was permeated with their delicate, sweet-scented smell, together with the smell of hot and decomposing dung in the cattle yard. Small clouds congregated, the dark blue sky took on a paler hue, the warm air and those smells of putrefaction became still more delicate and sweet. All the balmy warmth of this vernal paradise hummed drowsily and blissfully with honeybees and bumblebees, who burrowed into its curly ambrosial snow. And repeatedly, with beatific tedium, diurnally, now here, now there, first one then another nightingale gave a metallic chirp.

The tree-lined avenue ended far in the distance, at the gates of the barn. Far to the left, at the corner of the earthen wall that enclosed the garden, there was a dark spruce grove. Two peasant girls were visible beside that grove, splotches of color amidst the apple trees. As usual, Mitya turned at the midpoint of the avenue and walked towards them. Bending over, he made his way through ramifications of low branches, which touched his face with feminine delicacy, redolent of honey and of something like lemon. And, as usual, one of the girls, the thin ginger-haired Sonka, had barely caught sight of him when she began laughing and screaming wildly.

"Oy, the master's coming!" she screamed in sham alarm, and jumping down from the thick pear bough where she had been resting, she rushed to her spade.

The other girl, Glashka, responded in just the opposite way, pretended not to have noticed Mitya at all; leisurely, firmly implanting on the iron spade her soft black-felt galosh, white petals clustered within its top, she dug the spade into the ground with an energetic thrust, and turning over a slice of earth, she burst out singing loudly, in a strong pleasant voice: "Hey, my garden, garden of mine, who do you flower for!" She was a strapping wench, purposeful and always solemn.

Mitya walked up and sat in Sonka's place, on the bough of the old pear tree, where the bole split into branchings. Casting her bright eyes upon him, Sonka asked loudly, with affected off-handedness and gaity:

"Oh-ho, now, just got up? Look out you don't sleep yourself into trouble!"

She was fond of Mitya and she made every effort to hide it but could not; she behaved awkwardly around him, babbled whatever came into her head, always, however, hinting at something, vaguely surmising that there was some basis for the distracted state he was in as he wandered incessantly here and there. Suspicious that he was living with Parasha, or that he was, at least, making dogged attempts to do so, she was jealous, spoke to him tenderly and sharply by turns, sometimes gazed at him languidly, openly displaying her feelings, sometimes coldly and with enmity. And Mitya was strangely pleased by all of this. There was no letter, still no letter, and he was not living now, but simply existing from day to day in ceaseless anticipation, languishing more and more in that anticipation, in the impossibility of sharing the secret of his love and torment with anyone, of speaking about Katya, about his hopes for the Crimea; Sonka's hints about some love in his life, therefore, were pleasant. These conversations, after all, somehow touched upon the inscrutable feelings that oppressed his soul. It was also exciting to know that Sonka was in love with him, was, consequently, his intimate to some degree, which made her somehow a secret participant in the amorous life he cherished within him, and sometimes he even felt a strange hope that perhaps in Sonka he could find either a confidante or a kind of surrogate for Katya.

Now, unaware of what she was saying, Sonka had touched upon his secret again: "Look out you don't sleep yourself into trouble!" He looked around. The brightness of the day made that solid mass of the dark-green spruce thicket before him seem almost black, and those bits of sky that filtered through the sharp tops of the trees were a special majestic blue. The vernal greenery of the lindens, maples and elms, bright throughout with the sun that pierced it from end to end, formed a buoyant, joyous canopy over all the garden, spread mottled shade and bright patches on the grass, the trails and clearings; the hot and balmy bloom, glowing white beneath that canopy, seemed porcelain, gleamed and shone in spots where it too was pierced by the sun. Mitya, smiling in spite of himself, asked Sonka:

"But what kind of trouble could I get into? There you've got my whole problem—I just don't have nothing to do."

"Hush now, don't you go swearing that on the Bible; I believe you!" Sonka shouted gaily, coarsely, once again affording him pleasure by her refusal to believe he had no love affairs. Suddenly she gave another raucous screech and shooed away the ginger calf with the white kinky tuft on his forehead; he had ambled out of the spruce grove, walked up behind her and began munching on the flounce of her cotton print dress:

"Ow, blast your eyes to the fires in hell! One more of His sons hath the good Lord sent us!"

"Is it true they're trying to marry you off?" said Mitya, at a loss for words but wishing to continue the conversation. "They say it's a rich farmstead and a handsome fellow, but you turned him down, won't listen to your papa..."

"Rich, all right, but dull as sin; ain't got molasses for brains," answered Sonka spryly, somewhat flattered. "Just might be I got me somebody else in mind..."

Without interrupting her work the solemn and taciturn Glashka shook her head:

"You do shovel it thick, girl, from the Don River to the ocean and back!" she said softly. "Just stand there gabbling all sorts of trash and you'll soon have a name for yourself in the village..."

"Shut up your cluck-clucking!" shouted Sonka. "I ain't no crow, I can hoe my own row!"

"And just who might be this somebody else you got in mind?" asked Mitya.

"Well, I'll own up!" said Sonka. "I done fell for that old grandpa-herdboy of yours. Just look at him and I go hot right down to my heels! I ain't no worse than you folks; I like riding old horses too," she said provocatively, hinting, apparently, at the twenty-year-old Parasha, who was already considered an old spinster in the village. Then all at once, with the audacity that she somehow was entitled to because of her secret infatuation with the young master, she threw down her spade and sat on the ground, stretching out and slightly spreading her legs in their old coarse half-boots and skewbald wool stockings, letting her arms drop feebly.

"Whew, I ain't done a thing and I'm dead give out!" she shouted, laughing. "They're worse for wear," her shrill voice rang out:

> They're worse for wear, these boots of mine,
> But on the toes they spark and shine,

and once again she laughed and screamed:

"Come off with me for a rest in the shed; I'm ready for anything!"

Her laughter was infectious. Smiling broadly and awkwardly, Mitya jumped off the bough, walked up to Sonka, and lay down with his head across her knees. Sonka pushed it away but he lay back again, his mind flowing with poetry, which he had been reading so much of for the last few days:

> Petals' scroll now brightly open,
> Blooming rose, of joy a token,
> Sprinkles, moistens all with dew.
> The abounding and unbounded,
> Aromatic, involuted
> World of love is mine anew...

"Don't you touch me!" screamed Sonka, now really alarmed, trying to lift his head and push it away. "I'll scream so loud all the wolves in the woods'll start howling. I ain't got nothing for you; it burned for a spell and then died out!"

Mitya closed his eyes and said nothing. The sun, shattering into fragments as it passed through leaves, branches and pear blossoms, formed hot varicolored patches, tickled his face. Tenderly and spitefully Sonka tugged at his wiry black hair—"Just like horsehair!" she cried—and pulled down his cap to shield his eyes. He could feel her legs beneath his head—more awesome than anything on earth, the legs of a female!—her stomach was touching him, he smelled her cotton print skirt and blouse, and all of this was mingled with the burgeoning garden and with Katya; the languorous chirping of nightingales both near and far, the perpetual, voluptuous, somnolent buzz of innumerable bees, the warm ambrosial air, and even the simple sensation of the earth beneath his back tormented him, produced an oppressive thirst for some superhuman happiness. And suddenly something began rustling in the spruce grove, began laughing gaily and maliciously, then gave a low resonant hoot—"coo-coo, coo-coo"—so balefully, so clearly, so near and so distinct that the rasp and the tremor of a sharp tongue were audible, and his desire for Katya, the desire and imperative that right now, at any cost, she must give him precisely it, that superhuman happiness, gripped him with such a fervency that, to the utter amazement of Sonka, he leaped up impulsively, and, stepping out with enormous strides, rushed away.

Together with that fervent desire, that demand for happiness, in accord with the low resonant voice that abruptly sounded with such awesome clarity right over his head in the spruce grove, that appeared to rive the bosom of all this spring world to its core, the thought had suddenly entered his mind that there would not be and could not be a letter, that in Moscow something had happened or was on the verge of happening, and that he was finished, lost!

XV

Back in the house, he stopped for a moment before the drawing room mirror. She's right, he thought; maybe my eyes are not Byzantine but, for all that, they are insane. And that thinness, the coarse and bony ungainliness, the sombre swarthiness of the brows, the hair's wiry blackness; is it really almost like horsehair, as Sonka said? Then he heard the quick tramp of bare feet behind him. Embarrassed, he turned around:

"Must be the young master's in love; he keeps on admiring hisself in the looking glass," said Parasha with affectionate drollery, running by on her way to the terrace with a boiling samovar.

"Your mama was looking for you," she added as she swept the samovar up on the table, set for tea, and turning around, she cast a quick keen glance at Mitya.

Everyone knows, they've all guessed! thought Mitya and forced himself to ask:

"Where is she?"

"In her room."

Having skirted the house, crossing already to the western sky, the sun peered translucently through pines and firs, which screened the terrace with their coniferous branches. The spindle shrubs beneath them also had an utterly summerish, glazy sheen. Covered with fine shade and spotted with hot patches of light, the tablecloth gleamed. Wasps were hovering above the basket that held white bread, above the cut-glass jam bowl and the cups. And this whole scene spoke of a lovely summer in the country and of how one could be happy and carefree. In order to forestall the appearance of his mother, who, of course, understood his situation no less than the others, and in order to demonstrate that he had no secret burdens whatsoever weighing upon him, Mitya left the drawing room and entered the corridor, which extended past the doors of his room, mother's, and two more rooms, occupied by Anya and Kostya in the summer. The light was dusky in the corridor, bluish in Olga Petrovna's room. This whole room was crammed snugly and cosily with the most antiquated furniture in the house: chiffoniers, commodes, a large bed, an icon case, the usual lamp burning in front of it, although Olga Petrovna had never shown any particular inclination to be religious. Beyond the open windows, on the neglected flower bed by the entry to the central avenue, there was a broad shady spot, and beyond that shade, directly facing it, the luminous garden glowed a festive green and white. Ignoring all this long familiar view, eyes in spectacles lowered over her knitting, Olga Petrovna, a large but spare, dark and solemn woman of forty, sat in an armchair by the window and rapidly plied her needles.

"Were you asking for me, mother?" said Mitya, stopping at the door of the room.

"No, no, I simply wanted to have a look at you. I almost never get to see you now, except at dinner," answered Olga Petrovna without interrupting her work, speaking in a special, immoderately calm tone.

Mitya recalled how, on the ninth of March, Katya had said that for some reason she was frightened of his mother, recalled the secret charming implication that was clearly there in her words... He muttered awkwardly:

"But did you, perhaps, have something to tell me?"

"Nothing, except that it seems to me you've got a bit bored these last few days," said Olga Petrovna. "Maybe you could take a little ride somewhere... over to the Meshersky manor, for example... They've got a house full of nubile young ladies," she added, smiling. "And, on the whole, I think they're quite a nice sociable family."

"In a few days I really might like to ride over there," answered Mitya with an effort. "But let's go have our tea; it's so pleasant out on the terrace... And we can talk there," he said, knowing full well that mother, with her penetrating mind and her reticence, would not resume that fruitless conversation.

They sat on the terrace until almost sunset. After tea mother continued knitting and speaking about the neighbors, about household matters, about Anya and Kostya—Anya had to take an examination over again in August! Mitya listened, answered now and again, but all this time he was feeling something similar to what he had felt just before his departure from Moscow; he was somehow stupefied again, as if in the throes of some grave disease.

For nearly two hours that evening he strode incessantly back and forth through the house, through drawing room, guest room, divan and library, up to the library's southern window, open onto the garden. In the windows of the drawing room and guest room the soft red of sunset glowed amidst branches of pines and firs; the voices and laughter of farm hands could be heard as they gathered for supper beside the workers' annex. Into the passages between rooms, through the library window gazed the even and achromatic blue of the evening sky, with one motionless rosy star hanging there; picturesquely sketched upon this blue was the green crown of the maple and the whiteness, somehow wintry whiteness, of everything blooming in the garden. And he kept striding, pacing, utterly unconcerned about how this would be interpreted in the house. His teeth were clenched so tightly that his head ached.

XVI

From that day on he stopped observing all the many changes that approaching summer was consummating around him. He saw and even felt them, those changes, but they had lost their discrete value, his delight in them was only a grievous delight; the better everything was, the more grievous it was for him. Katya had become an utter obsession; now Katya was in everything and behind everything to the point of absurdity, and since each new day was an ever more terrible confirmation that she no longer even existed for him, for Mitya, that now she was in the power of someone alien, was giving some other man herself and her love, which must needs be exclusively his, Mitya's, everything in the world began to seem unnecessary, grievous, and the more lovely it was, the more unnecessary and grievous it became.

He hardly slept at night. The captivation of those moonlit nights was incomparable. Quiet, ever so quiet lay the milky-white garden. Nocturnal nightingales sang assiduously, languished in indolent transports, contending with each other in the blithefulness and refinement of their songs, in purity, painstaking care, sonority. The silent, delicate, utterly pallid moon hung low above the garden, was accompanied invariably by the tiny, unspeakably captivating swell of pale-bluish clouds. Mitya slept with curtains undrawn, and the garden and moon peered in his windows all night. Every time he opened his eyes and looked up at the moon, immediately, like one possessed, he pronounced the word in his mind: "Katya!" And he said it with such rapture, such pain, that he himself realized how bizarre this was. How could it really be that the moon reminded him of Katya, but it did remind him all the same, reminded him of something, and, what was most amazing of all, there was even some visual resemblance! But ofttimes he simply saw nothing; his desire for Katya, the recollection of what had been between them in Moscow, enveloped him so forcefully that he shuddered all over in a feverish tremor and prayed to God—but, alas, always in vain—to see her right here, with him on this bed, at least in a dream. Once that winter he had gone with her to the Bolshoy Theater to hear Sobinov and Chaliapin in *Faust*. For some reason everything had seemed especially delightful that evening: the radiant chasm gaping beneath them, torrid and balmy with masses of people, the red-velvet, golden-fringed tiers of loges, overflowing with glittering raiment, the iridescent gleam of a gigantic chandelier above that chasm, the overture streaming out far below in accord with the conductor's gesticulations, its sounds now blaring, demoniacal, now infinitely tender and sad: "Once in far Thule there lived a good king..." After the performance, having accompanied Katya through the hard frost of that moonlit night to Kislovka, Mitya stayed with her later than ever, lost himself more than ever in the torpor of their kisses, and took with him the silk ribbon that Katya had used to tie up her braid for the night. Now, on these grievous May nights, he had come to the point that he trembled just to think of that ribbon, which lay in his desk.

In the daytime he slept, then rode on horseback to the large village where the railway station and post office were located. Fine weather continued. Sporadic rain would fall, thunderstorms, downpours would quickly come and go, and once more the hot sun would gleam, ceaselessly performing its rapid labor in the gardens, fields and forests. The garden had stopped flowering, lost its blooms, but continued to grow rampantly more dense and dark. The forests were now immersed in countless flowers, in high grass; their sonorous depths, steeped in the songs of nightingales and cuckoos, ceaselessly beckoned him into the marrow of their greenery. Now the bareness of the fields had disappeared—an opulence of grain shoots covered them throughout in variegated patterns. And for days on end Mitya lost himself in those forests and fields.

He was too ashamed to hang about every morning on the terrace or in the yard, waiting in sterile anticipation for the steward or a farm worker to arrive from the post office. And the steward or the worker would not always have time to ride eight versts for trifles. So he himself began riding to the post office. But he too would invariably return home with only an issue of the Orel newspaper or a letter from Anya or Kostya. His torments were becoming almost unbearable. The fields and forests through which he rode so crushed him with their beauty and their happiness that he even experienced physical pain in his chest.

Once, just before evening, he was riding from the post office through the deserted neighboring estate, which stood in the midst of an old park that blended into the birch forest surrounding it. He rode along the "festal prospect," as the muzhiks called the central avenue of this estate. Two rows of huge dark spruces lined the avenue. Majestically sombre, broad, covered with a thick layer of slippery rust-red needles, it led to an ancient manor house standing at the end of its corridor. The red, dry and calm light of the sun, which was sinking to his left, beyond the garden and forest, obliquely illumined the lower part of this corridor between the boles, glittered amidst the golden panoply of needles. And such spellbound silence reigned all around—only the nightingales were blaring their song from one end of the park to the other—there was such a sweet redolence of spruces, of jasmine bushes, which were clustered about the manor on every side, in all of this Mitya sensed such prodigious joy—someone else's, some pristine joy—and with such awesome distinctness did she suddenly appear to him on the huge decrepit terrace, amidst the jasmine bushes, Katya, in the image of his young wife, that he felt his face convulsed by a deathly pallor, and he said aloud, firmly, his voice resounding over all the avenue:

"If I don't get a letter in a week, I'll shoot myself!"

XVII

The next day he arose very late. After dinner he sat on the terrace, held a book on his knees, gazed at the pages covered with print and thought vacantly: "Should I go for the mail or not?"

It was hot; one behind the other, white butterflies hovered in pairs above the heated grass, above the glazy sheen on the spindle shrubs. Watching the butterflies, he asked himself again: "Should I go, or should I break off these shameful trips once and for all?"

From behind a rise the steward appeared in the gates, riding a stallion. He glanced up at the terrace and turned straight toward it. When he had drawn near, he pulled up the horse and said:

"A good morning to you! Still reading?"

And he looked around with a grin on his face.

"Is your mama sleeping?" he asked softly.

"I think she's asleep," answered Mitya. "Why?"

The steward was silent for a moment, then said abruptly, in a solemn tone:

"Look here, young master, I ain't got nothing against no books, but a man ought to know the right time for things. Why is it you're living like some kind of monk? Ain't there enough women or young wenches around?"

Lowering his eyes to the book, Mitya did not respond.

"Where have you been?" he asked, without looking up.

"Been to the post office," said the steward. "And, sure enough, there weren't no letters there at all, just this here paper."

"And why do you say 'sure enough'?"

"Because, what I mean is, somebody's still writing; they ain't finished yet," answered the steward coarsely and derisively, offended by Mitya's refusal to continue the conversation he had begun.

"If you please," he said, stretching out the newspaper to Mitya, and spurring his horse, he rode away.

I'll shoot myself! thought Mitya firmly, gazing at the book and seeing nothing.

XVIII

Certainly Mitya understood that there was nothing more savage and bizarre imaginable: to shoot oneself, to shatter one's skull, to cut off in a single instant the beat of a sound young heart, to break off one's thoughts and feelings, to go deaf, to go blind, to vanish from this unspeakably magnificent world, which for the first time only now had revealed itself to him in its entirety, to be deprived instantaneously and for all time of any share in the life that included Katya and the approaching summer, where there were sky, clouds, sun, warm wind, grain in the fields, villages, country hamlets, peasant girls, mother, manor, Anya, Kostya, verses in old journals, and some-where out there—Sevastopol, the Baidar Gates, torrid lilac-hued mountains with pine and beechen forests, the dazzlingly white, stifling highway, the gardens of Livadia and Alupka, scorching sands by the gleaming sea, suntanned children, suntanned women bathing—and once again Katya, wearing a white dress, beneath a white parasol, sitting on the shingle right beside the waves, which emit a blinding glare and provoke an unwitting smile of gratuitous joy...

He understood, but what could he do? Where could he go, how could he break out of that vicious circle, where the better everything was, the more grievous, the more unbearable it became? This, precisely this, was insufferable—the very happiness, with which the world was crushing him and which lacked something indispensable.

In the morning he would awaken, and the first thing to strike his eye was the joyous sun, the first thing he heard was the joyous pealing, familiar from childhood, of the village church bells—out there beyond the dewy garden, full of shade, glitter, birds and flowers; even the yellow wallpaper was joyous and dear, the same paper that had cast its yellowish gleam on his childhood. But immediately one thought would transfix his soul with rapture and horror: Katya! The morning sun sparkled with her youth, the crispness of the garden was lambent too with the beauty and the grace of her image; the wallpaper of his ancestors demanded that she share with Mitya the whole of this precious rustic antiquity, the life his fathers and grandfathers had lived till their deaths, here on this estate, in this house. And Mitya would throw aside the blanket, leap out of bed in just his open-necked nightshirt, long-legged, thin, but sound for all that, young, warm with sleep; quickly he would pull out the desk drawer, snatch up the cherished photograph and lapse into a stupor, gazing at it avidly, perplexedly. All the captivation, all the gracefulness, all the in-effable gleaming and beckoning something that comprises the maidenly, the female, all of this was in her slightly serpentine head, in her coiffure, in her faintly provocative, yet innocent gaze! But that gaze gleamed enigmatically, with inexorable gay muteness—where could he find the strength to bear it, so near and so remote, and now, perhaps, alien forever, the gaze that had re-vealed such unspeakable happiness in life and had so shamelessly, terribly deceived him?

On the evening when he had ridden from the post office through Shakh-ovskoe, that ancient deserted estate with its black spruce avenue, his outcry, which came as a surprise to Mitya himself, had expressed precisely the extreme state of enervation he had come to. Watching from the saddle at the postal window, waiting as the clerk rummaged in vain through a pile of newspapers and letters, he heard behind him the din of a train approaching the station, and that din, the smell of locomotive smoke, overwhelmed him with a happy recollection of the Kursk station and, on the whole, of Moscow. As he rode from the post office through the village, in each peasant girl of small stature who walked ahead of him, in the movements of her hips, he sensed some alarm-ing aura of Katya. Out in the fields he met someone's troika; in the tarantass, flying along at a brisk pace, he saw two hats flash by, one of them a girl's, and he nearly shouted it out: "Katya!" The white flowers on the boundary strip were linked in a trice with the thought of her white gloves, the blue "bear's ears" with the color of her veil... When he had ridden, by the light of the setting sun, into Shakhovskoe, the dry and sweet odor of spruces and the sumptuous odor of jasmine gave him such a keen feeling of summer and of someone's ancient summer life in this lovely and opulent estate that when he glanced at the red-gold twilight in the avenue, at the house standing in the evening shade, in the depths of the avenue's corridor, he suddenly saw Katya in the full bloom of female captivation, descending from the terrace into the garden, almost as distinctly as he saw the manor house and the jasmine. He had long since lost any concrete, true-to-life conception of her; with each passing day she appeared to him more singular, more transfigured. But on that evening her transfiguration had been so intense, so victoriously exultant, that Mitya was even more horrified than he had been that noon-day, when the cuckoo abruptly started hooting above his head.

XIX

He stopped going for the mail; by a desperate, extreme exertion of his will he forced himself to break off those trips. He also stopped writing. He had already tried everything, written everything: the frenetic protestations of his love, a love such as the world had never seen, the grovelling entreaties that she love him or at least be his "friend," the unconscionable tales about how ill he was, how he was writing from his sickbed—aimed at provoking at least her pity, at least attracting some attention—and even the menacing hints that there was, it seemed, only one recourse: to relieve Katya and his "more fortunate rivals" of his presence on the earth. Having stopped his writing and his dogged pleadings for an answer, forcing himself with all his strength to expect nothing (secretly hoping, nonetheless, that the letter would come precisely when he had deceived fate by shamming perfect indifference or when he really had managed to be indifferent), trying in every way possible to avoid thinking of Katya, searching in every way possible for some salvation from her, once again he began to read whatever he came across, to ride out with the steward into neighboring villages on matters concerning the estate, silently repeating over and over again: "It's all the same; what will be, will be!"

Then one day he and the steward were returning from a small farmstead, riding in the light drozhky, at a brisk pace as usual. Both sat astride the bench, the steward in front—he was driving—and Mitya in back, and both were being jounced about by the bumpy road, especially Mitya, who kept a firm grip on the cushion as he gazed by turns at the red neck of the steward and the bouncing fields before him. As they were approaching the manor house, the steward released the reins, let the horse go at a jog, and began rolling a smoke; smiling complacently, he looked into the open tobacco pouch and said:

"There wasn't no use for you to take umbrage at me back then like you did, young master. Wasn't it the truth I was telling you? I ain't got nothing against no books, why not do some reading when you got a minute or two, but books ain't going to run away nowhere; a man ought to know the right time for things."

Mitya flushed and answered in a tone that came as a surprise to him, with sham naivety and an awkward grin:

"But I don't see that there's anybody available..."

"How do you mean?" said the steward. "There's slews of women and wenches!"

"The wenches just tease," answered Mitya, trying to adopt the steward's manner. "You don't have no chance with wenches."

"They don't tease; you just ain't learned how to handle them," said the steward, switching to a preceptorial tone. "Then again, you're tightfisted. A empty sack don't stand upright."

"I wouldn't be tightfisted if things was set up so as to work out smooth, without any hitches," Mitya suddenly answered shamelessly.

"Don't you bother yourself none about that; everything'll be worked out just fine," said the steward, and lighting his smoke, he continued in a somewhat aggrieved voice: "It ain't no cash nor none of your presents I care about; I'd just like to give you a little cheer. Every time I look, there he is: the young master, sitting bored! I think to myself, No, I just can't let it go on like that. Ain't I always looked out for the masters? Nearly two years I been with you here, and, thank God, I ain't heard a bad word from you nor the madam. Take some, now, they don't give a damn for the master's livestock. Is them cows fed?—fine; they ain't?—the hell with'em. But I ain't like that. For me them cows means more than anything. That's what I tell the boys: you do what you like with me, but I want them cows fed right!"

Mitya had begun to think the steward was drunk when suddenly he dropped the air of aggrieved sincerity and said with a sidelong questioning glance:

"Well then, could we do any better than Alenka? A fine little piece, full of piss and vinegar, plenty young, and her husband's off at the mines... Course, you got to slip her a little gewgaw of some kind. It'll cost you, let's say, when all's said and done, a five. A ruble, let's say, on her treat, then hand her two more. And for me just a bit of something for tobacco..."

"That won't be any problem," answered Mitya, once again instinctively. "Only, what Alenka is it you're talking about?"

"Why, the forester's, naturally," said the steward. "Can't be you don't know her. Married the new forester's boy. I believe you may've seen her in church last Sunday... That's when it come to me outright: that-there is just the thing for our young master. Married less than two years, keeps right clean..."

"Well, sure, all right," answered Mitya with a grin. "Go on and get it set up."

"In that case, then, I'll give it a try," said the steward, taking up the reins. "I'll sound her out, then, in a day or so. And meantime you keep your eyes open too. Tomorrow she'll be out with the wenches fixing up the garden bank, so you just come on out in the garden... And them books ain't going to run away nowhere; could be you can still get a bellyful of reading in Moscow...''

He whipped up the horse, and once again the drozhky began to shake and bounce. Holding firmly to the cushion and trying not to look at the stout red neck of the steward, Mitya gazed into the distance, through the trees of their garden, at the willows in the village, which sat on a slope leading down to the river, to the meadows beside its bank. It was already half done, something bizarre and unexpected, absurd, something that, nonetheless, caused a chilling languor to pass through his body. And now in some new way, not as before, the bell tower, so familiar since childhood, its cross glittering in the early evening sun, jutted up in front of him, beyond the crowns of the garden's trees.

XX

The peasant girls called Mitya "wolfhound" because of his thinness; he was the type whose black eyes appear to be constantly dilated, whose moustache and beard hardly grow even in adulthood—something sparse and wiry just curls a bit. All the same, on the morning after his conversation with the steward he shaved, then put on a yellow silk shirt that gave his emaciated, somehow inspired face a strange and beautiful glow.

Shortly before eleven he walked slowly out into the garden, trying to adopt a kind of bored air, as if he were strolling about for lack of anything else to do.

He left the house from the main veranda, which faced north. To the north a slate-blue murk hung above the roofs of the coach house and cattle yard, above that part of the garden directly in front of the bell tower. There was a dimness about everything; steam and redolence flowed into the air from the chimney pipe of the workers' annex. Gazing at the sky and at crowns of trees in the garden, Mitya turned the corner of the house and set off for the linden avenue. From beneath the amorphous clouds gathering beyond the garden, from the southeast, a hot feeble wind was blowing. No birds were singing, not even the nightingales. There were only masses of bees, rushing soundlessly through the garden with their nectar.

The peasant girls were working by the spruce grove again, repairing the earthen wall, evening out the crannies left by cattle hoofs, filling them in with earth and with fresh and steamy, pleasant-reeking dung, which from time to time the farm hands carted in across the avenue from the cattle yard—the avenue was strewn with moist glittering dollops. There were about six of the girls. Sonka no longer was with them; they really had made a match for her now, and she was staying home, preparing for the wedding. There were several quite scrawny little girls, there was the stout comely Anyutka, there was Glashka, who seemed to have become even more austere and purposeful—and

100

Alenka. Mitya noticed her at once amidst the trees, he knew at once it was she although he had never seen her before, and he was taken unawares, the resemblance startled him like a flash of lightning, the something in common that he saw—or that he only fancied—between Alenka and Katya. He was so amazed that he even paused, momentarily dumbfounded. Then he walked toward her resolutely, keeping his eyes trained on her.

She too was small and agile. In spite of the dirty work she had come to do, she was wearing a pretty cotton print blouse (white with red polka dots), a black patent leather belt, a skirt of the same pattern, a pink silk kerchief, red wool stockings and soft, black galoshes, which suggested again (rather, her whole small lithe foot suggested) something of Katya, that is something of the womanly mixed with the childish. Her head was also small, and her dark eyes were prominent and gleaming in much the same way as Katya's. When he walked up she alone was not working, as if sensing that in some way she was special, different from the others; she stood on the earthen wall talking to the steward, resting her right foot on a pitchfork. Propped up on his elbows, the steward lay beneath an apple tree, smoking, his jacket with its torn lining spread beneath him. When Mitya walked up he politely moved over onto the grass, giving him his place on the jacket.

"Set down, Mitry Palich; have a smoke," he said in a friendly, offhand manner.

Mitya cast a quick stealthy glance at Alenka—the pink kerchief gave her face a lovely glow—then he sat down, keeping his eyes lowered, and lit a cigarette (many times that winter and spring he had given up smoking, but now he had started again). Alenka did not even greet him, appeared not to have noticed him. The steward continued telling her something that made no sense to Mitya because he had not heard the beginning of the conversation. She laughed, but in a way that indicated her mind and heart were not in the laughter. Contemptuously and derisively the steward kept throwing smutty allusions into every sentence. She answered him nimbly and also derisively, giving him to understand that in his pursuit of someone he had conducted himself stupidly, had been too brazen and at the same time chicken-hearted, afraid of his wife.

"Well, I see nobody's going to out-gabble you," the steward finally said, cutting short the argument on the pretense that it was all too wearisome and useless. "Better you come set with us a spell. The master's got something to say to you."

Alenka looked off to one side, tucked in the dark ringlets of hair on her temples, and remained standing in the same spot.

"I said get over here, you idiot!" said the steward.

Alenka hesitated for a moment, then suddenly made a nimble leap from the wall, ran up to within two paces of where Mitya lay on the jacket, and squatted on her haunches, staring at his face with a genial curiosity in her dark, dilated eyes. Then she began laughing and asked:

"Is it true you don't have no truck with women, young master? Like some kind of deacon in the church?"

"And how do you know he don't?" asked the steward.

"I just know," said Alenka; "I heard. No, he ain't allowed. He's got a little somebody in Moscow," she said with a mischievous gleam in her eyes.

"There ain't nobody here fit for him, so he don't live with nobody," answered the steward. "A lot you know about his business!"

"How do you mean, nobody?" said Alenka, laughing. "There's slews of women and wenches! Anyutka over there, now; you couldn't do no better. Anyut, come on over here, we got business for you!" she shouted in a ringing voice.

Anyutka, who had a broad fleshy back and short arms, turned around— her face was attractive, her smile kind and pleasant—she shouted an answer in her singsong voice and went back to working even harder.

"I said come on over here!" repeated Alenka, her voice ringing out still more loudly.

"No use me coming over; I ain't had no experience in that sort of business," sang out Anyutka merrily.

"We don't need Anyutka; we want something a little bit cleaner, more dignified," said the steward in a preceptoral tone. "We know exactly who we want."

He gave Alenka a very pointed glance. She was slightly embarrassed and blushed faintly.

"Oh no, oh no," she answered, hiding her embarrassment with a smile. "Anyutka, now, you won't find nothing better. And if it ain't her you want, well, there's Nastka; keeps herself right clean too, once lived in town..."

"That's enough, hush up," said the steward with unexpected coarseness. "Get back to what you're doing; you had your gabble and that's it. The madam's been on to me anyhow, says, 'With you all they do is get into mischief...' "

Alenka jumped up—once again uncommonly nimble in her movements— and grabbed the pitchfork. But just then a farm hand, who had finished dumping out the last cartload of manure, cried "Lunchtime!" Then, tugging at the reins he drove off smartly down the avenue, his empty cart bed thundering.

"Lunchtime, lunchtime!" screamed the girls in a variety of voices, throwing down their spades and pitchforks, leaping over the earthen wall, jumping down from it with their bare legs and multicolored stockings flashing, and running into the spruce grove to get their bundles of food.

The steward cast a sideways glance at Mitya, winked at him as if to say that things were starting to move, and raising himself a bit, he assented to the break with the pompous air of one in authority:

"Well, if it's lunchtime, I guess lunchtime it is..."

Splotches of color beneath the dark wall of spruces, the girls sprawled out gaily, haphazardly on the grass, began untying their bundles, removing their flat cakes and spreading them on the hem of their skirts between outstretched legs, began munching, drinking milk or kvass from their bottles, still talking loudly and rambunctiously, laughing out at every word and repeatedly glancing over at Mitya with curious and provocative eyes. Alenka bent toward Anyutka and whispered something in her ear. Unable to hold back a charming smile, Anyutka pushed her away roughly (choking with laughter, Alenka collapsed, head on knees), and with sham indignation she cried out in her melodic voice, which carried throughout the spruce grove:

"Idiot! Cackling away about nothing. What's so funny?"

"Let's get away from sin, Mitry Palich," said the steward. "Whew, just look there, they got the demons in their blood!"

XXI

The next day no one worked in the garden; it was a holiday, a Sunday.

Rain poured in the night, pounded its wet patter on the roof; now and then the garden was illumined by a pallid, but far-reaching, phantasmal glow. By morning, however, the skies had cleared again; once again all was simple, full of equanimity, and Mitya was awakened by the sunlit joyous peal of bells.

Leisurely he washed, dressed, drank a glass of tea, and set off for mass. "Your mama's done left," scolded Parasha affectionately; "you're like some kind of Tartar..."

One could reach the church either by way of the pasture, by going through the gates of the manor and turning right, or through the garden, along the central avenue and then to the left, by the road between the garden and barn. Mitya went through the garden.

Everything was quite summerlike now. Mitya walked down the avenue straight toward the sun, which cast a dry glitter on the barn and the fields. That glitter and the pealing bells blending somehow perfectly and placidly with it and with all this country morning, the fact that he had just washed, had just combed his wet, glossy black hair and put on his peaked university cap, all of this suddenly seemed so fine that Mitya, who had not slept all night again and who once again that night had experienced masses of the most discrepant thoughts and feelings, felt a sudden spasm of hope for some happy deliverance from all his agonies, for salvation, liberation from them. The bells gamboled and beckoned, the barn ahead of him was glittering with heat; a wood-pecker paused, perked up his crest, scurried up the rugged linden bole to its sunny bright-green crown, and velvet, black-red, purposeful bumblebees were burrowing into flowers in the blazing sun of the clearings, birds were flooding all the garden with their sweet and carefree song... Everything was just as it had been many, many times in his childhood, in his boyhood; this memory of all the captivation, the carefree former times was so vivid that suddenly he was sure God was merciful; perhaps it would be possible to live on earth even without Katya.

I really will go visit the Mesherskys, Mitya suddenly thought.

But then he raised his eyes—and not twenty steps from him he saw Alenka, who at that very moment was walking past the gate. She was wearing the pink silk kerchief again, a smart pale-blue dress with flounces, and new shoes with taps on the heels. Swinging her backside, she walked along rapidly, not seeing him, and he leaped aside impulsively, behind the trees.

When she was out of sight, he returned hastily to the house, his heart pounding. He suddenly realized that he had set off for church with the secret aim of seeing her, and he knew that he could not, must not see her in church.

XXII

While they were eating dinner, a special messenger from the station brought a telegram—Anya and Kostya had wired that they would arrive tomorrow evening. Mitya received this news with absolute indifference.

After dinner he lay on the terrace, supine on the wicker divan, eyes closed, feeling the hot sun approach the terrace, listening to the summery buzzing of flies. His heart was shuddering, the insoluble question was on his mind: What next in this Alenka business? When would it definitely be settled? Why hadn't the steward asked her outright yesterday: would she, and if yes, then where and when? And there was another torment as well: should he or should he not break his resolution to make no more trips to the post office? Couldn't he go once more today, for the last time? Wasn't this pathetic hope just another senseless self-torment? But what could one trip (really, just a simple ramble) add to his agony now? Wasn't it perfectly obvious now that for him everything out there, in Moscow, was finished forever? What, after all, could he do about anything now?

"Young master!" a soft voice suddenly rang out beside the terrace. "Young master, you sleeping?"

Quickly he opened his eyes. The steward was standing there in a new cotton print shirt and a new peaked cap. His face was festive, sated and slightly drowsy, drunken.

"Young master, quick, let's ride on out to the woods," he whispered. "I told the madam I had to see Trifon about them bees. Quick now, while she's still snoozing; she might wake up and change her mind... We'll pick us up something for old Trifon; after he's potted you get him to talking, and I'll sneak around and have a little whisper in Alenka's ear. Come on out quick, I done harnessed up the horse..."

Mitya jumped up, ran through the domestics' chamber, grabbed his cap and rushed out to the coach house, where a spirited young stallion stood harnessed to the light drozhky.

XXIII

The stallion tore off like a whirlwind and flew past the gates. They stopped for a moment at the shop opposite the church, bought a pound of lard and a bottle of vodka, and sped away.

Near a peasant hut that flashed by at the edge of the village they saw Anyutka, smartly dressed but having nothing better to do than stand there. The steward cried out something to her in a jocular but coarse tone; with drunken, senseless and malicious bravura he jerked aside the reins and used them to lash the stallion's croup. The horse dashed on at even greater speed.

Sitting there jouncing about in the drozhky, Mitya held on with all his strength. The back of his neck baked pleasantly in the sun, a warm breeze blew in his face, bearing the heat from the field, now redolent of rye breaking into bloom, of road dust and axle grease. The rye was swaying, flecked with silvery-grey ripples, like some kind of marvelous fur; skylarks were soaring continuously above it, crying out, skimming obliquely up and falling, and far ahead lay the soft blue of the forest...

In fifteen minutes they had reached the forest, and keeping up the same brisk pace, knocking against stumps and roots, they sped along its shaded road, which was joyous with patches of sun and countless flowers in the dense high grass on each side. Wearing her pale-blue dress, her legs in half-boots stretched out evenly, straight in front of her, Alenka sat embroidering amidst the oak saplings that were blooming beside the sentry hut. The steward barrelled past her, making a threatening gesture with his whip, and immediately reined in near the threshold. Mitya marvelled at the bitter and crisp scent of the forest and the vernal oak leafage; he was deafened by the ringing yelps of puppies, who surrounded the drozhky and filled all the forest with echoes. They stood there pouring out ferocious howls in all sorts of pitches and timbres, but their shaggy muzzles were kindly and their tails were wagging.

After they had climbed down, they hitched the stallion beneath the window, to a desiccate little tree that had been singed by lightning, and went into the hut through the dark entrance hall.

Inside it was very clean, cozy and snug, hot because the sun shone in both its tiny windows from beyond the forest and because the stove had been lit—they had been baking dodgers of bread that morning. Alenka's mother-in-law Fedosya, a neat respectable-looking old woman, sat at the table, her back to the sunny window, which was specked with small flies. When she saw the young master, she stood up and made a deep bow. They greeted her, sat down, and began smoking.

"Whereabouts is Trifon?" asked the steward.

"Having a rest in the storeroom," said Fedosya. "I'll go fetch him for you."

"Things is moving!" whispered the steward as soon as she had left, winking with both eyes.

But so far Mitya could see nothing moving at all. Everything so far was unbearably awkward; it seemed that Fedosya knew perfectly well why they had come. Once again the thought that had horrified him for three days flashed through his head: What am I doing? I'm losing my mind! He felt as if he were walking in his sleep, under the power of some alien force, moving faster and faster toward a lethal but relentlessly beckoning abyss. But he sat smoking, looking around the hut, trying to appear casual and calm. Especially shameful was the thought that any minute Trifon would come in, a man who was said to be testy and clever, who would immediately understand everything even better than Fedosya. But at the same time he was thinking of something else: where does she sleep? Right here on this plank bed or in the storeroom? In the storeroom, of course, he thought. A summer's night in the forest, the tiny windows of the storeroom, with no frames, no glass, the somnolent whisper of the forest all night long, and she sleeps...

XXIV

When Trifon came in he too bowed low to Mitya but said nothing and kept his eyes averted. Then he sat down on a bench by the table and began speaking with the steward in a dry hostile tone: what is it, what you here for? The steward hastened to reply that the madam had sent him, that she would like Trifon to come have a look at the apiary, that their beekeeper was a deaf old imbecile, and that he, Trifon, with all his cleverness and know-how, might be the top beeman in the whole province; thereupon he pulled out the bottle of vodka from one of his trouser pockets and the lard in its rough grey paper, now soaked with grease, from the other. Trifon gave him a cold, derisive glance, but rose from his seat and took a tea cup from the shelf. The steward served Mitya first, then Trifon, then Fedosya—with great relish she swilled hers down— and finally himself. Tossing off his drink, he immediately began to pour out another round, munching on a dodger of bread and puffing out his nostrils.

Trifon got drunk quite rapidly, but he maintained his dry manner, his hostile derisiveness. After only two glasses the steward grew extremely muddled. Outwardly the conversation took on the guise of friendliness, but the eyes of both men were mistrustful and rancorous. Fedosya sat in silence, looked on politely but discontentedly. Alenka did not appear. Having lost all hope that she would come, clearly realizing that now only a fool would dream of counting on the steward—on his managing to "have a little whisper" in her ear even if she did come—Mitya stood up and announced sternly that it was time to go.

"Directly, directly, there ain't no hurry!" responded the steward in a dour and insolent tone. "I still got something to tell you in private."

"Well, you can tell me on the way back," said Mitya, restraining himself but speaking even more sternly. "Let's go."

But the steward slapped his paim on the table and repeated with an air of drunken mysteriousness.

"Listen here, now, this is something that can't wait to be said going back! Come on out with me for a minute..."

Rising sluggishly from his place, he flung open the door to the entrance hall.

Mitya followed him out.

"Well, what is it?"

"Hush up," whispered the steward cryptically, staggering as he tried to close the door behind Mitya.

"Hush about what?"

"Hush up!"

"I don't understand you."

"Just hush up! Our lady'll be here! Take my word for it!"

Mitya pushed him away, went out of the entrance hall, and stopped on the threshold of the hut, not knowing what to do next. Should he wait a bit longer or drive home alone, or should he simply leave on foot?

Ten paces from him lay the dense green forest, now covered in evening shade, which made it even more fresh, pure and lovely. The kind of sun that goes with clear perfect weather was setting behind its crowns, radiantly spreading through them its carmine gold. And suddenly a melodic female voice rang out, low and resonant, reverberated through the forest depths, seemed to be somewhere far on the other side, beyond the ravines, its modulation so charming, so invocatory, as a voice sounds only in the forest amidst the evening glow of summer.

"A-ooo!" resounded the long-protracted cry of that girl, apparently amusing herself with forest echoes. "A-ooo!"

Mitya leaped down from the threshold and ran through flowers and grass to the forest. The forest descended into a rocky ravine. There in the ravine, chewing on cowslip stems, stood Alenka. Mitya ran to the edge and stopped. She gazed up at him in astonishment.

"What are you doing here?" asked Mitya softly.

"I'm hunting for our Maruska and the cow. Why?" she answered, also softly.

"Well, then, will you come?"

"Well, what am I supposed to do, come for nothing?" she said.

"Who said for nothing?" asked Mitya, now almost in a whisper. "Don't worry about that."

"When?" asked Alenka.

"Well, tomorrow... When can you?"

Alenka thought for a moment.

"Tomorrow I'll be going to shear sheep at my mama's," she said, after pausing and carefully surveying the forest on the knoll behind Mitya. "In the evening, soon as it's dark, I'll come. But where? Can't use the barn, somebody'd walk in... What about the shed, in the hollow of your garden? Only look out you don't pull no tricks—I won't do it for nothing... This ain't no Moscow," she said, gazing up at him with laughing eyes; "they say them women there pay for it theirselves..."

The journey back was chaotic.

So as not to feel indebted, Trifon had produced his own bottle, and the steward got so drunk that at first he could not mount the drozhky; he fell against it, causing the frightened stallion to lunge forward and nearly gallop off alone. But Mitya kept silent, looked at the steward insensibly, waited, patiently, while he took his seat. Once again the steward drove the horse with absurd ferocity. Mitya kept silent, held on firmly, looked at the evening sky, at the fields rapidly shuddering and bouncing before him. Above those fields, toward the sunset, the skylarks sang their last meek songs; in the east, now blue with the coming night, there were flares of the distant, placid heat lightning that promises nothing but fine weather. Mitya took in all this twilight captivation, but now it was utterly alien to him. There was only one thing on his mind and in his heart: tomorrow evening!

At home he was greeted with the news that a letter had come from Anya and Kostya, confirming their arrival tomorrow on the evening train. He was horrified; they would drive up in the evening, run out into the garden, possibly into the hollow, approach the shed... But immediately he recalled that they could not be driven here from the station until after nine, and then they would be fed, given tea...

"Are you driving in with me to meet them?" asked Olga Petrovna.

He felt himself go pale.

"No, I don't think so... I don't feel much like it... And there won't be any room..."

"Well, maybe you could ride in on horseback..."

"No, I don't know... What's the point, anyway? At least right now I don't feel like it..."

Olga Petrovna looked at him intently.

"Are you well?"

"Perfectly well," said Mitya in an almost rude tone. "I'm just awfully sleepy..."

And right after that he went to his room, lay down on the sofa in the dark, and fell asleep, still dressed.

In the night he heard torpid, faraway music and saw himself hanging above a huge, vaguely illumined abyss. It kept getting brighter and brighter, became ever more bottomless, ever more golden, more luminous, ever more swarming with masses of people, and then with utter clarity, with unspeakable sorrow and tenderness the words began sounding and resounding within it: "Once in far Thule there lived a good king..." He trembled with emotion, turned over on his other side, and went back to sleep.

XXVI

The day seemed interminable.

Mitya came out in a daze for tea and for dinner, then went back to his room again, lay down once again, took up a volume of Pisemsky that had been lying on his desk for ages, read without understanding a word, spent hours gazing at the ceiling, listened to the even, summerlike, satin hum of the garden in the sun beyond his window... Once he got up and went into the library to find a different book. But that room, captivating for its antiquity and its calm, for the view of the beloved maple outside one window and the bright western sky out the others, aroused such an acute reminder of those (now infinitely remote) spring days when he had sat in this room reading verses in old journals, and it all seemed so full of Katya that he turned and rushed back out. To hell with it! he thought in exasperation. To hell with all that poetic tragedy of love!

He recalled with indignation how he had intended to shoot himself if Katya did not write, and then he lay down again, once again took up Pisemsky. But just as before he understood nothing of what he was reading, and from time to time, as he gazed at the book and thought of Alenka, he would begin to shudder all over from a tremor in his stomach that grew more and more intense. And the closer it was to evening, the more often the tremor gripped him, churned within him. Voices and footsteps throughout the house, voices in the yard—now they were harnessing the tarantass for the trip to the station— everything had the kind of resonance it has when you are ill, when you lie alone and normal, humdrum life flows on all around, indifferent to you and therefore alien, even malign. Finally Parasha cried out from somewhere: "Madam, the horses are ready!" And the dry hollow mutter of harness bells became audible, then the tramp of hooves, the rustle of the tarantass rolling up to the veranda... "Ah, when will all this end!" muttered Mitya, beside himself with impatience, not moving, listening avidly to the voice of Olga Petrovna as she gave final instructions in the domestics' chamber. Suddenly the harness bells came alive, their hollow mutter grew ever more steady and categorical in accord with the din of the carriage rolling downhill, then began dying away...

Mitya quickly got up and went into the drawing room. That room was empty and bright with the clear yellowish sunset. All the house was empty, somehow strangely, terribly empty! With a strange, somehow valedictory feeling Mitya glanced into the open mute rooms—into the guest room, the divan room, the library, where through the window one could see the vespertine blue glow of southern sky above the horizon, the picturesque green crown of the maple, and, above it, the pink dot of Antares... Then he looked into the domestics' chamber to see if Parasha was there. Having assured himself that it too was empty, he grabbed his cap from the hook, ran back, into his room, and leaped out the window, throwing his long legs far out toward the flower bed. He froze dead still in that flower bed for an instant, then stooping, he ran across to the garden and veered immediately onto a secluded branch avenue, which was densely overgrown with acacia and lilac bushes.

Since there was no dew, the smells of the evening garden could not have been especially pungent. But for all the spontaneity of everything he did that evening, it seemed to Mitya that never in his life—with the exception, perhaps, of early childhood—had he encountered such strong and such diversified smells. Everything was redolent—acacia bushes, lilac leafage, currant leafage, burdocks, wormwood, blossoms, grass, earth...

When Mitya had taken a few quick steps, he was struck by a frightening thought: what if she tricks me and doesn't come? It seemed now that all of life depended on whether Alenka appeared or not; catching amidst the smells of vegetation another smell, that of evening smoke, which drifted over from somewhere in the village, he stopped once more and turned around for a moment. A twilight beetle was slowly floating and droning by not far from him, as if sowing quiet, tranquility and dusk, but everything was still bright from the evening glow, which enveloped half the sky with the even, long-undying light of early summer gloaming, and above the manor roof, visible in blotches through the trees, the skewed and sharp sickle of the newborn moon glittered high in transparent celestial emptiness. Mitya glanced at it, crossed himself with a brief perfunctory gesture below his chest, and strode out into the acacia bushes. The avenue led to the hollow but not to the shed—to reach it one had to go cater-cornered, to bear left. When he had strode through the bushes, Mitya began running headlong, amidst the low and extensive network of outstretched branches, sometimes bending, sometimes pushing them out of his way. A moment later he arrived at the designated spot.

Fearfully he plunged into the shed, into its darkness, which smelled of dry fusty straw, looked around attentively, and almost felt a surge of joy when he realized no one was there. But the fateful moment was drawing near; he stood beside the shed all keen sensitivity and strained concentration. The whole day long, nearly every minute he had experienced an extraordinary physical agitation. Now it had reached its utmost intensity. But strangely enough—even now, as throughout the day, it was somehow discrete, did not imbue the whole of him, possessed only his body, had not captured his spirit. But his heart was pounding terribly. And all around there was such staggering quiet that this was all he could hear—the pounding heartbeat. Soundlessly, tirelessly they hovered and whirled, the soft colorless moths in the branches, in the grey apple tree leafage, sketched in a variety of beautiful patterns against the evening sky, and these moths made the quiet seem even more quiet, as if the moths were spinning incantations and casting their spell upon it. Suddenly behind him there was a crackling sound; it jolted him like a thunderclap. He turned around wildly, gazed through the trees in the direction of the earthen wall— and beneath the apple boughs he saw something black rolling toward him. But before he had time even to think what it could be, this dark thing came swooping right up upon him, made some kind of sweeping movement—and proved to be Alenka.

She pushed down the hem of her short skirt made of black homespun wool, flung it away from her head, and he saw her frightened face, gleaming with a smile. She was barefoot, wearing only a skirt with a plain austere blouse tucked into it. Her girlish breasts stood up beneath the blouse. Its collar was cut wide, so that her neck and part of her shoulders could be seen; the sleeves were turned up above the elbows to reveal her rounded arms. Everything about her, from the small head, covered by a yellow kerchief, to the tiny bare feet, womanly and childish at the same time, was so fine, so lissome, so fascinating, that Mitya, who previously had always seen her smartly dressed, who for the first time saw her in all the captivation of that plainness, gasped inwardly.

"Well, hurry up, then," she whispered gaily and surreptitiously, and after a quick look around she darted into the shed, into its odorous dusk.

There she paused, and clenching his teeth to stop their chattering, Mitya hastily reached in his pocket—his legs were tensed, firm, like iron—and slipped a crumpled five-ruble note into her palm. Quickly she hid it in her shirt front and sat down on the ground. Mitya sat beside her and put his arms around her neck, not knowing what to do—wondering whether he had to kiss her or not. The smell of her kerchief, her hair, the oniony smell of her whole body, blending with the smell of a peasant hut, of smoke—it was all so lovely that his head spun, and Mitya could understand that, could sense it. Nonetheless, it was just the same as before. The awesome power of physical desire did not pass over into spiritual desire, into beatitude, rapture, into the sweet languor of all being. She pulled away and lay down on her back. He lay beside her, pressed against her, stretched out his hand. Laughing quietly and nervously, she took it and pulled it down.

"Absolutely not permitted," she said, half joking, half serious. She moved his hand away and held it tenaciously in her own small hand; her eyes looked through the shed's triangular window frame at the apple branches, at the now darkened blue sky beyond those branches and the motionless red dot of Antares, still hanging there in solitude. What did those eyes express? What was he supposed to do? Kiss her neck, her lips? Suddenly she put her hand on the short black skirt and said hastily:

"Well, hurry up, then..."

When they arose—and Mitya got up overwhelmed with disillusionment—putting her kerchief back on, straightening her hair, she asked in an animated whisper—now in the tone of an intimate, a lover:

"They say you been in Subbotino. Priest there sells sucking pigs cheap. Is that true or not? Ain't you heard?"

XXVIII

On Saturday of that same week the rain, which had begun as early as Wednesday, which had poured from morning to night, was still falling in torrents.

Time and again that day it intensified, showered down with a special vehemence and sombreness.

And all day long Mitya wandered endlessly through the garden, kept weeping so much all day that at times he himself was amazed at the force and abundance of his tears.

Parasha searched for him, cried out for him in the yard, on the linden avenue, called him for dinner, then for tea; he did not respond.

It was cold, piercingly damp, dark with storm clouds; against their blackness the thick greenery of the wet garden was prominent, especially dense, crisp and bright. The wind that gusted from time to time cast still another downpour from the trees—a deluge of spattering raindrops. But Mitya paid no attention to anything, saw nothing. His white peaked cap was drooping and had turned dark grey, his university jacket had gone black, his boots were muddied to the knees. He was a terrible sight, dripping water, soaked through and through, his face completely drained of blood, his eyes tear-blanched and insane.

He smoked one cigarette after another, walked with lengthy strides through the mud of the avenues, sometimes simply dashed off at random, headlong, into the tall wet grass amidst the apple and pear trees, stumbling against their skewed rugged boughs, splotched with sodden grey-green lichens. He would sit on the swollen, blackened benches, go out to the hollow, lie on the damp straw of the shed, in the very same spot where he had lain with Alenka. The cold and the icy dampness of the air made his large hands blue, his lips had turned mauve, his deathly pallid face with its gaunt cheeks had taken on a violet hue. He would lie on his back, legs crossed, hands behind his head, glaring savagely at the black straw roof, from which large rusty raindrops were falling. Then his cheeks went tense, his brows began to twitch. Impulsively he leaped up, pulled from his trousers pocket the stained and rumpled letter, which he had read over and over since receiving it late yesterday evening—the surveyor who came to the manor for several days on business had brought it—and once again, for the hundredth time, he devoured it avidly:

> Dear Mitya,
>
> Try not to think badly of me, forget, forget all that has been! I'm nasty, I'm repulsive, depraved, I'm not worthy of you, but I love art insanely! I've made my decision; the die is cast, I'm going away—you know with whom... You're sensitive, intelligent, you'll understand; I beg of you, my dear, don't torment yourself and me! Don't write me at all, it's no use!

When he had read to that point, Mitya wadded up the letter, and burying his face in the wet straw, clenching his teeth rabidly, he choked on his sobs. The incidental "my dear," which was such a terrible reminder of their intimacy and appeared even to restore that intimacy, which flooded his heart with unbearable tenderness—that was beyond human endurance! And right after this "my dear" came the firm declaration that even writing her now was no use! Yes, he knew it: no use! It was all over, finished forever!

Just before evening the rain, assailing the garden with tenfold greater force, and the sudden blasts of thunder finally drove him back to the house. Wet from head to foot, his teeth chattering from the icy tremor that had spread through all his body, he looked out from beneath the trees, and convinced that no one could see him, he ran up below his window, raised it from the outside—with its antiquated frame it could be opened by lifting the bottom half—and leaping into his room, he locked the door and hurled himself on the bed.

Darkness was quickly approaching. The din of the rain was everywhere— on the roof, all around the house, in the garden. It had a dualistic quality, that din, two disparate sounds—one sound in the garden, but by the house, in accord with the unremitting gurgle and plash of the gutters pouring water into puddles, another sound. That dichotomy of sound produced impalpable apprehension in Mitya, who had lapsed immediately into a lethargic torpor, and together with the fever that burned his nostrils, his breath, his head, it steeped him in something like narcosis, created what appeared another world, some other early evening in what appeared some other, some alien house, where there was a horrible presentiment of something.

He knew, he felt that he was in his own room, now nearly dark with the rain and approaching evening, that out there, at the tea table in the drawing room, were the voices of mother, Anya, Kostya, and the surveyor, but simultaneously he was walking through someone else's manor house, following, lagging behind a young nanny, and he was seized by impalpable, ever-growing horror, mixed, however, with concupiscence, with a presentiment of someone's intimacy with someone, an act that contained something unnaturally, grotesquely abhorrent, but in which he himself somehow was taking part. And he experienced all of this through the intermediary figure of a child with a large white face, whom the young nanny carried in her arms, leaning backward and rocking him to sleep. Mitya hurried to overtake her, overtook her and tried to look at her face—to see if she was Alenka—but suddenly he found himself in a dusky *gymnasium* classroom, its panes smudged with chalk. She who stood there at a mirror, in front of a chest of drawers, could not see him— he had abruptly turned invisible. She was wearing a yellow silk petticoat that tightly encompassed her rounded hips, high-heeled slippers, and sheer, black openwork stockings through which her body shone; sweetly timorous and shamefaced, she knew what was soon to occur. Already she had managed to hide the child in one of the drawers. Throwing her hair over her shoulder, she quickly began braiding it, and casting sideways glances at the door, she gazed in the mirror, at the reflection of her powdered face, her bare shoulders and small, milky-bluish breasts with their pink nipples. The door was flung open; looking around briskly and ominously, a gentleman in a dinner jacket came in, his face anaemic, clean-shaven, his hair black, short and curly. He took out a flat golden *porte-cigare* and began smoking with an air of free and easy

113

nonchalance. Her braiding now almost done, she looked at him timorously, knowing his intentions, then tossed the braid back over her shoulder and raised her bare arms... He put his arms around her waist condescendingly—and she embraced his neck, showing her dark armpits, nestled against him, buried her face in his chest...

XXIX

Mitya came to his senses, covered in sweat, with the astoundingly vivid realization that he was lost, that this world was monstrously sombre and hopeless, more than any netherworld beyond the grave could ever be. The room was full of murk, the dinning and spattering continued beyond the windows, and his body, which shuddered all over with chills, could not stand this din and this patter (unbearable for its sound alone). But most unbearable and horrible of all was the monstrous, grotesque unnaturalness of human coitus, which he himself and the clean-shaven gentleman seemed just now to have shared out between them. There were voices and laughter in the drawing room. They too were horrible and grotesquely unnatural in their estrangement from him, in the coarseness of life, its indifference, its mercilessness toward him...

"Katya!" he said, sitting up on the bed and throwing his feet to the floor. "Katya, what is this!" he said aloud, absolutely convinced that she could hear him, that she was there, that she was silent, unresponsive, only because she herself was crushed, because she herself understood the irremediable horror of all that she had done. "Ah, it doesn't matter, Katya," he whispered bitterly and tenderly, meaning that he would forgive her everything if only she would rush to him as she once had done, so that together they could be saved—could save their beautiful love in this most beautiful spring world that only so recently was like a paradise. But having whispered it—"Ah, it doesn't matter, Katya!"—he knew immediately that he was wrong, that it did matter, that salvation, a return to that wondrous apparition he had once been given to see at Shakhovskoe, on the terrace overgrown with jasmine, did not exist, could not be, and he began quietly weeping with the pain that was rending his chest.

It, the pain, was so intense, so unbearable, that without thinking what he was doing, without realizing what all this would lead to, passionately desiring only one thing, to escape from it at least for a moment and to avoid being engulfed again in that horrible world where he had spent the whole day and where he had just taken part in the most horrible and most abominable of all earthly dreams, he fumbled around for the drawer of his night table, pulled it out, found the cold and cumbersome lump of the revolver, and heaving a deep and joyous sigh, he opened wide his mouth, then vigorously, ecstatically, he fired.

14 September 1924. Maritime Alps.

114

ON THE NIGHT SEA

A steamer bound for the Crimea from Odessa docked in the night at Evpatoriya.

On the ship and beside it a scene straight from hell was played out. As winches rumbled the men taking on cargo and the others hoisting it up from an enormous barge below screamed ferociously; wrangling and shrieking, an Oriental rabble laid siege to the passenger ladder, stormed it with an incredible rush of frenzy, swarmed upward with bag and baggage; an electric bulb hanging over the ladder garishly illumined the dense, disorderly procession of filthy fezzes and bashlyks with turbans, goggling eyes, shoulders pushing forward, hands clutching handrailings convulsively. Below, beside the last steps, which the waves periodically inundated, there was still more clamor; there they also bawled and brawled, stumbled and clutched; oars thudded, boats full of people collided—they would fly high up on a wave, then plunge steeply, disappearing in the darkness under the broadside. And resiliently, as if on elastic, the dolphin-like bulk of the ship pitched now to one side, now to the other...

Finally things began to quiet down.

One of the last to board, a gentleman standing very erect, with straight shoulders, handed his ticket and bag to the porter at the first-class deckhouse; informed that there were no cabins left, he made his way back to the stern, which was dark. In one of the deck chairs, the only chair occupied, he could distinguish the black silhouette of a man, half reclining under a lap robe. The new passenger selected a chair several feet from him. The chair was low, and when he sat down the canvas stretched to form a comfortable and pleasant cavity. The ship rose and fell, slowly drifted, swung with the current. A soft breeze that was faintly redolent of the ocean wafted through the southern summer night. Summerish in its plainness and tranquility, with minute, modest stars in the clear sky, the night effused a soft transparent darkness. The distant lights were pale, and since the hour was late, they seemed drowsy. Soon everything on the ship was completely settled; now the placid voices of the crew were audible, the anchor chain clattered... Then the stern shuddered, rumbled with churning water and screws. Scattered low and flat on the distant shore, the lights floated away. The ship stopped swaying...

One might have thought that both passengers were sleeping, so motionless did they recline in the deck chairs. But they were not asleep; they were staring intently through the dusk at one another. And finally the first, the one whose legs were covered by the lap robe, asked simply and placidly:

"Are you going to the Crimea too?"

And the other, the one with the straight shoulders, answered unhurriedly in the same tone: "Yes, to the Crimea and then some. I'll be in Alupka, and after that in Gagry."

"I recognized you immediately," said the first.

"And I recognized you, and also immediately," answered the other.

"A very strange and unexpected meeting."

"Couldn't be stranger."

"In fact, it wasn't that I recognized you, but I seemed to have a pre-sentiment that for some reason you would appear—so that recognition was beside the point."

"I experienced exactly the same feeling."

"Yes? Very strange. Doesn't it force one to admit that life, nonetheless, has its moments—well, singular moments, so to speak? Perhaps life is not at all so simple as it appears."

"Perhaps. But then maybe there's another explanation: that just this minute you and I conjured up in our imaginations what we now take to be prevision."

"Perhaps. Yes, that's entirely possible. Even highly probable."

"Well, there you see. We philosophize, but maybe life is very simple. As simple as that clamor just now beside the ladder. Those fools, crushing each other; where were they all in such a hurry to get to?"

And the men fell silent for a moment. Then they began speaking again.

"How long since we saw each other? Twenty-three years?" asked the first passenger, the one under the lap robe.

"Yes, almost," answered the other. "Exactly twenty-three in the autumn. For you and me it's very easy to calculate. Almost a quarter century."

"A long time. An entire lifetime. That is, considering that life is nearly over for both of us now."

"Yes, yes. And so what? Are we really so terrified that it's over?"

"Hmm! Of course not. Hardly at all. It's all lies, after all, when we tell ourselves how terrifying it is; that is, when we try to frighten ourselves by saying, Look, you've lived out your life and in some ten years you'll be in the grave. And just think: the grave. It's no laughing matter."

"Absolutely right. And I'll tell you something even more interesting. You probably know how I am, so to speak, renowned in the world of medicine?"

"But who doesn't know that! Of course I know. And are you aware that your humble servant has also glorified himself?"

"Well, most certainly. One could say I'm your devotee, your faithful reader," said the other.

"Yes, yes, two celebrities. Well, what were you going to say?"

"That thanks to my celebrity, that is, to a certain erudition (God knows how much wisdom; the erudition, nonetheless, is substantial), I can be almost perfectly sure that I have not even ten years to live, but a few months. Well, at the very most a year. Both myself and my colleagues in the profession have diagnosed, with certitude, a terminal disease. And I assure you that, nonetheless, I am living almost as if nothing had happened. I only smile sarcastically. Imagine, if you please, I wanted to show up everyone with my knowledge of all the possible causes of death, to become renowned and to live magnificently; and my achievements collapsed on my head—I made the magnificent discovery of my very own death. They might have played the fool with me and deceived me: 'Hold on, old boy, we'll still get you through, what the hell!' But with me how can one lie and be deceitful? It's stupid and awkward. So awkward that they even overdo their candidness, which they combine with touching emotion and flattery: 'After all, dear colleague, there's no point in trying to bamboozle *you... Finita la commedia!'* "

"Are you serious?" asked the first.

"Absolutely serious," answered the other. "What, then, is the main point? Some Gaius once was mortal, *ergo* I too will die; but at some indefinite time in the future! Here, unfortunately, we have an entirely different matter: not at some indefinite time, but within a year. And is that very long, a year? Next summer you'll be sailing somewhere again over the ocean blue, and in Moscow, in the Novodevichy Cemetery, my noble bones will be resting. Well, so what? Just that in thinking of this I feel next to nothing; and what's even worse, this is not at all due to some fortitude that the students see in me as I expatiate to them upon my disease and its course, as something interesting from the clinical point of view; it's just some idiotic insensibility. And none of my acquaintances, who know that fatal secret, feel anything either. Well, take you, for example—are you afraid for me?"

"Afraid for you? No, I must confess, not really in the least."

"And of course not at all sorry for me."

"No, not sorry either. Besides that, I can't imagine you believe in those beatific realms where there's neither sorrow nor lamentation, but only paradisal little apples."

"Well, let's just say religious faith is not something that means a lot in your life or mine..."

Once again they both fell silent. Then they took out their cigarette cases and began to smoke.

"And also take note," said the first, the one under the lap robe, "that you and I are not putting on airs at all; we're not striking a pose for each other or for any imaginary audience. We're speaking really very simply, without any premeditated cynicism, without any caustic vainglory, in which there's always, all the same, a certain compensation: 'Will you kindly observe the plight we're in? No one else's problems can compare.' We're also conversing simply and falling silent without making the silence bear some meaning, without any stoic sagacity. Generally speaking, there is no more voluptuous animal on earth than man; the shrewd human soul can extort self-gratification from anything. But in our case I don't see even this. And that's all the more curious since one must add to our, as you express it, idiotic insensibility, all the singularity of our relationship. You and I, after all, are joined by a terribly intimate bond. That is, speaking more precisely, we should be so joined."

"Of course!" answered the other. "What horrors, in fact, I've caused you. I can imagine what you've gone through."

"Yes, and even much more than you can imagine. It's altogether horrible, all that nightmare experienced by a man, a lover or a husband whose wife has been taken away, won over, and who for days and nights on end, almost continuously, incessantly writhes in tormented pride, in terrible jealous visions of the happiness his rival is experiencing, and in hopeless, unremitting tenderness—or rather, tender sexual yearning—for the lost mate, whom at one and the same time he would like to strangle in a fury of hatred and shower with the most abasing professions of truly dog-like submissiveness and devotion. Altogether it's inutterably horrible. And besides that, I'm not an entirely ordinary man, but a highly sensitive and highly imaginative individual. So just think about what I experienced for years."

"Really years?"

"I assure you, not less than three years. And even for a long time after that a single thought of you and her, of your intimacy with her, would scorch me like red-hot iron. And it's understandable. Well, say a man, for example, wins over your fiancée—that's still tolerable. But your mistress, or, in our case, your wife! The one, excuse my frankness, with whom I've slept, whose every feature of body and soul I know like the back of my hand! Just think what scope there is here for the jealous imagination. How can you bear another's possessing her? It's all simply beyond human endurance. And for what did I nearly drink myself blind, for what did I wreck my health and aspirations? For what did I waste the time when my powers and talent were flourishing most brilliantly? Speaking without any exaggeration whatsoever, you simply broke me in pieces. I recovered, of course, but to what end? My former self, nonetheless, no longer existed and could not exist. You encroached upon the most sacred thing in all my existence! While seeking himself a bride, Prince Gautama beheld Yasodhara, who 'had the shape of a goddess and the eyes of a doe in spring'; in his passion for her, competing with the other young men, he performed the devil only knows what stunts; for example, he shot from his bow with such force that it was heard for seven thousand miles. And then he took off his necklace of pearls, entwined it about the neck of Yasodhara, and said, 'It is her I have chosen because she and I did play in the forest in times long past, when I was the son of a huntsman and she a forest maid. She lingers in the memory of my soul!' On that day she wore a gold-black mantle, and the prince cast his gaze upon her and said: 'She wears a gold-black mantle because myriads of years ago, when I was a huntsman, I saw her in the forests as a leopard. She lingers in the memory of my soul!' You'll forgive me for all this poetry, but it contains a profound, terrible truth. Just consider the sense of these remarkable words concerning the memory of the soul, and consider how horrible it is when an outsider transgresses upon this, the most sanctified encounter in the world. Who knows—perhaps I too would have shot with such force that it could have been heard for thousands of miles. But then suddenly you appeared..."

"Well then, what do you feel towards me now?" asked the man with straight shoulders. "Malice, loathing, craving for vengeance?"

"Just imagine: absolutely nothing. In spite of all the afore-cited tirade, absolutely nothing. Horrible, horrible. And there you have all the 'memory of my soul!' But then you know that perfectly well yourself; that is, you know I feel nothing. Otherwise you wouldn't have asked."

"You're right. I know. And that too is simply terrible."

"But we, nonetheless, aren't frightened by it. What sheer horror: that we're not frightened at all."

"Yes, in fact, not the least bit. They say: the past, the past! But it's all nonsense. Strictly speaking, people have no past whatsoever. Only a weak echo from some aggregate of all their previous lives..."

Once more the men lapsed into silence. The steamship shuddered, moved on; rising, then subsiding, slow and regular came the soft sound of a drowsy wave, sweeping along the broadside; behind the monotonous din of the stern, swiftly, monotonously swiveled the line of the log, which was ticking off something now and again with a delicate, cryptic chime: *dzeen...* Then the passenger with straight shoulders asked:

"Well, tell me... What did you feel when you heard of her death? Also nothing?"

"Yes, almost nothing," answered the passenger under the lap robe. "Most of all a certain astonishment at my own insensibility. I opened the morning paper—and gently it hit me in the eye: by the will of God, such and such a woman... For want of habit it's very strange to see the name of an acquaintance or intimate in that black frame, in that fatal part of the paper, printed ceremoniously in large type... Then I tried to grieve: as if to say, yes, it's that very same person, the one who... But:

> I heard the fatal tidings from dispassionate lips,
> And dispassionate was my response.

Not even any sorrow came of it. Only some sort of feeble pity... And this was the very one who 'lingers in the memory of my soul,' my first, cruel, long-enduring love. I knew her in her utmost charm and innocence, in that almost adolescent trustfulness and timidity that touches a man's heart ineffably—perhaps because all femininity must have this trusting helplessness, something childlike, a sign that a girl or a woman always harbors a future child within her. And it was to me, first of all, in some divine ecstatic horror, that she gave truly everything God had granted her; and I kissed her girlish body, the most beautiful thing on earth, truly millions of times in a frenzy that has no equal in all my life. And because of her I was literally out of my mind, day and night, for years on end. Because of her I cried, tore my hair, attempted suicide, drank, drove cabmen till their horses dropped, destroyed in a fury possibly my best, most valuable works... But then twenty years passed—and I looked numbly at her name in the mourning frame, numbly imagined her lying in a coffin... An unpleasant picture, but nothing more. I assure you, nothing more. But then, you now—you, of course—do you really feel anything?"

"I? Well no; what's there to hide? Certainly almost nothing..."

The ship moved on. Wave after wave arose hissing ahead, swept past splashing along the broadsides; the pallid snow-like wake that stretched behind the stern seethed and dinned monotonously. A lush breeze was blowing; a tracery of motionless stars lay high above the ship's black funnel, above the rigging, above the slender blade of the forward mast...

"But do you know what?" suddenly said the first passenger, as if having just come to his senses. "Do you know what's most important? That by no means could I connect her, the dead her, with that other person about whom I just spoke to you. No, by no means. Absolutely not. She, the other she, was a completely different person. And to say that I felt absolutely nothing for her, for that other her, is a lie. So then, what I said was inaccurate. That's simply not how it really is."

The other man reflected briefly.

"Well, then, so what?" he asked.

"Just that almost all our conversation has come to naught."

"Oh, come to naught, has it?" said the passenger with the straight shoulders. "That other she, as you express it, is simply you, your imagination, your feelings—in a word, something that is part of you. And so you've been moved and agitated by nothing more than your very own self. Think about it properly."

"You think so? I don't know. It could be... Yes, it could be..."

"And were you agitated for long even by your very self? Ten minutes. A half hour maybe. Well, a day at the most."

"Yes, yes. Horrible, but it seems you're right. And where is she now? Up there, in that lovely sky?"

"Only Allah knows that, my friend. Most likely nowhere."

"You think so? Yes, yes... Most likely..."

Tha plain of the unbounded sea lay like a black circle under the buoyant bright cupola of the night sky. And lost in that circular darkening plain, the little steamship numbly and steadfastly held its course. Stretching infinitely behind it was the sleepily seething, milkish-pale wake—to the distant point where the night sky merged with the sea, where in contrast to that milkiness the skyline seemed dark, melancholy. And the log line swiveled and swiveled, sadly and mysteriously ticking off something, severing now and again the delicate chime: *dzee-een...*

Having kept silent for a short time, the men said softly and simply to each other:

"Sleep well."

"Sleep well."

Maritime Alps. 1923.

120

THE CALF'S HEAD

A boy of about five, freckled, wearing a sailor-suit, stands in the butcher shop quietly, as if enchanted; papa has gone off to his job at the post office, mama to the marketplace, taking him with her.

"Today we're having a calf's head with parsley," she had said, and he had conjured up something small, attractive, beautifully garnished with bright greenery.

And now he stands there and gapes, surrounded on all sides by something that is huge and red, that has short, truncated legs hanging to the floor from rusty iron hooks and headless necks hulking up to the ceiling. The front of each hulk has a long, empty, gaping belly covered in nacreous ingots of blubber, and the shoulders and rumps glitter with fine pellicles of dried fatty meat. But his torpid gaze is concentrated upon a head, which has turned up right in front of him, lying on the marble counter. Mama looks at it too as she haggles fervently with the shop's proprietor, who is also enormous and fat, wearing a coarse white apron horribly stained on the belly with what looks like rust, girded very low by a broad belt that hangs with thick greasy scabbards. Precisely it, the head, is the object of mama's haggling; the meatman is screaming something angrily and jabbing the head with a pulpy finger. All controversy is centered upon it, but it lies immobile, apathetic. Its bovine brow is flat and placid, the turbid-blue eyes are half closed, the large lashes drowsy, and the nostrils and lips so dilated that they have an impudent, disgruntled look... And all of it is bare, flesh-grey and resilient, like rubber...

Then with one terrible blow of his axe the meatman cleaved it into two halves, and he flung one half, with one ear, one eye and one thick nostril, in mama's direction, onto a piece of cotton-thread paper.

1930

THE IDOL

It was teeming and animated that winter too, as winters always were in the Moscow Zoological Gardens. Music was played at the skating rink from three o'clock on, and there were throngs of people arriving, swarming about, skating. But on the way to the rink they all paused for a moment to gaze curiously at something attracting their notice in one of the pens by the road. All the rest of the pens, together with the many artificial grottos, huts, and pavilions scattered about on the snowy meadows of the zoo, were deserted, and like everything deserted, they were doleful. All the strange beasts and birds who populated the zoo were wintering in warm lodgings, but this pen was inhabited; it contained something even more exotic than any pelican, gazelle, or duckbill platypus: an Eskimo tent of skins and bark and a big bearded dun reindeer with smooth rump and dock tail, crowned by the high and heavy blades of grey antlers—a powerful beast who was somehow all firm and rigid, like everything northern, polar; he was meandering about, striking the snow periodically with the hoof of his slender leg, searching for something beneath it. And beside the tent, sitting right on the snow, his short legs in skewbald fur stockings crossed and tucked under him, his bare head protruding from indurate sacking of reindeer hide, was what appeared to be some living idol, but it was simply an effeminate, beardless, savage muzhik, who had almost no neck, whose flat skull was striking for its brawn and for the thickness of the coarse and straight, resinous-black hair upon it, whose copper-yellow face, with broad cheeks and narrow eyes, was marked by inhuman obtuseness, which, however, appeared somehow blended with sorrow. From three o'clock until late evening this idol did nothing but sit there in the snow, paying no attention to the people swarming in front of him, but from time to time he gave a performance. Between his knees there were two wooden basins—one containing pieces of raw horseflesh and the other black blood; he would extend his short arm for a piece of the horseflesh, dip it into the blood and stuff it in his fish mouth, swallow, and lick clean the fingers, which were completely out of keeping with everything else: they were small, slender, even beautiful...

That winter, among those who often went to the skating rink at the Moscow Zoological Gardens and who, in passing, looked upon such an astounding specimen of humanity were a young man and his fiancée, both university students. And the image of those happy days remained in their memories forever: snowy grounds, frostiness, trees in the Zoological Gardens incrusted with curls of rime as if with grey coralline rock, the bars of a waltz drifting over from the rink, and him, sitting there, incessantly stuffing in his mouth the pieces of sopping meat black with blood, absolutely no expression in his dark narrow eyes, on his flat, yellow, iconic face.

1930

122

THE ELEPHANT

A thin, lively-eyed little girl resembling a fox cub, uncommonly charming in her pale-blue ribbon, which grips the platinum hair in a bow on the crown of her head, stands in the menagerie, gaping at the oblique scabrous hulk of an elephant, obtusely and majestically facing her with his large, broad-browed head, ratty ears like burdocks, starkly protruding tusks and thick, hummocky tube of the low-hanging proboscis with black-rubbery funnel at its tip. In a very soft voice:

"Mama, why are his legs swelled up?"

Mama laughs. But the elephant himself is laughing. Inclining the broad-browed head, he too looks at the girl, and there is clearly a glitter of something sly and merry in his porcine little eyes. He sways back and forth with pleasure, begins twitching the proboscis—and suddenly, out of pathetic helplessness, unable to express his feelings and thoughts any other way, he raises it up at a sharp angle, revealing the moist-fleshy pulp of its underside, the horns of his bared tusks and the absurdly small mouth between them, in anguished rapture he lets roll out of his terrible viscera a hollow thunderous rumble, then emits a joyously doltish, mighty bellow that shakes the whole menagerie.

For dinner a special dish of cauliflower was served and there were guests—a plumpish, but still youthful and attractive lady with a black-eyed boy, who was very quiet and attentive.

Mama told about the elephant, how the little girl had asked about his legs. And the girl understood that she had said something funny, that she was the source of admiration, and she started twisting and turning, rolling her head round and round, then burst out with excessively loud guffaws.

"A lovely child!" said the lady in a pensive way, gazing at her unabashedly.

And kicking out with her dangling feet, she repeated archly:

"No, mama, really: why *are* his legs swelled up?"

But mama's smile was no longer spontaneous; she was talking with the lady about something else now, something of absolutely no interest. Then, casting a sideways glance at the boy, the little girl fidgeted out of her chair, ran up to the buffet, and, in order to get their attention again, she started guzzling water right from the mouth of a carafe, sputtering, burbling, and spilling it down her chin. And when she had spilled it all over herself and had choked, she stopped and burst into tears.

1930

SEMPITERNAL SPRING

...And, what's more, my friend, life has taken a remarkable turn for me. In June I went out into the countryside, to the provinces (visiting an acquaintance of mine). Of course, I still recall that there was a time when these journeys were not considered the least bit extraordinary. I suppose that even at present they are not considered as such by you in Europe. But many are the things that we once had here and that one still has in Europe! Two or three hundred versts is no laughing matter for us now. In Russia, which has reverted to ancient Muscovy, the distance between points is, once again, enormous. And nowadays the Moscow humanoid does not go in much for travelling. Of course we have every sort of unlicensed freedom here now, more than we know what to do with. But don't forget that all of this "freedom," which we couldn't imagine we would ever live to see, began only quite recently.

In a word, something out of the ordinary occurred, something I had not experienced for many years. One fine day I took a cab and set off for the railway station. In the letter that you somehow got through to me you wrote that your conception of Moscow nowadays, even of its external appearance, is "insufferable." Yes, it is repulsive. And that feeling was especially acute as I rode along to the station, exhilarated by the peculiarity of my position, by my role as a traveller, in the sort of cab that once appeared only in the most abysmal backwoods regions and charged not a billion rubles, but twenty kopecks for the ride. What Asiatic multitudes of people! How many hawkers there are, peddling from trays in all sorts of flea markets and "nookies," to use that vile idiom that's becoming ever more fashionable here! How many buildings in ruins! How full of ruts the roadway is, and the foliage on the trees that remain has run rampant! On the squares in front of the railway stations there are also "nookies," constant selling and buying, mobs of the lowliest rabble, speculators, thieves, street women, vendors of assorted culinary slop. In the stations they have snack counters open again and they have waiting rooms for different classes, but all of these are nothing but barns, befouled to the point of utter hopelessness. And always so many people—such a struggle to push one's way through. Trains are infrequent; the wholesale confusion and all the red tape makes buying a ticket a difficult business, and you've really done something if you make it into a coach, which, of course, is also of backwoods quality, with the wheels corroded to a rusty red. Many people show up at the station as early as the evening of the day before their departure.

I arrived two hours before the train left and came near paying for my audacity since I barely managed to get a ticket. But by some means or other (that is, by bribery, of course) the matter was arranged; I received a ticket, got into a coach, and even found a seat on a bench instead of on the floor.

And then the train was off, Moscow was left behind, and I saw the fields, forests and villages I had not seen for ages; a deeply rooted day to day existence had resumed here after that little holiday of dissipation by which *Rus* had amused herself at such an incredible price. Soon almost everyone packed into the coach began nodding, lolling back and snoring, open-mouthed. Opposite me sat a muzhik with light brown hair, big, self-assured. At first he smoked and kept spitting on the floor, making a rasping sound by rubbing across it with the toe of his boot. Then he took a milk bottle from the pocket of his *poddyovka* and started drinking in protracted gulps, breaking off only to avoid suffocation. Having drunk all his milk, he too flopped back, reclined against the wall, and started snoring like the others; and the rancidity that wafted from him began virtually driving me crazy. Unable to bear any more, I gave up my place and went out to stand in the corridor. And there in the corridor I came upon an acquaintance whom I had not seen for some four years, a former professor, a former rich man; he stood there swaying with each sway of the coach. I hardly recognized him; he had become a hoary old man with something of the pilgrim who wanders about sacred places. His shoes, his sleazy coat and hat were ghastly, even worse than my own trappings. Unshaven for ages, grey hair down to his shoulders, he had a sackcloth bag in his hand, another on the floor by his feet. "I'm on my way home," he said, "to the country; they've given me a plot of land attached to my former estate, and, you know, I'm living just like that Muscovite turned rustic whom you're on your way to see. I feed myself by the sweat of my brow, but my free time is devoted to my former work—a broad historical study, which, in my opinion, could inaugurate a whole new scholarly era..." By now the silvery disk of the sun was floating low beyond the boles of trees, beyond the forest. A half hour later the founder of a new era disembarked at his cloistral substation—and began hobbling along with his sacks in the cold twilight, by the green path of a cutting through that birch forest.

When I arrived at my destination, it was already after ten, and dusk had set in. Since the train was late, the muzhik who came for me had waited for a while, then took off for home. What could I do? Sleep in the station? But they lock up the station at night, and if they did not lock it up there would be no divans or benches left there—"They ain't no more masters nowdays, my friend"—and even for "Soviet" subjects sleeping on the floor is not always a pleasant prospect. Hire some other peasant in the settlement by the station? But that's an almost impossible undertaking these days. By the entrance to the depot sat a mournful and apathetic muzhik who had come for the early morning train to Moscow. I spoke with him. He dismissed the whole idea with a wave of his hand. "Who's going to drive there now! Ain't hardly no horses, all the rigs is wore out... Wheel axle costs two billion, makes me sick even to talk about it..." "What about going on foot?" I asked. "You got far to go?" I told him where. "Well, that ain't no more than twenty versts. You'll make it." "But then, I'd have to go through the woods, and what's more, on foot." "Why, that don't mean nothing, going through the woods! You'll make it."

But immediately after that he told me about how two "peoples" of some sort had hired somehow "this here fellow" in their village last spring, and then both he and they had vanished completely: "Never seen no more, not them, nor him, nor the horses, nor the rig... So that nobody ever did find out who done in who—them him or him them... No sir, it ain't like old times no more!"

Naturally, after hearing such a story, I lost all desire to travel by night; I decided to wait until morning and to ask for a night's lodging in one of the taverns by the station. "We got here altogether two of them," the peasant had said. But it turned out that spending the night in the taverns was also impossible—they would not take me in. "Now if you want a little tea, we're at your service," they said in one place. "We got tea on the menu here..." I sat for a long time in that barely illumined *chambre* drinking tea, that is, something nauseating made from well-stewed grass. Then I said: "At least let me sit on the porch until morning." "But you'd be uncomfortable out on the porch..." "Not more uncomfortable than on the road!" "You unarmed?" "Search me, be my guest!" I turned out all my pockets and unbuttoned my coat. "Well maybe on the porch is all right—otherwise, ain't nobody going to let you in their shacks; they're already all of them sleeping now anyway..." Soon after I had gone out and sat down on the porch, the light in the tavern was extinguished—the adjacent tavern had long since been dark—and night, sleep, silence set in... How long that night lasted! In the distant sky beyond the dark of the forest the scumbled sickle of the moon was rolling. Then it too disappeared, and in its place summer heat lightning began to glimmer... I sat, strode about in front of the porch along the dim white road, sat again, smoked home-grown tobacco on an empty stomach... At some time after one o'clock I heard the alternating modulation of wheel spokes, the thrust of naves on axles down the road—and a short time later someone drove up to the adjacent tavern, stopped, and began to tap on the window in a kind of stealthy, prearranged manner. First a head peered out from the passageway; then the proprietor cautiously emerged, a barefoot dishevelled old man, the very one who had refused my request for lodgings with such astounding spite and rudeness, and a mysterious operation commenced. Something resembling sheepskins was repeatedly dragged out of the passageway and loaded into the newcomer's cart, and all this took place in the glimmer of heat lightning, which illumined the forest, shacks, and road with increasing intensity. The wind had turned cooler now, and thunder rumbled threateningly in the distance. I sat there admiring the spectacle. Do you remember those thunderstorms in the dead of night at Vasilevsky? Do you remember the fear they inspired throughout our household? Just imagine, I no longer have any sensation of fear. And that night on the porch of the tavern the dry storm, which came to naught and brought no rain, aroused only feelings of delight. But towards the end of my vigil I felt a horrible weariness. I also felt downhearted. How is one to walk twenty versts after a sleepless night?

But at sunrise, as the storm clouds beyond the forest began to pale and thin out and all my surroundings began taking on a humdrum diurnal aspect,

I ran into some unexpected good luck. A carriage swept past the tavern and stopped at the station; a commissar had come for the Moscow train, the man who now managed Prince D.'s former estate, located right in the region where I was bound. The tavern keeper, who had awakened and stuck her head out the window, informed me of this, and I rushed up to the coachman as he left the station for his return trip; it was even strange how readily he agreed to let me go with him. He turned out to be a fascinating man, a childishly naive giant who kept repeating as we drove along: "Rather not even look; can't see nothing for the tears in my eyes!" Meanwhile the sun was rising, and the swayback, broad-rumped white stallion, crazed and deafened with age, carried us briskly and lightly down the forest roads, in the carriage that was also quite old but was marvelous, as soothing as a cradle... Many a year had it been, my friend, since I last rode in a carriage!

The friend whom I visited for a few days in this forestland is a very curious man in some ways; self-taught, half educated, he had always lived in Moscow, but last year he abandoned the city and returned to his birthplace, the village and manor that had belonged to his ancestors. Since he hates the new Moscow vehemently, he used to send me glowing descriptions of the beauties of his region, insisting that I come to him for a rest from that Moscow. And it's true, the region is astonishing. Just imagine: a thriving settlement, peaceful, picturesque, looking as if there had never occurred not only everything that has occurred, but even the abolishment of serfdom or the French invasion. All around are pristine forest preserves, remoteness and silence unparalleled. The forest, which is gloomy and resonant, consists primarily of pines. Walking through the depths of that forest in the evening I sensed an aura not of olden times or antiquity, but of eternity itself. The evening glow shows only in bits and pieces; here and there the red of the slowly expiring sun behind the tree tops breaks through. The balsamic warmth of the pine needles, heated throughout the day, mingles with the pungent crispness that wafts from the marshy depressions and the narrow but deep river, with its mysterious convolutions, which emits a cold haze in the evening. One hears no birdsong, just a death-laden muteness and a few nightjars flitting about. There's one and the same interminable sound, like the sound of a spindle. When it is completely dark and stars have appeared over the pine forest, the hoarse, blissfully grievous shrieks of eagle owls begin sounding all around, and in those shrieks there is something still inchoate, pretemporal, where a mating call, the baleful anticipation of coitus, blends the sounds of laughter and sobbing, rings out with the horror of some abyss, of dissolution. And so, in the evening I wandered in the pine forest beneath the incantations of the nightjars, in the dead of night I sat on the little portico listening to the owls, and I devoted my days to the captivating world of the former manor house—truly "former" since not a single one of its noblemen-lords remains alive... It's an unspeakably beautiful place.

The days were sunny and hot. On my way to the manor house I walked through alternating patches of sun and shade, down a sandy road, amidst the stifling sweet fragrance of pine needles, then along the river through the undergrowth by its bank, flushing kingfishers and looking at the open backwaters, which were covered over with white water lilies and dotted with dragonflies, at the shady rapids where the water was transparent as a tear, although it seemed black as well, where tiny fish gleamed like silver and some sort of blunt green snouts gazed goggle-eyed... Then I crossed the ancient stone bridge and ascended to the manor grounds.

By some fortunate chance the manor has remained untouched, unplundered, and it has everything that is usually associated with such estates. There is a church, built by a famous Italian; there are several marvelous ponds; there is a lake called Swan Lake and on it an island with a pavilion, where fetes were often held in honor of Catherine the Great, who used to visit the manor; farther on there are gloomy ravines full of firs and pines, so enormous that your hat nearly falls off when you gaze at their crowns, which are burdened with the nests of kites and of some other large black birds with funereal fans on their heads. The house, or rather the palace, was built by the same Italian who built the church. I entered the grounds by way of the huge stone portals upon which two contemptuously somnolent lions reclined, surrounded by something growing dense and wild, truly the grass of oblivion. Most often I would make my way directly to the palace and enter its vestibule, where all day long a one-armed Chinaman with a short rifle across his knees was seated in an ancient satin armchair; the palace is now a museum, you see, "the people's property," and must be guarded. Of course, only someone with the temperament of a Chinese could bear to sit there like an idiot in a completely empty building; there was something even eerie about that idle vigil. But the one-armed, short-legged dolt with the yellow-wooden visage sat placidly, smoked cheap shag, occasionally whined something old-womanish and plaintive in an indifferent tone, and looked on with indifference as I went past him.

"Don't be afraid of him, master," the coachman had told me in the voice one uses to speak about dogs. "I'll let him know about you; he won't bother you."

And so it was; the Chinaman did not bother me. If he had been ordered to bayonet me, then of course he would have done so without blinking an eye. But since there was no need to bayonet me, he merely looked at me askance, and I made myself at home, was free to pass hours on end in the *chambres* of the palace. And endlessly I wandered through them, endlessly looked about me, lost in private thoughts... The ceilings sparkled with gilded ornamental festoonery, with gilded coats of arms, with Latin apothegms (If only you knew how unaccustomed my eyes had grown not only to beautiful things, but even to simple cleanliness!). Priceless furniture was reflected in the lacquered floors. In one *chambre,* under a red satin canopy, there was a towering bed made of some dark wood; there was also a Venetian chest, which opened to mysterious mellifluent music. In another room the entire wall between the windows was occupied by a clock with chimes; in a third stood a medieval organ. And

128

everywhere busts and statues gazed down upon me, portraits and more portraits... Lord, the beauty of the women in those portraits! And what handsome men in full-dress uniforms or camisole-waistcoats, in wigs and brilliants, with bright cerulean eyes! But the brightest and most majestic of all was Catherine. With what beneficent good humor she stood resplendent, regnant in that sumptuous circle! And, strange to behold, on a small escritoire in one of the studies was a brown wood plank containing a golden disc, engraved with the information that this was a portion of the flagship "St. Eustasia," which had perished in the Battle of Cheshme "with glory and honor to the Russian Realm..." Yes, with glory and honor to the Russian Realm... That sounds strange now, doesn't it?

I also spent a good deal of time in the assembly chambers downstairs. You know my passion for books; well, in those vaulted chambers below there was a book repository. It was cool there, perpetually shadowed, the windows had thick iron bars, and through the bars one could see the joyous greenery of bushes, the joyous sunny day, still the same, exactly the same as a hundred or two hundred years ago. Book shelves were built into niches in the walls and on these shelves glimmered the lustreless gold of ten thousand book spines, nearly all of the most important achievements in Russian and European thought over the last two centuries. In one room there was an enormous telescope, in another a gigantic planetarium, and on the walls, once again, there were portraits, extremely rare engravings. Once I pried apart the pages of a magnificent little tome from the beginning of the last century and read these lines, printed on the rough paper:

> Be not consumed by mad desire;
> Rebellious spirits pacify.
> O shepherd lad, damp down the fire,
> Bestill thy reedpipe's doleful sigh.

And for a long time I stood there enchanted. What rhythm and what charm, what grace and dancing modulation of feelings! Now, when only "nookies" remain of the glory and honor of the Russian Realm, they write differently: "The sun, like a mare's-piss puddle..." Another time I came upon a first edition of Baratynsky, and, as if by design, opened the book at these verses:

> So be it; let all past times away like fleeting dreams,
> Still beautiful, wasteland Elysium, art thou;
> Thy puissant grace resplendent gleams,
> Becalms my soul as I gaze on thee now...

Just before my departure I visited the famous church. Pale-yellow, circular in structure, it stands in the forest on the edge of a hollow, its golden crown sparkling in the blue sky. Inside there is a circle of yellowish marble columns supporting an airy cupola full of sunshine. In the circular gallery between the columns and walls there are paintings of saints with the stylized countenances of those who are buried in the familial crypt under the church. And through the narrow windows one sees how the wind sways the shaggy crests of the pines, which stretch their wild majestic limbs from the hollow to reach the same level as the windows, and one hears the singing and the roaring of that wind. I descended into the pitch-darkness of the crypt, using the red flame of a wax candle remnant to illumine the enormous marble coffins, the enormous iron lucernes, and the scabrous gold of mosaics along the arches. The chill of the netherworld wafted from those coffins. Could it be that indeed they were here, those handsome men with cerulean eyes who stood so regnant in the palace *chambres?* No, I could not reconcile myself to that... Later I ascended again to the church and gazed for a long time through the narrow windows at the wild and somnolent agitation of the pines. Somehow joyously and sorrowfully that temple, forgotten, forever deserted, revelled in the sun! A dead silence reigned within it. But beyond its walls the summer wind roared and sang—the same, the identical wind that blew a hundred or two hundred years ago. And I was alone, absolutely alone, not only in that bright and dead temple, but, so it seemed, in all the world. Who could have been with me, with a person who by some truly miraculous circumstance had been spared amidst the vast concourse of the dead, amidst the gross and swift collapse of the Russian Realm, a collapse without equal in the history of man!

And that was my last visit to the manor. On the following day I departed...

Now, as you see, I am back in Moscow again. More than a month has passed since my return, but I'm still experiencing the keen, and, what's more, indescribably strange emotions that I brought back with me. And I doubt that they will ever leave me. You see, what I began to feel and understand so vividly and acutely during my trip had already been ripening within me long before that. And I cannot foresee, there just cannot be anything in the future that could alter my present state of mind. They, these people of the so-called new life, are right—there is no return to former times, to the past, and the new way now reigns firmly, is now setting in and becoming the everyday norm. In my present state of mind I constantly feel as if the very last link between me and the world surrounding me is corroding or being ripped apart, that I am withdrawing from it more and more and retiring into that world to which I have been linked not only all my days, from childhood and infancy, from birth, but even before birth. I am retiring to "Bygone Elysium," as if into some dream that glitters with the semblance of the bright and strikingly vivid realm where those dead men with cerulean eyes are now transfixed, in the empty palace in the woods near Moscow.

It goes without saying, you see, that a miracle has occurred: a certain someone, already mouldering in the stench of a burial pit, turns out not to have perished entirely, like the thousands of others who were dumped with him into that pit. To his own great astonishment he begins gradually recovering his senses, finally makes a complete recovery, and even finds it possible to raise himself up and make his way back out into the wide world. Now he is back amidst the living, he acquires once more the familiar habit of being; like everyone—ostensibly like everyone—he sees the city again, the sky, the sun, concerns himself again with nourishment, clothing, shelter and even with worldly circumstances and endeavors. But, my friend, can a person pass through death, even a temporary death, unscathed? And the most important thing is how much it changed, how incredibly that very wide world itself changed while we, who survived by some miracle, were abiding in the grave! I repeat, such a rapid collapse, such a transformation of the whole face of the earth over a period of some five years is unprecedented. Imagine the almost instantaneous ruin of all the world of antiquity; and imagine a few people buried beneath the debris, beneath an avalanche of barbaric hordes, people who suddenly come to life after two or three centuries. What must they feel? God, above all else what loneliness, what ineffable loneliness! So, you see, a certain obsession has long been growing within me. The more I become accustomed to the fact that my ascension from the dead is not a dream, but is utter reality, the more I am struck by a sensation of the terrible upheaval that has taken place on earth— I speak, of course, not of external changes, although even in externals we must confront a baseness so unparalleled that the situation will not be rectified for centuries. And I have begun looking around me more and more intently, recalling my life before the grave more and more vividly... The obsession has grown and grown. No, for me the former world to which I once belonged is not the world of the dead; it is reviving more and more, becoming my soul's single, ever more joyous refuge, my private abode, inaccessible to anyone else!

Yes, on my way out of Moscow, riding through her streets, I felt with a special intensity something I had long been feeling. I realized to what extent I am a man of another time and age, and how alien to me are all Moscow's "nookies" and all that new brand of offal that rolls along her streets in automobiles! And then, think about the station from which I departed, the coach where I found a seat, my travelling companion who was drinking milk right from the bottle... Think about the professor with his sackcloth bags, his scholarly fancies, and that forest cutting through which he hobbled away—all alone, terribly alone... How touched I was as the train stood at the substation where he got off—those first impressions of silent fields, forest remoteness, the smell of birches, flowers, evening crispness! My God, my God, once again— after a thousand years of the most terrible travail on earth!—once again that pure sacred stillness, the setting sun beyond the forest, the distant expanses, the vista at the other end of the forest cutting, bitter and crisp aromas, the sweet chill of evening glow... And my sense of alienation from this "Soviet" coach on whose platform I stood and from the brown-haired muzhik who was sleeping in it suddenly struck me so deeply and intensely that tears of happiness welled up in my eyes. Yes, by some miracle I have survived, have not perished like the thousands of others who were butchered or tortured, who disappeared without a trace, who shot themselves or hanged themselves; once again I am living and even travelling. But what do I have in common with this new way of life, which has devastated my whole universe? I am living—and sometimes, as at this very moment, am even in a mood of rapturous bliss—but with whom and where am I living?

And the night that I spent on the tavern porch was also just a part of my past. For could I perceive it as a night in June in the year nineteen hundred twenty three? No, that night was a night out of my previous life. The heat lightning and the thunder and the crisp wind that blew in with the approaching storm also came out of the past... They carried me away completely into the world of the dead, blissfully ensconced for all time in their unearthly cloister. And now that sunny regnancy of the summer days hangs before me incessantly, that pine forest and fairyland-somnolent palace lost and forgotten in the pines, those portals with lions and the tall weeds growing above them, the sombre ravines full of firs, shallow ponds with flocks of wagtails on their grassy banks, the lake, overgrown with sedge, the forever-deserted church and empty glistening assembly chambers full of the visages of the dead... I cannot describe to you the marvelous feeling that never seems to leave me; how terribly alive they are for me!

Do you remember that Baratynsky poem from which I quoted several lines and which harmonizes so well with what predominates in all my present life, with what lies secreted in the inmost recesses of my soul? Do you remember how it ends, that elegy devoted to a presentiment of the Elysium that Baratynsky apprehended under the burden of his bereavement and sorrow? Amidst the desolation of my native domain, amidst the debris and the graves I feel, he says, the hidden presence of some Spectre; in reference to that "Lethean Shade," that "Spectre," he writes:

> And it prophecies with suasion an abode divine,
> Where a *sempiternal spring* shall lull me for all time,
> Where I shall not remark the lost destroyed design,
> Where e'er unwithering oaks cast down their blitheful umber,
> And streams flow on unceasing, without number.
> There that sacred Shade I'll meet, that world make mine...

The desolation that surrounds us is indescribable; countless, without end are the ruins and the graves. What do we have left except "Lethean Shades" and that "sempiternal spring" to which, "with suasion," they are calling us?

Maritime Alps. 5 October 1923.

THE COLD FALL

In June of that year he was a guest at our estate—he always had been considered one of the family; his late father had been a friend and neighbor of my father. On June fifteenth Francis Ferdinand was killed in Sarajevo. They delivered the newspapers from the post office on the morning of the sixteenth. Holding the Moscow evening paper, father came out of his study into the dining room, where he, mama and I were still drinking tea, and said:

"Well, my friends, it's war! They've killed the Austrian crown prince in Sarajevo. That means war!"

On Saint Peter's Day we had a number of guests—for father's name day—and at the dinner table our engagement was announced. But on July nineteenth Germany declared war on Russia...

He came in September but stayed only a day and night—to say good-bye before his departure for the front (at that time everyone thought the war would end soon; our marriage was postponed until spring). And so we were spending our last evening together. After supper, as was customary, they brought in the samovar, and looking at the windows, all misted over with its steam, father said:

"An incredibly early and cold fall!"

We sat quietly that evening, merely exchanging meaningless words from time to time, exaggeratedly calm, concealing our secret thoughts and feelings. Even father's remark about the autumn was full of feigned homeliness. I walked up to the door of the terrace and wiped the glass with a handkerchief; out in the garden clear icy stars were glittering brightly and distinctly in the black sky. Leaning back in his easy chair, father smoked, absently gazing at the hot lamp hanging over the table; mama sat under its light in her spectacles, diligently sewing up a small silk pouch. We understood its purpose—and felt both touched and frightened. Father said:

"So you want to go in the morning all the same, and not after lunch?"

"Yes, with your permission, in the morning," he answered. "Sad to say, I still haven't arranged everything at home."

Father let out a brief sigh.

"All right, my dear boy, whatever you think. But in that case it's time for mama and me to get some sleep; we certainly want to see you off tomorrow..."

Mama stood up and made the sign of the cross over her future son; he bent to kiss her hand, then father's. Left alone, we stayed for a time in the dining room—for some reason I decided to lay out a game of solitaire. He paced silently from corner to corner, then asked:

"Want to take a little walk?"

Feeling more downhearted than ever, I responded impassively:

"All right..."

Putting on his coat in the anteroom, still in a pensive mood, he recalled Fet's verses with a sweet ironical smile:

> The autumn's so frosty this year!
> Wrap up in your shawl and capot...

"I don't have a capot. How does it go after that?"

"Can't remember. Like this, I think:

> Look there, in the pine wood, my dear;
> The forest's on fire; see the glow?"

"What kind of fire?"

"The rising moon, of course. There's a sort of rural autumn charm in those lines: 'Wrap up in your shawl and capot...' The days of our grandfathers and grandmothers... Oh God, my God!"

"What's wrong?"

"Nothing, dear. It's sad, all the same. Sad and good. I love you so very much..."

When we had put on our coats, we went through the dining room, onto the terrace, then down into the garden. At first it was so dark that I had to hold on to his sleeve. Then the ever brighter sky began revealing black branches, strewn with the mineral glitter of stars. Pausing for a moment, he turned toward the manor house.

"Look how the windows of the house are shining in some absolutely special way, in an autumn way. I'll remember this evening as long as I live, forever..."

I turned to look, and he embraced me in my Swiss wrap. I pushed aside the downy kerchief from my face and let my head fall back so he could kiss me. After we had kissed he looked in my face.

"How your eyes are gleaming," he said. "Aren't you cold? The air is quite wintry. All the same, if I'm killed, you won't forget me right away?"

I thought, And what if he is killed? Could I really forget him in a short time all the same—for isn't everything forgotten in the end? And frightened by my thoughts, I answered hurriedly:

"Don't say that! I could never go on living if you died!"

After a brief silence he said slowly:

"Well then, if I'm killed, I'll wait for you there. You just live, enjoy your life on earth, then come to me."

I burst out crying bitterly...

In the morning he left. Mama hung the ominous little pouch that she had sewn the previous evening around his neck—it contained a golden icon, worn by her father and grandfather in time of war—and in a paroxysm of desperation we made the sign of the cross over him. Watching as he rode away, we stood on the porch in that state of torpor that one always experiences when seeing off someone for a long separation, feeling only the amazing incongruity between us and the joyous sunny morning all around, with its glistening rime frost on the grass. We stood there awhile, then went back into the emptiness of the house. I walked through the rooms, hands behind my back, not knowing what to do with myself, whether to start sobbing or to sing out as loud as I could...

He was killed—what a strange word!—a month later, in Galicia. And thirty whole years have passed since then. And I have lived through so much, so very much during those years, which seem to have lasted for ages when you think about them attentively, when you turn over in the memory all that magical inscrutable something, a mystery to both the mind and heart, that is called the past. In the spring of 1918, after father and mother had both passed on, I was living in Moscow, in the cellar of a trader-woman from the Smolensk market, who always used to mock me: "Well, now, your excellency, how's your life expectancy?" I too was engaged in huckstering. Just as many others were doing at that time, I was selling what few things I still possessed to soldiers in Caucasian hats and unbuttoned greatcoats—some sort of ring, or a small cross, or a moth-eaten fur collar. And there, huckstering on the corner of Arbat and the market, I met a rare, beautiful person, an elderly retired military man, whom I soon married and with whom I went away in April to Ekaterinodar. It took us nearly two weeks to get there. We travelled with his nephew, a boy of about seventeen, who was working his way south, to the volunteer forces—I went as a peasant woman in bast shoes; my husband wore a tattered Cossack smock and let his black and grey-streaked beard grow out—and we remained in the Don and Kuban regions for more than two years. In a winter storm we sailed with a huge mob of other refugees from Novorossisk to Turkey, and during the voyage, at sea, my husband died of typhus. After that I had only three relations left on all the earth: my husband's nephew, his young wife, and their daughter, a baby of seven months. But soon the nephew and his wife sailed away to the Crimea to join Wrangel's forces, leaving the baby in my hands. There they disappeared without a trace. After that I stayed on for a long time in Constantinople, earning a living for myself and the child by the most burdensome iow labor. Then, as did so many others, she and I began wandering here and there and everywhere: Bulgaria, Serbia, Czechoslovakia, Belgium, Paris, Nice... Long since grown, the girl remained in Paris, became altogether French, quite comely and absolutely indifferent to me. She worked in a chocolate shop near the Madeleine; her sleek hands with the silver nails wrapped boxes in satiny paper and tied them up with thin golden twine. And I lived and still live in Nice on whatever the Lord happens to send me... I had first been to Nice in 1912—and in those happy times I never could have imagined what it would become for me some day!

So I went on living after his death, having once rashly sworn that if he died I could never go on. But in recalling everything that I have lived through since then, I always ask myself: what, after all, does my life consist of? And I answer: only of that cold fall evening. Was there ever really such an evening? Yes, all the same, there was. And that's all that there ever was in my life—the rest is a useless dream. And I belive, I fervidly believe that somewhere out there he's waiting for me—with the very same love and youthfulness as on that evening. "You just live, enjoy your life on earth, then come to me..." I've lived, I've had my joy; now I'll be coming soon.

3 May 1944

LIGHT BREATHING

In the graveyard, above a fresh clay mound, stands a new cross made of oak, sturdy, ponderous, smooth.

April, grey days. The tombstones here, in this spacious provincial graveyard, can be seen from afar through the bare trees, and a cold wind keeps jangling and rattling the porcelain wreath at the foot of the cross.

There is a large, convex porcelain medallion set into the cross, and the medallion contains a photographic portrait of a schoolgirl with joyous, strikingly living eyes.

This is Olya Mesherskaya.

As a small girl she was indistinguishable from all the others in that mass of brown school frocks; what could be said about her except that she was one of those comely, rich and happy little girls, that she was a capable student but was mischievous and tended to be quite indifferent to the exhortations of her form mistress? Then she began blossoming out, developing in leaps and bounds. At the age of fourteen her waist was slender, her legs well-formed, and already clearly defined was the shape of her breasts and all those other curves whose charm has never been expressed in the human word; at fifteen she had acquired a reputation for beauty. How attentive were some of her girl friends to their coiffure, how well-groomed they were, how devoted to the demureness of their every bodily movement! But she was afraid of nothing— neither inkstains on her fingers nor a blush somewhat too florid, neither hair in disarray nor a knee that was bared as she fell on the run. Without any effort whatsoever on her part, somehow imperceptibly, it all came to her, everything that so distinguished her from all the others at the school during those last two years: elegance, stylishness, grace, the clear gleam of her eyes... No one could dance at the school balls as Olya Mesherskaya could, no one could skim along on ice-skates in quite the same way, no one at the dances was ever so ardently pursued as she, and, for some reason, no one was more adored by the lower-form schoolgirls. Imperceptibly had she become a young lady and imperceptibly had her name achieved renown at the school, and already there were rumors in the air, that she was capricious, that she could not live without admirers, that the schoolboy Shenshin was madly in love with her, that she was said to love him too but was so inconstant in her treatment of him that he had attempted suicide...

In that last winter of her life Olya Mesherskaya, so they said at the school, was out of her mind with gaity. The winter was snowy, sunlit, frosty; the sun set early behind the tall fir trees in the snowy schoolyard and the weather was invariably fine, radiant, holding the promise of more frost and more sunshine tomorrow, of strolls along Sobornaya Street, skating at the municipal gardens, of a rosy tinge in the evening sky, music, and masses of people glissading about that rink in all possible directions, amidst whom the one who appeared most carefree and happy of all was Olya Mesherskaya. But then one day, during the noon recess, as she dashed like a whirlwind across the school assembly hall, pursued by a mob of blithefully shrieking first-form girls, she was suddenly called to the office of the headmistress. She stopped on the dead run, breathed just one deep sigh, straightened her hair with a brisk womanly gesture that was now quite natural for her, hitched up the straps of her apron on her shoulders, and ran upstairs, her eyes glistening. The headmistress, a woman still young, but grey-haired, sat calmly plying her knitting needles, at a desk beneath a portrait of the tsar.

"Good day, *Mademoiselle* Mesherskaya," she said in French, not raising her eyes from the knitting. "Unfortunately, this is not the first time I've been obliged to summon you here in order to have a word with you concerning your behavior."

"Yes, *madame*," answered Olya as she approached the desk, looking at her with those clear and lively eyes but without any expression on her face; then, with the delicacy and grace peculiar to her and her alone, she dropped a curtsey.

"You'll pay scant attention to my words; unfortunately I've become convinced of that," said the headmistress. She raised her eyes and tugged up on the knitting, making the ball of wool spin on the laquered floor so that Olya looked down with an inquisitive glance. "I have no intention of repeating myself; I shall not speak at length," she said.

Olya was very fond of this uncommonly clean and large office, which, on such frosty days, wafted the lovely warmth of the sparkling Dutch stove and the crisp fragrance of lilies-of-the-valley on the desk. She sat silently and expectantly, glancing at the full-length portrait of the young tsar, who was standing in the middle of some lustrous drawing room, at the even parting in the milk-white, neatly permed hair of the headmistress.

"You are no longer a little girl," said the headmistress in a momentous tone, holding back her irritation.

"Yes, *madame*," answered Olya simply, almost gaily.

"But not yet a woman," said the headmistress with still greater moment in her tone, and her sallow face reddened slightly. "First of all, what sort of hair style is that? It's a grown woman's hair style!"

"It's not my fault, *madame,* that I have nice hair," answered Olya, lightly touching both hands to her beautifully done coiffure.

"Ah, so that's it, not your fault!" said the headmistress. "The hair-do is not your fault, those expensive combs are not your fault; it's not your fault that you're ruining your parents with spending twenty rubles on shoes! But, I repeat, you simply fail to take into account that you're still a mere school-girl..."

But at that point Olya interrupted, maintaining her simple, calm and polite manner:

"Excuse me, *madame,* you're mistaken; I'm a woman. And do you know whose fault it was? Papa's friend and neighbor and your brother, Aleksei Mikhailovich Malyutin. It happened last summer in the country..."

And within a month after that conversation a Cossack officer, ugly and plebian in appearance, having utterly nothing in common with the set to which Olya Mesherskaya belonged, shot her on the platform of a railway station, amidst a whole throng of people who had just arrived on the train. And the incredible confession of Olya Mesherskaya, which had so astounded the head-mistress, proved to be absolutely true. The officer declared to the investigator for the prosecution that Mesherskaya had led him on, had been intimate with him, had sworn to be his wife, but at the railway station on the day of the murder, as she was seeing him off for Novocherkassk, she suddenly told him that the idea of loving him had never even entered her head, that all the talk of marriage was just her way of mocking him; and she let him read the page in her diary describing the episode with Malyutin.

"I quickly scanned the lines while she promenaded about, waiting for me to finish reading, and then, right there on the platform, I shot her," said the officer. "You have that diary here; please examine what was written on the tenth of July of last year."

The entry in the diary read as follows:

"It's past one in the morning. I fell into a deep sleep but awakened immediately... Today I've become a woman! Papa, mama and Tolya, all of them went off to the city; I was left on my own. I was so happy to be alone! In the morning I strolled about in the garden and openlands, went out into the forest; it seemed to me that I was the only one in the whole wide world, and never in my life had my thoughts been so clear. I also dined alone, then played the piano for a whole hour; the sounds of that music made me feel as if I would live forever and would be happier than anyone on earth. After that I fell asleep in papa's study, and at four o'clock Katya woke me up and said that Aleksei Mikhailovich was there. I was very pleased to see him, it was so nice to receive him and entertain him. He was driving a pair of Vyatka-breed horses, very beautiful, and they stood out by the porch the whole time. He stayed on because it started to rain, and he was hoping the roads would be dry by evening. He was sorry he hadn't caught papa in, was quite animated, and behaved with me like a gallant young admirer, kept joking about how he had long been in love with me. When we went for a stroll in the garden before tea, the weather was lovely again, the sun was glistening throughout the wet garden, though it had turned quite cold, and he took me by the arm and said that he was Faust with his Margarete. He's fifty-six years old but still very handsome and always well dressed—the one thing I didn't like was that he was wearing one of those coats with a cape. He smells of English cologne and has quite young, black eyes and an absolutely silvery beard, elegantly parted into two long halves. For tea we sat out on the glassed-in terrace, I felt as if I were not so well and lay down on the ottoman, and he smoked, then sat down beside me, began paying me some sort of compliments again, then taking my hand

and kissing it. I covered my face with a silk handkerchief, and he kissed me several times on the lips through the silk... I don't understand how that could have happened, I was out of my mind, I never thought I could be that sort! Now there's only one way out... I feel such revulsion for him, I just can't live through this!"

Over the course of these April days the city has turned clean and dry, its cobblestones have taken on a white hue, and one walks along its streets with a pleasant sense of buoyancy. Every Sunday after mass a small woman in mourning attire, in black kid gloves, carrying an umbrella with an ebony handle, makes her way along Sobornaya Street, which leads her out of the town. On the way she crosses a muddy square full of smoke-blackened smithies, where the crisp air from the openland blows. Further on, between the monastery and the dungeon, one meets the white, cloud-strewn slope of the sky and the grey spring fields, and then, after getting past the puddles beneath the monastery wall and turning left, one sees what appears to be a large low-lying garden, enclosed by a white fence, above whose gates are written these words: "The Assumption of the Holy Mother of God." The small woman crosses herself perfunctorily and walks, as if accustomed to the path, down the central avenue. When she has reached the bench opposite that oak cross, she sits there in the wind and the spring cold for an hour, for two hours, until her feet in the light boots and her hands in the narrow kid gloves are frozen through and through. As she listens to the birds of spring, blithefully singing on despite the cold, as she listens to the jangling of the porcelain wreath in the wind, she sometimes thinks that she would give half her life if only that dead wreath were not hanging there before her eyes. That wreath, the mound, the cross of oak! Is it possible that she lies there beneath it, the one whose eyes shine so immortally from the convex porcelain medallion on the cross, and how can one reconcile the pure gaze of those eyes with all the horrible things now associated with the name of Olya Mesherskaya? But in the depths of her soul the small woman is happy, as are all people who dedicate their lives to some passionate dream.

This woman is the form mistress of Olya Mesherskaya, a spinster no longer young, who has lived for years in some fantasy world that takes the place of her real life. The first of her fanciful creations was her brother, a poor and utterly undistinguished junior officer; all of her most cherished thoughts were of him, his future, which, for some reason, she imagined to be full of sparkling promise. After he was killed in the Battle of Mukden, she tried to convince herself that her work was her sacred mission. Now the death of Olya Mesherskaya has inspired yet another captivating dream. Olya Mesherskaya is the object of her every thought and feeling. On every day off work she visits her grave, spends hours staring at the oaken cross, conjuring up the pallid face of Olya Mesherskaya in her coffin amidst flowers, and she recalls a conversation she once overheard. One day, while strolling about the schoolyard during the noon recess, Olya Mesherskaya had been speaking in a quick rapid patter to her favorite classmate, the tall plump Subbotina girl:

"Once I was reading one of papa's books—he has scads of curious old books—and I read what a woman must have to be truly beautiful... Well, you know, there was so much there that I can't remember it all, but, of course, it said black eyes, smouldering like pitch—really and truly, that's what it said: smouldering like pitch! Then, eyelashes black as the night, a gentle blush about the cheeks, a slender form, hands somewhat longer than the usual—you understand? A bit longer than ordinary! A small foot, a moderately large bosom, a calf that is rounded just so, a knee the color of seashells, sloping shoulders— I learned a lot of it almost by heart, it's all so perfectly right! But the main thing, you know what the main thing is? Light breathing! And I've got it, you know. Just listen how I can sigh... It's true, I've got it, don't I?"

Now that light breathing has dissolved anew in the vapors of the world, in the cloud-strewn sky, the cold spring wind.

1916

NIGHT OF DENIAL

A sombre stormy night near the end of the rainy season; darkness, raging winds and cloudbursts.

The shores of the sacred Isle of the Lion, black forests that extend to the very edge of the ocean, which seems about to engulf them.

A tremendous roar of waves, advancing relentlessly upon the island in frothing, inwardly glittering masses to cover not only the littoral sand-bars, where glutinous rings of starfish lie emitting a cryptic glow and thousands of susurrous crabs are writhing about, not only the shoreline cliffs, but even the feet of the palms, which bow down, looking like serpents as their thin trunks curve back from those shoreline bluffs.

From time to time the damp and warm tempest blows through with redoubled vehemence, with incredible force, so majestic and powerful that the fierce rumble rolling out of the forest toward the sea is no less terrible and harsh than the rumble of the sea itself. Then the palms, swaying from side to side, like living creatures tormented by a vexing somnolence, suddenly bend far over before the storm winds that have come tearing up to the shore, fall in unison toward the vale, and myriads of dead fronds tumble noisily down from their tops, and heady fragrances pervade the air, wafted from the interior of the island, from its cryptic wooded heartland.

Glutted and bleak, as they were on the nights of the Flood, the storm clouds hang still lower above the ocean. But in the boundless expanse between them and that watery abyss there is a certain semblance of light: to its secret depths the ocean is replete with the secret flame of innumerable lives.

The billows on the sea, with their fiery-roiling manes, roll roaring toward the shore, then flare up with such brilliance just before collapsing that a man who is standing in the forest above the shore is illumined by the green light they reflect.

The man is barefoot, dressed in the tatters of an anchorite, his head shaved, his right shoulder bared.

Amidst the majesty surrounding him, he is small of stature, like a child, and could that have been horror that shone for a fleeting second upon his emaciated face in the lustre and din of that collapsing wave?

Overcoming the din and the blended rumble of forests and tempest, he proclaims in firm and sonorous tones:

"Glory to Thee on High, the Hallowèd One, the All-Seeing-Most-Lucidly, the Subduer of Desire!"

Whirling in with the raging winds, what appear to be myriads of fiery eyes spark in the dark murk of the forest. And the voice of the man who stands on the shore resounds ecstatically:

"All in vain, Mara! In vain, Thousand-Eyed One, dost Thou tempt me, soaring above the earth in life-giving storms and cloudbursts, fecund and fragrant anew with the putrescence of graves, which give birth to new life out of dust and rot! Get thee hence, Mara! As a drop of rain runneth down and away from the taut leaf of a lotus, even so doth Desire glissade from my soul!"

But the vortex of innumerous fiery eyes whirls triumphantly amidst the downpour of tumbling fronds, eyes that illumine what seems a gigantic graven image sitting on the ground beneath the dark canopy of the forest, its head towering up to the very tops of the palms.

Its legs are crossed.

Wound about it from neck to loins are the grey coils of a snake, which puffs out its rose-colored throat, stretching its flat narrow-eyed head above the head of the image.

Despite the prodigious weight of those serpentine coils, he who sits is unconstrained and stately, erect and majestic.

On the crown of his head is the divine excrescence, the pointed lump. The blue-black, curly but short hair is like the blue in the tail of a peacock. The rubicund visage is regally serene. The eyes are gleaming like semi-precious stones.

And his terrible voice, a voice that rings with untrammeled freedom, that is like the thunder in its force, rolls majestically out of the depths of the forest toward the man who is standing on the shore:

"Verily, verily I say unto thee, my disciple: again and yet again wilt thou deny me for the sake of Mara, for the sake of that sweet deceit that is mortal life, on this night of earthly spring."

Paris. 1921.

Abbreviations: *Sob. soch.*—Ivan Bunin, Sobranie sochinenij [Collected Works] (9 volumes) Moscow, 1965-1967.

Lit. nasled.—Ivan Bunin. Literaturnoe nasledstvo. (2 volumes), ed. by V. R. Shcherbina, et al. Moscow, 1973.

THE GRAMMAR OF LOVE

"a certain Ivlev"—In describing the origins of this story, Bunin mentions that he used the beginning letters of his own name (Ivan Alekseevich) to form the surname Ivlev. See *Sob. soch.,* IX, 369. Ivlev also appears in other stories, such as "A Winter Dream" (1918) and "In a Far Distant Land" (1923).

tarantáss—A low four-wheeled carriage with two long poles connecting front and rear axles. The carriage body rested on these poles, which served as springs. In snowy weather the body was mounted on a sledge.

Khvóshinsky—the man; Khvóshinskoe—the name of his estate. At one point the peasant lad calls the estate, or the village located near it, Khvóshino.

"There is a state, but by what name..."—First four lines of a long poem by E. A. Baratynsky, "The Last Death" (1827).

IN A FAR DISTANT LAND

Pushkin's Pskov exposé *(pskovskaja povest' Pushkina)*—A nonsense phrase that reflects the dreamlike atmosphere of the story. Its sounds are more important than any meaning the words may express. Alexander Pushkin is the author of the play *Boris Godunov.* The mention of Godunov (Russian tsar from 1598 to 1605) later in the story together with the mention of Pushkin here suggests that Ivlev may have derived some inspiration for the imagery of his dream by reading Pushkin before going to bed.

AN UNKNOWN FRIEND

This story was inspired by Bunin's correspondence with a certain Natalya Esposito over a two-year period (1901-1903). Mrs. Esposito first wrote him from Ireland in 1901, but, unlike the author in the story, Bunin answered her. In one of her letters she uses the expression *l'ami inconnu,* which, in Russian, became the title of the story; many other passages from her letters are cited almost verbatim in "An Unknown Friend." See *Lit. nasled.,* II, 412-23. Bunin may have begun the story before his emigration or, at least, made extensive notes for it, since the Esposito letters were left behind when he emigrated and he could not possibly have remembered so many detailed passages from them in the year the story was written (1923).

NOOSIFORM EARS

Nevsky Prospect—Main thoroughfare of St. Petersburg, now Leningrad. For descriptions of many of the Petersburg place names, bridges, cathedrals and other landmarks mentioned in "Noosiform Ears," see *S.-Peterburg. Putevoditel' po stolitse* (No compiler listed). Izd. S.-Peterburgskogo gorodskogo obshchestvennogo upravlenija, 1903.

"the statue of Alexander III"—Unveiled in 1909. Sculptor— P. P. Trubetskoj.

144

"munched on pink peppermint sweets"—The peppermint was thought to disguise the smell of alcohol on one's breath.

"I'm what they call a degenerate"—The English word 'degenerate' has its origins in *de* + *genus* ("that departs from its race or kind"). The Russian word *vyrodok* has the same etymological basis and the same meaning but has an additional (archaic) meaning surely known to Bunin: "the very worst or *the very best* of a given category of persons, having no similarity to any of them; unique, original" (17 vol. Academy Russian Dictionary; my italics). On Bunin's treatment of degeneracy in a variety of works, see James Woodward, *Ivan Bunin. A Study of His Fiction* (Univ. of North Carolina, 1980), p. 108.

"By the ears, for example"—In his rather ironic discussion of "noosiform ears" Sokolovich seems to be mocking the theories of Cesare Lombroso (1835-1909), the famous Italian psychiatrist and criminal anthropologist, who considered criminal behavior atavistic and listed various physical stigmata associated with different criminal types. Murderers were supposed to have cold glassy eyes, long ears, dark hair and canine teeth. On Lombroso see *Encycl. Britannica* (15th edition) and *Bol'shaja sovetskaja èntsiklopedija* (2nd edition). Although Lombroso's theories have now been rejected, they had some influence on Bunin, who was always inclined to judge a person's character according to physical features. See, e.g., James Woodward, p. 109, citing a statement by Bunin (on the physical features of natural criminals) that seems to come directly from Lombroso or his disciples.

"I read Dostoevsky's *Crime and Punishment*"—Much of "Noosiform Ears" is a polemic with Dostoevsky and a parody of *Crime and Punishment,* Sokolovich being a travesty of Raskolnikov and Korolkova a travesty of Sonya Marmeladova.

"a trip to Sakhalin Island"—Allusion to the trip made by Anton Chekhov in 1890 (and his subsequent book). Sakhalin Island was the location of a notorious penal settlement.

"a Vilnius acquaintance . . . Yanovsky"—The real name of Nikolai Gogol was Yanovsky; in "Noosiform Ears" Bunin's polemical tone is directed not only at Dostoevsky, but also at Gogol. The passage a few paragraphs later (beginning, "Nevsky Prospect in the dead of night...") is, in part, a take-off on Gogol's famous description of Nevsky in the story "Nevsky Prospect."

"Korolkova, who called herself simply 'kinglet' "—Her surname resembles the Russian word for a type of bird, the kinglet *(korolëk).*

"the horrible stout horse"—Another reference to the equestrian statue of Alexander III.

REMOTE

the Arbát—At one time a prosperous district of Moscow; by the time of this story (early twentieth century) it had long since fallen into decline. The main street of the district is also called Arbat. For detailed notes on the Moscow streets and landmarks mentioned in "Remote," see I. A. Bunin, *Rasskazy (Selected Stories),* ed. by Peter Henry (Letchworth, Hertfordshire: Bradda Books, 1962), p. 114-121.

"the title of prince"—See note to "A Passing."

Strastnóy (=Strastnoy Bul'var), Petróvka, Kuznétsky (=Kuznetsky most)—Famous Moscow streets; see notes to "The Consecration of Love."

"pneumatics"—Inflated rubber tires, recently introduced at the time the story is set.

"vats of bay leaves stood at the entrance of the Prague"—The Prague Restaurant still operates today in the Old Arbat district. The bay leaves are used for flavoring certain soups.

Trinity Monastery, New Jerusalem Monastery—Famous Russian Orthodox monasteries near Moscow, much visited by Russian believers on pilgrimages.

INDULGENT PARTICIPATION

Imperial Theatres—The connection of the "former artiste" with the Imperial Theatres emphasizes her ostensible ludicrousness and obsoleteness since at the time this story is set (second decade of the twentieth century) these state-run theatres were considered bastions of conservatism. The new mode in theatre was exemplified by the Moscow Art Theatre, established by Stanislavsky and Nemirovich-Danchenko in 1898.

Fifth Moscow *Gymnasium*—Located on Povarskaya Street (now renamed Vorovsky St.), this school was known for the philanthropic concerts that it regularly organized.

The Lower Depths—Maxim Gorky's famous play. Staged by Stanislavsky at the Moscow Art Theatre in December, 1902.

The Blue Bird—Written by the Belgian symbolist Maeterlinck, this play was very popular in Russia in the early twentieth century and still sometimes appears at the Moscow Art Theatre, where Stanislavsky staged it in 1908.

The Three Sisters—Anton Chekhov's famous play, first performed at the Moscow Art Theatre on January 31, 1901.

Chaliápin (F. I. Shaljapin, 1873-1938)—World-famous bass, he sang the role of the miller in *Water-Nymph (Rusalka)* by A. S. Dargomyzhsky, an opera based on Pushkin's poem of the same title.

Sóbinov, L. V. (1872-1934)—Renowned Russian tenor.

Snow-Maiden (Snegurochka)—A folklore fantasy by the playwright Alexander Ostrovsky. Rimsky-Korsakov's opera based on it was first staged by the Mamontov opera in 1882.

Shor, Krein, and Erlich—Moscow chamber musicians. Still a popular trio in post-revolutionary years.

Zimin's opera—A Moscow opera house that functioned between 1904 and 1917. Founded by S. I. Zimin (1875-1942).

Igor Severianin [pseud. of I. V. Lotarev (1887-1941)]—Futurist poet who was extremely popular when this story is set. Bunin despised him for his modernist pose and his neologisms. In fact, Bunin disliked most of the works mentioned here. The whole passage has a subtle irony that culminates with the reference to a writer whom Bunin considered the quintessence of early twentieth-century modernist vulgarity.

etheric-valerian mixture—Valerian drops were (and are) a common remedy for nerves. They supposedly have a calming effect on the heart and central nervous system.

Hoffmann's drops—A remedy for nerves or upset stomach; after the German doctor Friedrich Hoffmann (1660-1742).

lilies-of-the-valley—Drops made from the lily-of-the-valley are taken for a heart condition.

"the Lord has sent us to a sink-tuary here"—This pronunciation of the word 'sanctuary' reflects the artiste's old-fashioned, pseudo-aristocratic style. In a diary note Bunin mentions that his first wife Anna Tsakni once played this song for him in the days before their marriage. See *Ustami Buninykh,* ed. by M. Grin (Frankfurt: Posev, 1977), I, 33.

A PASSING

the prince—"Prince" *(knjaz')* is a title granted within the Russian landed nobility and does not imply any connection with royalty.

chetverik—Old Russian dry measure=26.239 litres.

"Praise ye the Lord from the heavens"—Psalm 148.

tarantass—See note to "The Grammar of Love."

In one of his early stories, "The Golden Pen" (1920), the Soviet writer Valentin Kataev gives an ironic portrayal of Bunin in Odessa in the process of writing what was to become "A Passing" as the revolution raged around him.

NIGHT

In this story Bunin quotes extensively (but seldom with exactitude) from the Bible. In my translation I have attempted to retain the inexactness of quotations. Notes below refer to the Biblical passage in the King James Version.

"And I decided to seek and search out..."—*Ecclesiastes* 1:13.

"God hath made man reasonable..."—*Ecclesiastes* 7:29.

"Be not righteous over much..."—*Ecclesiastes* 7:16.

"In days to come all will be forgotten..."—*Ecclesiastes* 1:11.

"Also their love, and their hatred..."—*Ecclesiastes* 9:6.

"Eat thereof and ye shall be as God"—*Genesis* 3:5.

"God is in heaven, and we upon earth"—*Ecclesiastes* 5:2.

"Shroud of Christ"—A large rectangular piece of cloth on which the body of Christ in his coffin is depicted. Used in Russian Orthodox church rituals.

"The fool sitteth idly..."—*Ecclesiastes* 4:5.

"He that observeth the wind..."—*Ecclesiastes* 11:4.

"Royal Portals" (or "Royal Gates")—Central doors in iconostasis of Russian Orthodox churches.

"All is vanity of vanities..."—*Ecclesiastes* 1:2-3.

"The sleep of a labouring man is sweet!"—*Ecclesiastes* 5:12.

"And there is nothing better for a man..."—*Ecclesiastes* 2:24; 5:18; 9:7.

"once, myriads of years ago, I was a goat yeanling"—Metempsychosis (transmigration of souls) is important in both Hinduism and Buddhism; in the 550 births of the Buddha, he supposedly appeared not only as human, but also as animal, vegetable, and divine.

"the one who made this statement"—Gautama Buddha.

"The fits of Mohammed, when the angels revealed to him..."—This experience has been called the analogue of the Christian Transfiguration or the coloquy of Moses on Sinai. See James Hastings (ed.), *Encyclopedia of Religion and Ethics* (New York: Charles Scribner's Sons, 1917-1927), VIII, 878.

Maya (Māyā)—'illusion,' 'appearance.' A Hindu philosophic term, "applied to the illusion of the multiplicity of the empirical universe, produced by ignorance . . . when in reality there is only One." (*Encyclopedia of Religion and Ethics,* VIII, 503.) "Māyā causes a state of *moha* . . . 'delusion,' in which consciousness of the ultimate reality is lost, and bewildered men believe in the reality of the manifest world presented to their senses. It is a cosmic delusion which draws a veil across men's perception, leading them to error and infatuation with the world and the flesh, obscuring from the mind the vision of their true destiny." Benjamin Walker, *The Hindu World* (New York: Praeger, 1968), II, 53-54.

"Nothing perishes—all things are but altered."—"*Omnia mutantur, nihil interit.*" Ovid, *Metamorphoses.*

"Withdraw from the Chain"—Allusion to the Buddhist concept of continuous reincarnation and the idea of withdrawal from the chain of incarnations to attain Nirvana, which is referred to in an earlier published version of the story (under the title "Cicadas"): "Nirvana with its eternal bliss, which is sad, nonetheless, for the mortal, who never on earth can completely renounce Maya, the sweetness of 'being.'"

147

"Sun, stand thou still!!"—*Joshua* 10:12.

"Night unto night passeth knowledge."—*Psalm* 19:2.

TRANSFIGURATION

On the Transfiguration *(Preobrazhenie)* of Jesus Christ, which is celebrated on August 6 in the Russian Orthodox Church, see Matthew 17:1-13; Mark 9:2-9; Luke 9:28-36. The Russian verb from the same root *(preobrazit'sja)* is also a high-style word for 'to die'; therefore, the Russian title has the additional connotation 'death.' It is clear that Christ's Transfiguration is directly applicable to the meaning of Bunin's story if one reads certain commentary on this miraculous event. See, e.g., Joseph Campbell, *The Hero With a Thousand Faces* (Princeton University, 2nd ed., 1968), p. 229-30, 236-37. Campbell (as Bunin) sees the Transfiguration in terms of Eastern religious concepts.

On the history and design of the Russian peasant hut, see *Bol'shaja sovetskaja èntsiklopedija* (2nd ed.) vol. 17, p. 352-3. See also Genevra Gerhart, *The Russian's World* (Harcourt Brace Jovanovich, 1974), p. 60-68.

THE CRANES

drozhky—A low, open four-wheeled carriage with a long narrow bench, which the riders straddle.

poddyovka—A man's light coat, gathered tightly at the waist, its skirts reaching below the knees.

verst—About 2/3 mi. (1.067 km. or 3500 ft.).

Avian symbolism is common in Bunin's works (see e. g., in this collection, the stork in "First Love" and the owls, skylarks and nightingales in "The Consecration of Love"). Migratory birds, in particular the crane, are especially dear to the Russian folk psyche. Bunin once remarked: "The migration of birds is caused by an internal secretion: in autumn by a deficiency of a hormone, in spring by an excess of it... This agitation in birds may be compared to the time of sexual maturity and to periods of 'seasonal stimulation of the blood' in human beings...

I've been just like a bird all my life!"

Cited in A. Baboreko, *Ivan Bunin. Materialy dlja biografii* (Moscow, 1967), p. 61.

THE CONSECRATION OF LOVE

The mention of skylarks returning, bringing warmth and joy, alludes to certain songs sung and rituals observed by peasant girls or children as invocations to spring. The skylarks supposedly bring spring with them when they return on March 9.

Tverskóy Boulevard—Probably the most famous and surely one of the most beautiful boulevards in Moscow; it now runs into Gorky Street at the Pushkin Monument.

Strastnóy Monastery—Once located on Pushkin Square; demolished in Soviet times.

Pushkin Monument—Famous monument erected in 1880. Now located on Gorky Street across from the termination of Tverskoy Blvd. Sculptor—A. M. Opekúshin.

Strélna—A fashionable restaurant in pre-revolutionary times.

"Betwixt us there's a slumbrous secret"—I have not found a source for these lines; Bunin himself may have written them in imitation of poor symbolist poetry.

Kuznétsky=Kuznétsky most—Then and now a main thoroughfare and important commercial street in Moscow.

Moscow Art Theatre—See notes to "Indulgent Participation." Bunin, who disliked this theatre for its modernism, often criticizes it subtly (or not so subtly) in his works.

Kislóvka—Two streets near the center of Moscow were called Kislovsky Lane. Upper Kislovsky Lane *(Bol'shoj pereulok)* is now Semashno Street; Lower Kislovsky Lane *(Malyj pereulok)* is now Sobinov Street.

Molchánovka—This Moscow street is located off Prospect Kalinina near the large bookstore "Dom Knigi." Also mentioned in "Indulgent Participation."

The Soviet critic Baboreko has pointed out a possible prototype for the director of Katya's drama school. Just before the beginning of W.W.I a certain A. I. Adashev, an actor at the Moscow Art Theatre and founder of his own private drama school, departed hastily for the provinces after the press devoted a number of articles to his scandalous behavior with his female students. See V. Afanasev, *I. A. Bunin* (Moscow, 1966), p. 297.

Rules of the Household (Domostroj)—A document of the 16th Century containing a detailed list of rules for social, religious, and especially home and family conduct. According to *Domostroj,* the exemplary family was patriarchal, ruled firmly by the male lord and master.

"In the church choir a young girl sang."—First line of a famous untitled poem (1905) by the symbolist poet Alexander Blok. In making another of his frequent critical allusions to modernist art, Bunin chooses a poem that was extremely popular all over Russia among girls like Katya.

Miskhor—Seaside resort on the Crimean Peninsula near Yalta.

"young Werther from Tambov"—The allusion is to Goethe's *Sorrows of Young Werther.* Tambov is a Russian city often taken as symbolic of backwoods provincialism.

"your body is the highest reason"—The following well-known quotation expresses the Nietzschean idea: "Body am I entirely, and nothing else; and soul is only a word for something about the body" ("On the Despisers of the Body." *Thus Spoke Zarathustra*—tr. by W. Kaufmann).

"Junker Schmidt..."—Here is a literal, non-poetic translation of the poem, entitled "Junker Schmidt":

> The leaf fades. The summer passes.
> Rime-frost sparkles silver.
> Junker Schmidt with a pistol
> Wants to shoot himself.
> Wait, you madman, once again
> The verdure will come alive!
> Junker Schmidt! Word of honor,
> Summer will return!

The author of the poem, Koz'ma Prutkov, is a parodic invention of A. K. Tolstoy and the Zhemchuzhnikov brothers, poets of the nineteenth century. The poem is one of Prutkov's most famous parodies of the romantic pose, and Junker Schmidt himself "has become the archtypal Prutkovian romantic hero" (Monter). Although "Junker Schmidt" was once printed with the sub-title "From Heine," it has not been determined precisely which Heine poem is parodied. See B. H. Monter, *Koz'ma Prutkov. The Art of Parody* (The Hague: Mouton, 1972), p. 80-81. Monter also includes a poetic translation—p. 80.

The Asra—A romance by the Russian pianist and composer Anton Rubenstein (1829-1894), based on the words of a Heine poem ("Der Asra," 1846). Bunin, who was much impressed by this romance as a young man, mentions it in at least one other work,

"Without Kith or Kin" ("Bez rodu-plemeni"). See *Sob. soch.* V, 525, and II, 504. The phrases and lines quoted in Russian differ somewhat from the original Heine poem.

Kursk—Mitya takes the train bound for southern and south-western points; it departs from the Kursk Station, located east of the Kremlin near what is now the main or outer ring road (Sadovoe kol'tso). Mitya changes trains in Orel, takes a train through the town of Verkhov'e (west and slightly south of Orel), and debarks, presumably at a small station between Verkhov'e and Elets, the town where Bunin himself attended *gymnasium.* The setting of Mitya's estate in the Orel District is obviously based on Bunin's own knowledge of manor life there.

Annunciation Day—March 25 by the pre-revolutionary calendar.

Spanish blister flies or blister beetles—A pharmaceutical preparation called *cantharides,* commonly called Spanish fly, is made from these beetles. It is used as a blister-inducing agent and is also one of the principal aphrodisiacs recognized by modern medicine.

Sarafan—Sleeveless dress, buttoning in front, worn by Russian peasant women; tunic dress.

drozhky—See note to "The Cranes."

"The household sleeps,..."—First two lines of untitled poem by A. A. Fet (1820-1892).

"Over smooth and tranquil river..."—From a poem by Ivan Turgenev, "Prizvanie" ("An Invocation"—1844); quoted by Bunin inexactly. The first line is not in the Turgenev poem at all.

"I don't have nothing to do"—In speaking with the peasants or the steward, Mitya often uses substandard locutions in an attempt to approximate their speech patterns.

"They're worse for wear, these boots of mine"—In an earlier published version Bunin used all four lines of this *chastushka* (folk ditty). Here is a loose translation that is more directly vulgar than the original but that makes the meaning clear:

> They're worse for wear, these boots of mine,
> But on the toes they spark and shine;
> Married, single, fat, two-faced:
> All girls are the same below the waist!

"Petals' scroll now brightly open"—From the Fet poem entitled "The Rose" (1864). The quotation is not exact.

Sóbinov and Chaliápin—See note to "Indulgent Participation." In Gounod's opera *Faust* (staged at the Moscow Bolshoy Theatre, beginning September 24, 1899) Chaliapin played Mephistopheles, Sobinov played Faust. This detail establishes the exact chronology of the novel's action (all dates old style):

> December, 1899—Mitya and Katya meet.
> March 9, 1900—Mitya's "last happy day in Moscow."
> One week before Easter, 1900—Katya's examination.
> Late April, 1900—Mitya leaves for the country.
> Early June, 1900—Mitya's suicide.

"Once in far Thule there lived a good king"—This same line from Gounod's *Faust* is sung by the rakish officer Petritsky, a friend of Vronsky, in Tolstoy's *Anna Karenina* (Part II, Ch. 20).

eight versts—One verst=1.067 km. This indicates only one way; the round trip to the station is sixteen versts.

Sevastopol—Crimean city made famous by the siege of English, French and Turkish forces during the Crimean War.

Baidar Gates—A pass between the principal range of the Crimean Mountains, extending from the Baidar Valley to the Black Sea coast.

Livadia—Small Crimean city located on the Black Sea three kilometers from Yalta.

Alupka—Crimean resort located 17 km. southwest of Yalta.

Shakhovskoe—According to Bunin's wife, V. N. Muromtseva-Bunina, Shakhovskoe was modelled on the estate Kolontaevka, located in Bunin's native district.

Mitry Palich—Mitya's name and patronymic (Dmitry Pavlovich) in the steward's pronunciation.

sentry hut—The forester's family lives in a sentry hut or guard hut *(karaulka)* since it is his job to protect the trees in the forest from timber thieves.

storeroom *(klet')*—Room in peasant hut used as storage room and summer sleeping room.

Pisemsky—A. F. Pisemsky (1820-1881), Russian novelist and dramatist.

Antares = Mars—Brightest star in the constellation Scorpio.

ON THE NIGHT SEA

Evpatoria—Seaport on the western Crimean Peninsula.

Alupka—see notes to "The Consecration of Love."

Gagry (Gagra)—Resort on the Black Sea about 80 km. NW of Sukhumi.

"Some Gaius once was mortal"—Gaius = Gaius Julius Caesar. This is a paraphrase from a syllogism in a textbook of logic by J. G. Kiesewetter (1766-1819), a book widely used in nineteenth century Russian schools. Bunin most likely recalled Tolstoy's prominent citation of the same passage in "The Death of Ivan Ilich" (Ch. 6).

Novodevichy Cemetery—Probably the most well-known cemetery in the country, burial place of some of the most famous Russians of the nineteenth and twentieth centuries.

Prince Gautama = Gautama Buddha. Yasodhara was his legendary wife.

"I heard the fatal tidings from dispassionate lips"—Slightly misquoted lines from Alexander Pushkin's famous elegy on the death of Amalia Riznich, "Beneath the Blue Skies of her Native Land." This poem expresses much the same feelings experienced by the writer in Bunin's story—indifference upon hearing of a former mistress' death. The same two lines are quoted in Ivan Turgenev's *First Love.*

THE IDOL

In Russian the title of this story is especially appropriate since the Russian word *idol* has two meanings: (1) idol, image of a divinity, and (2) callous or obtuse person, blockhead.

SEMPITERNAL SPRING

poddyovka—See note to "The Cranes."

The Battle of Cheshme (Çeşme)—Naval battle on the Aegean Sea during the Russo-Ottoman War of 1768-74. Fought in early July, 1770, it resulted in a decisive victory over the Turks.

"The sun, like a mare's-piss puddle"—Parody of two lines from a poem by the Soviet poet Sergej Esenin, "Mare Ships" ("Kobyl'i korabli," 1919):

> Even the sun freezes, like a puddle
> Pissed full by a gelding.

"So be it; let all past times away like fleeting dreams"—Inexact citation from the poem by E. A. Baratynsky, "Desolation" (1834), which provided Bunin with the title for his story (see the concluding lines of this poem cited at the end of "Sempiternal Spring").

THE COLD FALL

The Austrian Archduke was assassinated in Sarajevo on June 28, 1914 (Gregorian calendar). All dates in this story are based on the old, pre-revolutionary Julian Calendar.

Saint Peter's Day—June 29, old style.
Ekaterinodar—Renamed Krasnodar in 1920.
"The autumn's so frosty this year!" (literal trans.: "What a cold fall!")—Bunin quotes
   the first stanza of a two-stanza poem by A. A. Fet; the quotation is slightly incorrect.

LIGHT BREATHING

The Battle of Mukden—The final and greatest battle of the Russo-Japanese War, fought
   February 19-March 10, 1905.

"Light Breathing" is foreshadowed in a Bunin poem of 1903, "The Portrait," which describes a graveyard and a portrait of a girl with "large clear eyes" and a "coquetishly simple hair style." See *Sob. soch.,* I, 178-9. In choosing his title, which furnishes the musical tonality for the entire story, Bunin may also have been influenced by the sounds in the first line of a famous poem by Fet, "Whispers, Timid Breathing" ("Shjopot. Robkoe dykhan'e," pub. in 1850). For Bunin's note on the origins of this story, see *Sob. soch.,* IX, 369.

NIGHT OF DENIAL

Mara (Māra)—In the Buddhist scriptures Mara is the sovereign of the world, god of death
   and god of the living. "Māra is Kāma, 'Desire,' since desire is the *raison d'être* of
   birth and death; and, because Buddha is the deliverer from death and birth, Mara is
   the personal enemy of Buddha . . . Māra embodies desire, the universal fetterer,
   the sensual life both here and in the other world." *Encyclopedia of Religion and
   Ethics,* VIII, 406-07.
"the divine excrescence"—This protuberance on the skull of the Buddha is also mentioned
   in "Night."

H E R M I T A G E   Publishers of New Russian Books

2269 Shadowood Dr., Ann Arbor, MI 48104
ISBN Prefix: 0-938920   Tel. (313) 971-2968

Aksenov, Vasily. ARISTOFANIANA S LIAGUSHKAMI. Col. of
plays. Illustr. by E. Neizvestny. 1981, 384 pp. 5½" x 8½".
-06-5   Cl. $ 20.00   -07-3   Pbk. $ 11.50
Aksenov, Vasily. PRAVO NA OSTROV. Col. of stories. 1983.
200 pp. 5" x 8".   -34-0   Pbk. $ 6.50
Aranovich, Felix. NADGROBIE ANTOKOLSKOGO. Docum. essay
on Russian-Jewish sculptor. 80 ill. 1982. 180 pp. 6" x 9".
                                              -16-2   Pbk. $ 8.50
Armalinsky, Mikhail. POSLE PROSHLOGO. Col. of poems. 1982.
110 pp. 5½" x 8".   -30-8   Pbk. $ 5.50
Averintsev, Sergey. RELIGIA I LITERATURA. Col. of articles.
1981, 140 pp. 5½" x 8".   -02-2   Pbk. $ 7.00
Brackman, Rita. VYBOR V ADU. A study on Solzhenitsyn. 1983.
144 pp. 6" x 9".   -20-0   Pbk. $ 7.50
Chertok, Semen. POSLEDNYAYA LYUBOV' MAYAKOVSKOGO.
A lit. study. 1983. 128 pp. 5½" x 8½".   -31-6   Pbk. $7.00
Dovlatov, Sergei. ZAPOVEDNIK. A novel. 1983, Sept. 140 pp.
5½" x 8".   -39-1   Pbk. $ 7.50
Dovlatov, Sergei. ZONA. A novel about prison camp. 1982. 128 pp.
5½" x 8".   -23-5   Pbk. $ 7.50
Efimov, Igor. ARKHIVY STRASHNOGO SUDA. A novel. 1982.
320 pp. 5" x 7½".   -25-1   Pbk. 10.50
Elagin, Ivan. V ZALE VSELENNOY. Col. of poems. 1982. 212 pp.
4½" x 6".   -24-3   Pbk. $ 7.50
Ezerskaya, Bella. MASTERA. Col. of interviewes with Rus. artists in
exile. 1982. 112 pp. 15 ill. 5" x 8".   -10-3   Pbk. $ 8.00
Genis, Alexander. Vail, Peter. SOVREMENNAYA RUSSKAYA
PROZA. 1982. 192 pp., 23 ill. 5½" x 8½".   -28-6   Pbk. $ 8.50
Girshin, Mark. UBIYSTVO EMIGRANTA. A novel. 1983. 150 pp.
4½" x 6".   -29-4   Pbk. $ 7.00
Guberman, Igor. BUMERANG. Col. of satirical poems. 1982. 120 p.
4½" x 4½".   -15-4   Pbk. 6.00
Kleyman, Ludmila. RANNYAYA PROZA SOLOGUBA. A study.
1983, Sept. 220 p. 6" x 9".   -41-3   Pbk. $ 14.00
Korotyukov, Aleksey. NELEGKO BYT' RUSSKIM SHPIONOM.
A novel. 1982. 140 pp. 5½" x 8½".   -18-9   Pbk. $ 8.00
Lungina, Tatiana. VOLF MESSING. An essay on great Rus. psychic.
1982. 270 pp., 15 ill. 5½" x 8".   -12-X   Pbk. $ 12.00
Mikheev. Dmitry. IDEALIST. A novel. 1982. 224 pp. 6" x 9".
                                              -14-6   Pbk. $ 8.50
Neizvestny, Ernst. O SYNTEZE V ISKUSSTVE. An article and an
album of drawings. In Rus. and in English. 1982. 96 pp., 60 ill.
8½" x 11".   -22-7   Pbk. $ 12.00
Ozernaya, Nataliya. RUSSKO-ANGLIYSKY RAZGOVORNIK.
1982. 170 pp. 6" x 6½".   -21-9   Pbk. $ 9.50
Paperno, Dmitry. ZAPISKI MOSKOVSKOGO PIANISTA. A me-
moirs. 1983. 200 pp, 30 ill. 6" x 9".   -26-X   Pbk. 8.00
Popovsky, Mark. DELO AKADEMIKA VAVILOVA. A study on
famous scientist killed by Stalin. 1983, Aug. 280 pp. 25 illustr.
6" x 9".   -33-2   Pbk. 10.00
Rzhevsky, Leonid. BUNT PODSOLNECHNIKA. A novel. 1981.
240 pp., 5½" x 8".   -01-4   Pbk. $ 8.50
Shturman, Dora. ZEMLYA ZA KHOLMOM. Col. of political articles.
1983, July. 256 pp. 6" x 9".   -32-4   Pbk. $ 9.00

Suslov, Ilya. RASSKAZY O TOV. STALINE. Col. of stories. 1981.
140 pp. 5½" x 8".   -03-0   Pbk. $ 7.50
Suslov, Ilya. VYKHOD K MORYU. Col. of stories. 1982. 230 pp.
6" x 9".   -19-7   Pbk. $ 8.50
Svirsky, Grigory. TRETIY EXODUS. A docum. novel on the emigr.
of Jews from USSR. 1983. 520 pp. 6" x 9".   -44-8   Pbk. $ 19.00
Ul'yanov, Nikolay. SCRIPTY. Col. of articles on the Rus. history.
1981. 235 pp. 5½" x 8½".   -05-7   Pbk. $ 8.00
Volokhonsky, Henri. STIKHI. Col. of poems. 1983, Aug. 160 pp.
6" x 9".   -45-6   Pbk. $ 8.00
Zernova, Ruth. ZHENSKIE RASSKAZY. Col. of stories. 1981.
160 pp. 5½" x 8½".   -04-9   Pbk. $ 7.50

BOOKS IN THE ENGLISH LANGUAGE

FROM   HERMITAGE

Barsch, Karl-Heinrich. PUSHKIN AND MERIMEE AS SHORT
STORY WRITERS. A study. 1983. 90 pp., 5" x 8".
                                                           -35-9   Pbk. $ 7.00
Bunin, Ivan. IN A FAR DISTANT LAND. Col. of stories. Transl.
from Russian by Robert Bowie. 1983. 172 pp., 6" x 9".
                                                           -27-8   Pbk. $ 8.50
Debreczeny, Paul. TEMPTATIONS OF THE PAST. A novel.
1982. 110 pp., 4½" x 6½".   -17-0   Pbk. $ 6.50
Efimov, Igor. METAPOLITICS. Philosophical-historical study.
Transl. from Russian by Isabel Heaman. 1983. 230 pp., 5" x 8".
                                                           -36-7   Pbk. $ 9.50
Kaverin, Veniamin. A SCHOOL PLAY. Two novellas transl. from
Russian by Alice Nichols. 1983. 210 pp. 5" x 8". -37-5   Pbk. 8.00
Monahan, Barbara. A DICTIONARY OF RUSSIAN GESTURE.
50 ill. 1983. 110 pp., 4½" x 6½".   -38-3   Pbk. $ 9.00
Neizvestny, Ernst. ON NTHESIS IN ART. An article in English and
in Russian, and an album of drawings. 1982. 96 pp., 60 ill.,1983.
8½" x 11".   -22-7   Pbk. $ 12.00

TERMS OF SALE

INDIVIDUALS are to pay in advance, adding $1.50 for post-
age and handling (regardless of number of books ordered). There is
a 20% discount on orders of 3 or more books.

BOOKSELLERS ordering 10 or more books receive a 40%
discount (shipping costs to be paid by purchaser) and 90 days
credit. Firms in Europe and Asia have 120 days credit. On orders
of fewer than 10 books the discount is 30%.

On orders of 50 copies of one title, the discount is 45%, and on
orders of 100 copies and more—50%. No returns.

LIBRARIES have 90 days credit.

The prices of books scheduled for publication in 1983 might
vary somewhat. Dates are approximate.